WILDE IN HIS ARMS

A Dark Horse Dive Bar Novel

Jennifer Ryan

For you, the reader. Thank you for your support, reviews, and your time.

It is no small thing that you choose my books to read. I hope they offer you an escape, a treat, a means to relax and enjoy the ride that you know will always end with a happy ever after – even if I make my characters really work for it.

I love this job. And I get to do it because of you!

Chapter One

Aria groaned at the knock on her door at the unforgivably rude hour of 9:43 a.m. Everyone she'd actually answer the door for knew she didn't get up before noon. Not when her shifts ended at two a.m. or later most nights. Since she hadn't gone to sleep until four, she burrowed into her pillow, hoping the asshole at her door left, so she could get some more sleep.

The knock came again, this time more insistent and persistent.

She ignored it again, until she heard a gruff voice shout, "Aria! It's me."

Yeah, that voice made her belly quiver with anticipation and her heart leap. It made her conjure one dirty thought after the next of what the man who owned that voice could do to her body. And right now, it made her tighten her thighs as heat bloomed between her legs.

"Ar-i-a!" Another round of pounding on her door. This time with a dose of irritation.

Yeah, well she had reason to be upset, too, even if she still desperately wanted him.

Stupid hormones!

She'd texted him sixteen days ago. Sixteen! And heard nothing back.

All of a sudden he can't wait to see me.

It wasn't uncommon for them to go days between a text or call. They lived in different states. Worked long hours. But sixteen days. It was the punctuation mark on their long-distance relationship.

If you could call it that anymore.

This past stretch of no communication was the longest, but certainly not the only time they'd gone without speaking for days or even more than a week.

She threw off the covers and sat up, finger-combing her hair away from her face.

Nick had a demanding job with the FBI. He lived in Montana. He traveled for work.

Well, she had a demanding job, too. She lived in Wyoming. Her family and business were here. And because of that, and the fact that Nick's brother Mason was married to Aria's sister, Lyric, it meant that Nick came to town to see her when he had time and wanted to visit his brother, too. In the beginning, he found the time to come often. A few times a month. It gave them time to get to know each other in between having the best sex ever. Because they gave in to their desires so easily. And after those mind-blowing moments, they whispered secrets in the dark. She'd never shared so much of herself, or been so desperate to learn everything about someone else.

She stood and headed for the door.

After a bad breakup with her ex—because the asshole cheated on her—she hadn't wanted anything serious. The spark that ignited between her and Nick when they met was all she thought she needed. Well, that and the fireworks in the bedroom. She loved losing herself in his arms. He wanted her. He treated her like she was the sexiest woman he'd ever seen. Like he needed her to blot out all the bad he saw on the job with the amazing way she made him feel. He made her feel that way, too. Their stolen moments a day here, two days there, were enough.

Until they weren't even close to what she thought they could have if they truly committed to each other.

She started catching feelings that very first night they snuck off together. Feelings that grew each and every time he showed up and smiled that smile and looked at her like she was his every dream come true. In the beginning, she wanted to believe it was just sex. A bit of fun. But he blew her mind each and every time.

Multiple orgasms do that to a girl.

But there was something more there in the morning-after that first time, when they stood in her open front door and he turned to say goodbye and instead said, "I don't want this to be a one-time thing, and I can't make any promises because I don't live here and my job is crazy-demanding. I don't want to go, but I can't stay."

She'd fallen for his open heart and blatant honesty. "Then I'll see you when I see you." She had delivered that line with a sexy smile, letting him know she'd be there when he came back, happy to take him into her arms for however long it lasted.

But now...months later, her sister married to his brother and pregnant, Jax married and expecting a baby, too, and Melody, her baby sister, about to be the next one down the aisle, and she and Nick were still in the same place they always were—always happy to see each other and fall into bed but never any closer. No promises made. No plans for the future.

What the hell were they doing?

What were they to each other? Lovers, yes. Friends? Sorta. They mostly lived in the moment.

And when she opened the door and stared into his tired eyes and handsome face, she knew this was the last time they'd be together like this. Because damn he looked good. But she couldn't keep doing this to herself. Because every time he left, he took a piece of her with him. Soon, there'd be nothing left of her.

This time had to be goodbye.

Because she still wanted to be a wife and mother. More than that, she wanted a man who loved her like the air he breathed. And while she felt that kind of connection to Nick, he'd never shared his feelings.

Neither had she. She'd done that once and got burned. But he had to know. Right?

Did Nick know she loved him?

Probably not. They didn't talk about such things.

She knew he cared about her. He couldn't fake that in bed. He wasn't using her. He genuinely enjoyed being with her. And she felt the same about him. But being the person who gave him comfort and connection and orgasms didn't fulfill her desire to be someone's everything.

"Please don't be mad at me." Those words burst out of Nick's mouth the second she opened the door and took in his rumpled thermal long-sleeve shirt, black jeans, scuffed work boots, and the shiny badge at his waist. He wasn't wearing his gun, but she bet he had it locked up in his car.

And if he was wearing the badge, she bet he was here for work, not necessarily just to see her. Which made this a happy (mostly) coincidence, or something.

She wasn't really fully awake or thinking clearly with her hormones on a rampage, begging for her to drag him to her bed.

And, oh yeah, why would his being here make her mad?

"Um...good morning." She scratched her head and wondered if her long, dark hair was as messy as it felt.

Nick stepped close, cupped her cheek in one hand, and kissed her softly. "Morning. You look good enough to eat and I'm so hungry." Nick looked her up and down, then backed her into her living space above the bar, kicking the door shut, his eyes devouring her from head to toe in her simple black tank top and purple lace-trimmed panties.

He bent his knees, wrapped his arms around her back, lifted her up, and she wrapped her legs around his waist as he kissed her like he would never stop. He walked them to her bed on the other side of the apartment, kneeled on the edge of the bed, then fell forward with her. They hit the mattress with a bounce, Nick making sure he didn't crush her by taking most of his weight on his forearms as his impressive erection pressed against her soft center. "Fuck. You feel good." He rubbed his long length against her soft folds, making them both groan with pleasure.

In between kisses she asked, "What are you doing here?"

He kissed her again, his tongue thrusting in her mouth in time to the way he rocked his cock against her. "Last night," he said between deep, penetrating kisses. Then he lifted his head and looked down at her. "Your sister was kidnapped."

"What!" Aria gasped, her eyes going wide, as she attempted to jump up and go find her sister, even though she didn't even know which one.

Nick held her down beneath him. "Melody is fine. I swear it. She's in the hospital. Just for observation," he added quickly, kissing her forehead, her cheek. "She's asleep right now. You can see her in a couple of hours."

He paused, searching her eyes. "Until then, be here with me?" He kissed her again. "Please." That really did sound like he was begging. "I need you so much." He kissed her again, his tongue sliding against hers. "Then I'll tell you everything." He dove back in for another kiss as Aria tried to wrap her head around everything he'd just said through the haze of lust and need he made her feel as he trailed kisses down her neck and chest to her breasts, where he sucked her tight nipple into his mouth over her tank.

"Nick. Please." She wasn't sure what she was begging for at the moment. More information about her sister, or more of his mouth. Both.

He looked up at her from between her legs. "You and me now. Talk later. I swear she's safe and okay."

She gave in the second he tore her panties down her legs, then dove into her pussy with his tongue like a man on a mission. And the only thing he seemed to want was her writhing on the bed. She could get behind that, knowing he'd never lie about her sister's condition. She sank her fingers into his golden hair, holding him to her as he licked and sucked her clit exactly the way she liked it.

He slid one finger, then two into her wet channel, stroking her as he circled her clit with his tongue, once, twice, and then setting off the orgasm he'd so masterfully built inside her.

And he wasn't done. He shucked off all his clothes, tossing them to the floor, and she recovered enough to enjoy the show as he revealed every chiseled muscle in his shoulders, arms, chest, and abs. That V leading to his groin always made her mouth water. And his thick, hard cock made her pussy clench, like it couldn't wait to be wrapped around him.

She didn't want to give that up.

She didn't want to give *him* up.

But he'd made it clear his job came first. He was here now, but she knew he'd be leaving again. So she'd hold on to him and this moment as long as she could.

He pulled her tank over her head, then planted his hands on either side of her shoulders and looked down at her, his eyes filled with appreciation and desire. "God, I've missed you." He gently ran his fingertips down her sternum and between her breasts as he watched his fingertips glide over her skin. "I think about you all the time. You're a distraction and my every fantasy."

She gaped at him. "You think about me?"

His head snapped up and his hazel eyes met hers. "Yes. Always."

Yet he hadn't texted or called in sixteen days.

He quirked up an eyebrow. "Don't you think about me?"

She met his gaze and gave him the truth. "I try not to. It makes me sad you're not here." Still, she thought about him all the time, which made her sad all the time because he wasn't here. But she didn't tell him that.

"Let's make the most of our time together right now."

That's all they'd done for months.

His lips closed over her breast. He licked and sucked her tight nipple, making her moan and arch up, offering his greedy mouth everything he wanted. His hands clamped around her thighs and pushed them wide. "You taste so good." He planted one hand next to her head as he leaned over her. "But right now I need to be inside you." He notched the head of his cock at her wet entrance, kissed her softly, and thrust into her to the hilt. "Fuck, you feel so good. Like you were made just for me."

She felt like he'd been made for her, too. But even his words didn't make her feel like he'd claimed her, because she already knew he wasn't staying. All they had was right now.

So she took full advantage, locking her legs around his waist, holding him close with her hands on his back, her nails digging in.

She soaked up every brush of his skin against hers, every breath they shared as they kissed, every stroke of his cock gliding in and out of her tight channel, every sigh and moan, every sultry, needy look they shared. And when the climax hit them both, and for a single moment time stopped as their bodies hit that perfect peak, she knew that nothing would ever be as good, or enough without him.

But that didn't mean she didn't deserve more than just these perfect moments they shared.

She loved them.

She loved *him*.

But she couldn't keep him.

And she couldn't keep hurting herself and denying what she really wanted.

Nick nuzzled her neck and kissed her softly behind her ear. "I've missed you."

She still had her legs wrapped around his waist and her arms over his shoulders. She hugged him hard. "I miss you, too." *Every second of the day.*

Nick rolled to his side and pulled her with him, so she ended up resting her head on his shoulder as he held her close to his side with one strong arm.

No condom cleanup needed. They'd talked about her having an IUD and them both being tested. Her after she found out her ex had cheated on her. Him at his last physical. They had total trust and faith in each other that they weren't seeing anyone else while they were seeing each other. Though sometimes she wondered if he did see other people when the silences between them grew so long. But knowing her history, he wouldn't do that to her. He'd promised after the first night they were together. He told her he saw too many people doing bad things in his job and he'd never hurt her like that when all he had to say was it was over to spare her that betrayal.

"Tell me," she prompted, demanding the details he'd put on pause.

He held her tighter. "Fox called Mason last night to tell him that someone kidnapped Melody. Most likely for a big ransom. Mason got the police involved and called me for backup, in case we were dealing with someone dangerous."

Which she translated to someone willing to kill Melody if they didn't get their money.

Fox owned his own software company and had opened two adult learning centers for people aging out of the foster care system who needed to learn a skill fast so they could get a decent job and support themselves. She knew he had money. But enough to make someone kidnap Melody for a ransom?

"Who kidnapped her?"

"You probably know Brian and Josh from the bar. Fox's mom used them, and a woman who worked with

Fox—Amy, a chef teaching at the center—to kidnap Melody."

"Oh God." This had all happened a couple of hours ago.

She leaned up on her elbow and stared down at him, one hundred percent believing her little sister would try to kick some ass if someone got out of line with her.

Nick brushed the hair away from her face and behind her ear. "Don't worry. We got to her in time. And Fox clocked Josh for touching Melody." He brushed his fingers through her hair again. "Melody was checked out by a doctor. Mason went home to be with Lyric and fill her in. I came here to see you before I head back to work. I wanted you to hear it from me."

"And you didn't want me to find out you were here helping Mason and didn't come to see me."

Nick rolled to his side and looked her in the eyes. "I couldn't wait to see you." His smile always warmed her heart. Like Mason, he didn't smile enough.

"How long can you stay?" The hope in her heart died a quick death when Nick checked his watch and frowned.

"My helicopter ride will be at the airport in an hour." Which meant he needed to leave soon because it was a forty-minute drive.

She fell back on the pillow and stared up at the ceiling. "I guess you better get going then."

Nick leaned over her. "Don't be like that." He nuzzled his nose against her cheek, trying to coax her back to happy so that when he left everything between them was good.

But it wasn't.

"Don't be like what, Nick? Disappointed? Sad? That's how I feel. You came running when Mason called. And I appreciate it because it was for my sister. I'm sure last night was scary as hell for her and everyone else trying to find her. But for me, you show up acting like you can't stand not to have me in your arms the second I open the door after you haven't called or texted in more than *two weeks*. You're not even trying anymore to pretend this isn't just sex. When you're back home in Montana, I'm out of sight, out of mind."

Nick stared down at her, his eyes filled with anger and what she hoped was regret to go with the heaping dose of frustration coming off him. "Is that what you think of me? That I'd treat my brother's wife's sister like some...booty call. Seriously?"

Brother's wife's sister? Not girlfriend. That said a lot.

"Why haven't you contacted me at all for the past two weeks? What the hell am I supposed to think when I get nothing but silence from you? When our whole...whatever this is we're doing, revolves around *you*. Your schedule. Your job. Your availability to see me."

Nick turned it right back on her. "Why haven't you contacted me to say you missed me? That you wanted me to come? That you were willing to drive up to see me?"

"Now we're playing games with each other?" She rolled out of bed, found her tank on the floor, and pulled it on.

Nick sat on the edge of the bed and stared over it at her. "I'm not playing games. I'm asking you why you stewed on this instead of simply calling me."

She pulled on her panties, crossed her arms under her breasts, and stared at the floor. "Because your silence spoke volumes. And I want more. I deserve more."

Nick dragged on his boxer briefs, then his jeans, and let out a frustrated breath. "You're right. You do. I was busy on a new case. One that is taking up a lot of my time.

And that's no excuse." He put on his socks and shoes. "I just…every time I wanted to reach out, it was late at night and I knew you were working at the bar. I kept telling myself, I'll call her tomorrow at lunch when she wakes up, but then…"

"You got busy and time got away from us."

"Yes."

She pulled on a pair of leggings. "I get that your job is important. Lives are on the line. And yeah, I'm just a bartender."

He stopped in the middle of putting on his shirt, his arms in both the sleeves in front of him, and turned to pin her in his gaze. "You're more than that," he growled.

"Fine. But the thing is, Nick, I have no idea what we are to each other. Whatever this is that we're doing, isn't enough. My sisters and brother have found their someone, who will never let them go. I want that, too. But all I am is lonely."

He pulled on his shirt and adjusted his belt and badge. "I know this isn't easy. But we have something good here."

"We have amazing chemistry. What we've shared has been more than I've ever had with anyone."

He held his arms out to his sides. "I feel the same way."

"But I want more."

His arms dropped.

She poured out everything she'd held inside too long. "I want everything. Marriage, the house, the kids, a dog, and the love of my life by my side. But you're so dedicated to your job, you think that's a life. And if you're happy with that, that's fine. But for me…I want more." *I want it with you.* She couldn't seem to bring herself to give him that last desperate piece of herself.

Nick's phone buzzed with a text. He checked it quickly and sighed. "That's the pilot. He's running early."

Meaning they were out of time. He had places to go, people to arrest, others to save. "How is your cousin, Hawk?"

"He's...the same. He spends too much time alone." Nick frowned at her. "So do I. That's why you and I..." He shook his head. "If I don't leave now, I'm going to be late. And I—"

"Have a meeting," she finished for him, because he always had a meeting to get to.

Her heart ached. She really wanted to know what all the missing words were in those half sentences. But she knew the drill. "You should try to get some sleep, too. You look tired."

"Aria." God, the way he said her name. With regret and longing and something more. A plea.

She wanted to give him everything.

But how could she when he was always walking out the door.

He took two steps toward her. So close, but not touching. "I wasn't expecting this when I came to see you." His gaze dropped to the tangled sheets on the bed.

"Yeah. I know. But it's been coming for a while." She looked up at him, wanting so desperately to wrap her arms around him and hold him here with her. "As much as I love our time together, I can't do this anymore." Her throat closed as she held back a sob. She wasn't going to fall to pieces. Not now. Not in front of him.

His shoulders slumped. "Don't say that. Not when I've got zero time and I'm walking out the door."

"That's an answer in and of itself. You've got a helicopter waiting for you, a meeting to get to, bad guys to arrest, people to save. I understand. I really do. But I just can't keep having sex with you, no matter how good it is, and holding myself back from finding what I really want."

He took her hand and squeezed it. "We have more than great sex."

"Do we? Because from where I'm standing, and from how you showed up today and we ended up in bed and now you're walking out the door, I can't see that we have anything else." Tears welled in her eyes. She tried to blink them away, but this broke her heart.

He winced when he saw her tears. "Can we please just hit pause and talk about this when I come back?"

Not exactly a set date or time coming out of his mouth.

"I don't see what's going to change, Nick."

He cupped her face, brushing away a tear with his thumb. "I care about you. You have to believe that."

"I do. That's not the issue."

His phone beeped again. "Fuck. I don't have time for this." He released her and ran his fingers through his hair in frustration.

"Exactly."

His gaze snapped to hers. "That's not what I meant. I want to stay and fix this."

"I know. But we can't deny the truth. And I'm not picking a fight with you. I'm not asking you for anything. I'm simply telling you, I can't do this anymore. It breaks my heart to watch you walk out the door again and again and nothing changes. I wish I could say I'll pack up my life here and move to be closer to you, but I can't do that.

Melody is leaving with Fox. Lyric and Layla are pregnant. It's going to be up to me to keep the bar open."

Nick put his hand over the back of his neck. "I know." He checked his watch again. "I don't want to leave like this."

"It's the same way we always say goodbye. I'll see you around, Nick. It just won't be like this anymore."

Nick hooked his hand at the back of her neck, leaned in, and pressed his forehead to hers. "We're not over. I can't accept that."

She didn't say anything.

Nick gave her a quick kiss and walked toward the door.

She followed him all the way and stood in the doorway as he made his way down the stairs and to his car, opened the door, then turned back to her and just stared at her leaning against the frame, tears rolling down her cheeks.

"We're not over," he declared again, then got in his car and drove off, leaving her alone and brokenhearted.

"Yes, we are," she told the wind, because he was long gone.

Chapter Two

Nick called his brother the second he drove away from Aria's place. Of course Mason picked up right away.

"What's up?"

"I fucked up. Big time. She dumped me."

Silence.

"Mason?"

"I heard you. I'm waiting to hear what you're going to do about it. She's the best thing that ever happened to you and I know you're not stupid enough to let her go, even if you have neglected her and the relationship."

Nick rolled his eyes, frustration eating at him. "Tell me how you really feel."

"I think you're an asshole for using work as an excuse. The same way I was an asshole for not going after Lyric the second I saw her and wanted her. So I say again. What are you going to do about it?"

"Fuck! I don't know." His job was his life.

She'd gotten that right.

But he loved being with Aria. She fit him. Understood him.

"The job is the job. But it's not everything. It's not the same as having someone in your life who sees you, knows you, loves you. It's nothing compared to really living."

Mason would know. He'd been undercover and alone for years until Lyric brought him back to life. Back into the family.

He was a new man because of her. A better man.

Nick wanted to be the man for Aria. "You think I should quit my job to be with her?"

"Is that the answer that feels right to you? Or, my brilliant brother, is there another solution? One you haven't considered. One that would mean you were fulfilled and allowed you to be with her. If that's even what you really want."

"Of course I want to be with her. She's fucking amazing."

"Yeah. These Wilde women are something."

Nick heard Lyric's muffled voice, then his brother's soft groan. He bet they were kissing. They were always kissing.

And Nick had that same chemistry with Aria.

He understood that she wanted more. She was the oldest, the one who looked out for all her siblings. And yeah, maybe it stung to see them all happily settling down and starting families. He sometimes got jealous when he watched Mason and Lyric together. He envied their connection, the easy way they were together, the lightness that came over his brother when Lyric was in the room with him. Mason smiled more now than he had in the last five years. It was because of her.

They were a family now.

Nick wanted that, too. He just let other things get in the way.

While his job was based in Montana, that didn't mean he couldn't figure something out. Mason did when he quit undercover work and started training other agents and overseeing cases.

"I can't lose her."

"Then don't. And for what it's worth, I don't think she wants to lose you either."

"She wants more, and I get that because it's what I want, too. I just thought I had more time to figure this out." Which was why he had put it off, thinking he and Aria would eventually make plans. Instead he focused on work and lost track of how many months he'd delayed making plans with her. Or even letting her know he wanted to make plans with her.

Nick rubbed his hand against his chest. "I can't believe she ended things."

Mason sighed. "Bro, I know you haven't gotten any sleep, so you're not thinking clearly. But you need to get your head in the game. Start with figuring out how to spend more time here with her. If this is really a forever thing, you've got to make her believe in that and you before you pop the question. And, hey, if we both end up having kids, they'll grow up with each other and be as close as us."

The picture Mason painted was everything he wanted. He loved all the Wildes. They always made him feel like he belonged. With all the shit he saw on the job, he'd love to come home to his gorgeous wife and kids and have the kind of normal Mason found with Lyric.

He didn't want work to be his whole life, even if that's how he'd been living for the past decade. He'd worked hard to achieve his goals in the FBI. He was proud of his accomplishments and record.

He turned into the airport and spotted the helicopter waiting for him. "I have to go. Thanks for the ear and advice."

Mason chuckled. "Yeah, no problem. Just fix this fast before my wife sends me after your ass for hurting her sister."

"That's the last thing I want to do. Tell Lyric I'm sorry I didn't get to see her. And kiss her."

Mason growled.

It was something their cousin Hawk had started with his brothers and Nick had joined in just to rile Mason. Every time they saw Lyric, they kissed her on the forehead. It drove Mason nuts. He was so possessive, but he took it all in stride because he loved them. He knew they loved her for loving Mason.

And Lyric was a good sport. Especially because she'd declared herself Hawk's best friend. She spoke to him more than any of them and they appreciated her tenacity with their ex-military, gruff, intense, broody cousin.

Oh, Hawk had every reason to be the way he was, but nothing they said or did seemed to help. More often than not, he simply didn't show up; instead he'd hide away in his house. Alone. Lost in the horrific memories of the past and the crash that left him scarred, body and soul.

Fuck. He was thinking about Hawk just so he didn't have to think about the shit-show he'd turned his own life into with Aria.

He loved her.

He wanted her back.

And he better figure out a way to do that before he lost her forever.

Chapter Three

Javier Lopez stood just outside the private plane that would take him to Idaho to deliver his product. The kids better keep quiet. The last thing he needed was a bunch of sniveling brats giving him a headache.

Or alerting anyone that they weren't a bunch of kids from a group home, traveling for a class trip as he'd told airport staff when they arrived.

He was just about to board the plane when he spotted the man rushing toward a waiting helicopter. He was a good distance away, but Javier would know that asshole anywhere. A shot of adrenaline and rage swept through Javier at just the sight of the man who'd betrayed him.

The fucking bastard had pretended to be his friend, his right-hand man, then stabbed him in the back. Javier had narrowly escaped getting arrested and locked up for the rest of his life. He'd had to go underground for some time and rebuild his business in the shadows after that fucking FBI agent got one over on him.

The bastard.

He wanted to take him down right now, but there were too many witnesses.

Javier had been searching for him since the day he discovered the asshole's treachery. No one got away with double-crossing him.

Nick would pay.

But Javier couldn't do anything now. Not with a plane full of kids he was auctioning off tomorrow.

Fuck.

The helicopter took off. Javier braced himself as the wash from the rotors blew over him.

One of the airport workers must have seen the fury on his face and rushed over. "Everything okay?"

Javier shook his head. "My friend Nick just boarded that helicopter. I just missed him. Any idea where he's headed?"

The guy grinned. "Agent Gunn is in and out of here a couple times a month.

Which meant he had a reason to be here. Family maybe?

"He's headed back home to Montana. They'll be landing in Bozeman soon." The helpful airport worker kept smiling.

Satisfaction soothed Javier's fury down to a simmer. "Thank you." Javier ducked into the small plane and nodded to his pilot, his mind filled with retribution. "Let's go." He had to drop the kids in Idaho with his people, then he needed to get to Montana to kill Nick Gunn.

Fucking undercover agent.

He was going to pay with his life for crossing Javier six years ago.

CHAPTER FOUR

Aria walked into Melody's hospital room with a bouquet of pink and white alstroemeria lilies late in the afternoon. She hoped they cheered up her sister, who looked tired, sitting in the bed, Fox in a chair beside her, their hands clasped together. Lyric and Mason stood on the other side of the bed. Lyric had brought homemade double chocolate cookies. Melody's favorite. Which meant that while Mason was out helping to find and rescue Melody, she'd been home stress-baking.

"You should have called me," Aria scolded Lyric, then pinned Mason in her death glare. "Not cool."

"Yeah, we already heard it from Mom, Dad, and Jax." Lyric at least looked contrite. "We didn't want to worry everyone when Fox had a fairly good idea who took Melody."

Aria walked over to Fox and gave him a quick hug. "Thank you for getting her back."

"I'm really fine," Melody said as Aria set the flowers on the table beside the bed, then squeezed her sister's arm.

Aria looked back to Mason. "Thank you, for what you did to help."

He nodded, then studied her for a second. "You okay?"

Of course he knew about her and Nick. They were close and didn't keep anything from each other.

She didn't know how she felt. But he could probably see her bloodshot eyes from crying. "I should have thanked him before he left. Would you please tell him I appreciate his help?"

"He'd rather hear you say it."

"Yeah, well, then he should have answered my text two weeks ago."

Mason winced at her words and angry tone.

She sucked in a breath, shaking her head at Lyric's unspoken, *Do you want to talk about it* look.

She dropped her shoulders and sighed. "I'm sorry. I'm a little raw." She turned to Melody. "But I'm here for you. Whatever you need."

"I said I'm fine." The tone said otherwise and so did the concerned look Fox gave Melody, though she didn't acknowledge that either. "What's up with you and Nick?" Melody obviously wanted the spotlight off her.

"I ended things."

Lyric obviously knew, since she and Mason shared a concerned look.

Melody clasped her hand. "I'm sorry to hear that. You two seemed so happy together."

"Yeah. When we were together. And that was the problem. We spent way more time apart. The long-distance thing was never going to work. He loves his job. I love my life here. So...that's it."

Mason looked like he wanted to say something, but Lyric squeezed his arm to keep him from speaking up.

Aria nodded for Mason to go ahead and speak his mind.

"All I'll say is that he's wrecked that you ended it. And he wants to make it right. Just…give him a chance to make it right."

She held his earnest gaze for a long moment, wanting so badly to believe Nick would change his whole life for her. "I didn't ask him for anything. I want him to be happy."

"He is. With you. You're the best thing in his life. He knows that. We all know that."

Her eyes welled with tears. "There's barely any room in his life for me and I was drowning in loneliness. I can't do it anymore."

Lyric hugged Mason the second she saw the pained look on his face. He'd been where Nick was now. His whole life about the job. Until he met Lyric and everything changed. He changed his life to be with her.

Lyric's gaze turned to her. "You deserve to be with someone who puts you first."

She appreciated her sister's support, but right now, she didn't want to talk about Nick. It hurt too much.

To shift things away from her and Nick, she turned to Fox. "I bet you haven't left Melody's side. What can I get you from the cafeteria? Coffee? A sandwich?"

"I'm fine," he said as Melody said, "He needs coffee and something to eat," at the same time.

Aria backed toward the door. "I'm on it." She turned to Mason and Lyric. "Can I get both of you something?"

"We're heading out in a few minutes. I need to start cooking at the bar. Mason has a call he needs to be on later."

Aria nodded. "If I'm not back before you leave, I'll see you at the bar. Mason, good to see you."

"You, too. And things are going to work out. I know it, because I know my brother. He's not going to give up."

Then he shouldn't have walked away this morning. He should have stayed and told me how he really feels and what he really wants instead of leaving for work like that mattered more than me.

Lives are on the line.

Yeah. Her head got it, but her heart wanted her to come first.

Chapter Five

Nick rounded the block one more time, driving in circles as he looked for a spot to park on the busy street. He'd called in an order for lunch to take back to the office for himself and several colleagues. He spotted the black Charger coming around behind him again. He wasn't the only one looking for someone to give up their parking space.

A silver Toyota pulled out in front of a hair salon and Nick quickly parallel parked, barely glancing at the Charger as it passed.

Sorry, buddy. This one is mine.

Nick climbed out of his car and headed around to the front to walk up the block to the Italian place he ordered from at least once a week. But before he hit the sidewalk, he spotted the florist and stopped short, thinking of Aria and sending her flowers to say he was sorry how they left things and that he wanted a second chance.

The crack of gunfire split the air and the windshield of his car burst into a spiderweb of shattered glass. Nick spun around, crouching low and pulling his gun at the same time, his heart pounding with adrenaline. The Charger had stopped in the street. A man stood next to the open driver's side door. Their eyes locked for one brief second and recognition dawned in his mind.

Javier Lopez.

The scumbag dove back into the car and sped away before Nick could get off a clean shot, wheels peeling out on the pavement.

The people on the sidewalk had stopped and stared, unsure what really happened in those few split seconds.

That's all the time Nick needed to know who had taken a shot at him.

That was too damn close for comfort.

Relief joined the rush of adrenaline coursing through his system.

If he hadn't stopped midstride...

Fear hit him all at once, along with the realization he could have been killed.

He didn't want to think about just how close he'd come.

He couldn't believe the past had caught up to him like this.

The last time he had seen Javier, he was standing over an FBI agent he'd just executed during a raid. Nick was undercover and the second he'd rushed forward to help the dying agent, Javier knew Nick had betrayed him and was an undercover agent. Javier had shot at him, betrayal written in his eyes. Nick managed to scramble out of the way of the bullet, giving Javier just enough time to slip through the agents swarming the warehouse and get away.

Nick swore that one day he'd put Javier behind bars for his heinous crimes and for killing his fellow agent.

How did Javier find me? Why now?

Nick didn't know. But he needed to report the shooting and start looking for Javier Lopez. If he was in Montana, more than likely he was back in business, and Nick needed to stop him before he hurt or killed anyone else.

Nick walked up onto the curb and behind a pillar to give himself cover in case Javier came back to take another shot at him. He called his boss, giving what little information he knew to his superior, including the partial plate number he'd managed to glimpse before the car sped away.

Then he waited, contemplating how close he'd come to dying while on a lunch run for the office. It showed how dangerous his job really was and that someone could come after him at any time, any day. He was getting too old to be chasing bad guys through the streets. That's why he'd gotten out of undercover work and oversaw the guys out in the field. It still left him traveling a lot and missing out on family time here at home.

He thought about being able to see Aria every day, lying beside her every night. He wanted to see her right now, to hold her in his arms and tell her about his shit day and how fucked up it was to be shot at on the street and how if he'd died he'd have regretted every second he spent away from her.

Fucking near-death experience gave him a whole new perspective.

He needed to make some drastic changes in his life. Now. Before it was too late.

The cavalry showed up and he tried to focus on the job and not his desperate desire to call Aria. As much as he wanted to hear her voice, she probably wouldn't take his call and that would sting even more.

It took some time to give his statement and for the forensic team to do their thing. They found little evidence, besides the bullet recovered from the passenger side headrest in his car.

Once he was done with everything at the scene, he called his cousin Hawk to come pick him up. The bureau would assign him another car tomorrow. He just wanted to go home to Aria.

If only he could.

While he waited for Hawk, he picked up the food he'd ordered, then pulled out his phone, found a florist in Blackrock Falls, Wyoming, and called in an order to surprise Aria and let her know he was thinking about her.

"And what should the card say, Mr. Gunn?"

"You saved my life today. We're not over. XO Nick."

"Yes, sir. We'll have that delivered in the next two hours. Anything else I can do for you?"

"No, thank you." Now all he had to do was wait and see if the flowers made her want to talk to him again, because he desperately needed her. But first, maybe he needed to think about exactly what he wanted to say. More importantly, what he wanted to do and how he would make it happen.

Chapter Six

Aria was setting up the bar for the night when Patsy from Patsy's Petals walked in carrying a huge bouquet of flowers in a gorgeous cobalt-blue vase.

"Someone found a keeper." Patsy set the bouquet on the bar. "Sorry, sweetie, I didn't know your favorite flowers, so I gave you the best of what I had on hand."

The pink roses, white carnations and mums, sprigs of pink stock, and red gerbera daisies mixed with greenery were lush and smelled amazing as she sank her face into the blooms and inhaled.

Patsy gave her a sly smile. "So, tell me about him."

She'd known Patsy forever. When she was a kid and her mom took her into town, she loved to stop by Patsy's shop and just smell all the flowers. "Who are they from?" Her heart wanted them to be from Nick, but her head told her that she had a date tonight with a guy who'd asked her out practically once a week for the last six months. She'd always told Mark she was seeing someone, but last night when he asked for a date, she'd finally said yes. Because she deserved to go out on a date and have some fun. If she was going to have that something good in her life, she needed to get out there and find the man she was looking for.

You already found him. He's just not that into you.

Was that it? Nick just enjoyed the amazing chemistry they shared and didn't want more?

He doesn't have time for you, or more.

Ugh! She'd been thinking these thoughts since he left the other day.

"You don't know who they're from." Patsy rubbed her hands together. "Now things are getting interesting."

Aria waved her off. "Stop. It's just...I ended something recently with someone who didn't want things to be over and I'm maybe starting something tonight with someone new."

"Well, color me impressed. Don't settle for anything less than what you deserve. And you deserve the best, sweetie."

Aria pulled the card from the bouquet and read the note.

You saved my life today. We're not over. XO Nick.

Patsy's knowing grin widened. "I don't know about you, but I like a guy who knows what he wants and goes after it." She shrugged. "But that's me."

Aria was still stuck on what the note said.

She desperately needed to know if he was all right. In his line of work, anything could have happened to him. She pulled out her phone and called him.

Nick picked up on the third ring. "Hey, sweetheart, I was just walking in the door."

She spoke over him. "Are you okay? Why are you home so early? Did you get hurt?"

"Hey now, slow down. I'm okay. Just had a close call today."

Her heart pounded even harder. "What are you talking about? What happened?"

He didn't often talk about his work. Most of it he had to keep secret because he had men undercover. "I just wanted you to know I'm thinking about you. About us."

"Nick." She put enough warning in her tone for him to get that she wanted a real explanation.

He huffed out a breath. "I was out picking up lunch. I saw a car following me, but thought it was just someone looking for a parking spot on the busy street, just like me. I got out of my car to walk to the restaurant and I stopped short when I spotted a florist and thought I've never sent you flowers and I should. I should do a lot of things for you."

"Nick." She said his name for a whole other reason and this time her tone conveyed how much he was in her heart.

"In that split second that I stopped, someone took a shot at me, barely missing me."

She gasped. "What? Why? Are you okay?"

He chuckled. "I'm talking to you, which means I'm better than okay."

"Who tried to kill you?" She couldn't believe that sentence came out of her mouth. Or that Nick had probably faced that deadly situation more than once on the job. Especially when he'd worked undercover.

"A man I tried to take down a couple of years ago when I was working undercover."

"Are they going to put you in protective custody?"

"No. I'm a trained agent. I'll be fine."

She wasn't so sure about that. "Someone needs to watch your back."

"I love it that you still care."

"Of course I do."

"Then don't end this. Us. We can figure this out." Desperation infused his plea.

She didn't see how anything would change when he was so tied up in his job. "Nick... I have a date tonight."

"What? No." A deep rumble of a growl came from deep in his throat.

"I love the flowers. Thank you for thinking of me and sending them. And I'm more than glad you're okay. I don't know what I'd do if something happened to you."

"If that's how you feel, then don't go out with whoever you're seeing tonight. Give me a chance to make things right."

Her heart wanted to give in but her head won out. "It's better this way, for both of us."

"It's not better for me, sitting here, thinking about you out with someone else. You know you want it to be me. I want to be the only one you're with."

"And when would that be? Tomorrow? A week from now? Two weeks? A month? When will you have time to work me into your busy life?"

"Does it count at all that I want to be there with you right now? I know things have to change for us to make this work. I need some time to figure it out."

"You've had more than six months to figure it out. I want someone in my life who is going to be there making memories with me, building a life with me."

"I don't want to lose you. Don't go on the date."

"I'm going, Nick. I can't keep waiting for you."

He did that growly thing again. "You're going to be looking at him and knowing that I'm the one you want. I'm the one who makes you crave to be touched, because you know how I make you feel. I know how you like my lips and tongue on your skin, my cock buried deep inside you, filling you up, pounding into you until you forget everything but my name falling from your lips. You know I'm the one who loves to spend hours making you come, making you feel good, letting you know how much I love hearing you fall apart beneath my hands."

A flush of desire raced through her as her heart longed for him. "Nick."

"That's right. Me. The one who always reminds you why we're so good together. And we could be so much more if you just give us a chance."

She didn't know what to say. "I have to go." Because if he kept talking like this, she'd give in and find herself six months down the road still waiting on him to find the time to be with her and still deciding what he wanted.

Her heart clenched with the thought of even doing it. But she disconnected the call, then folded her arms on the bar, and laid her head on them, tears gathering in her eyes.

A warm hand landed on her shoulder and squeezed. "Those are some beautiful flowers." Lyric's soft voice coaxed her to say something.

"*He* sent them."

"Nice. So why are you upset?"

Aria raised her head and let her sister see her tear-filled eyes. "Because he wants me. And I want him. And that doesn't seem to change anything between us. How can we be so drawn together and yet always feel so far apart?"

"Long-distance relationships are hard."

"Exactly, and that's not going to change. We want different things. That's why I'm going on a date tonight."

Lyric gaped at her. "You're serious about moving on."

It wasn't really that. "I love my life. I love working here with you and everyone else. I'm happy just being me. But being with Nick...it made me see that I could be even happier with someone I love in my life. The days that he was here, or I spent with him in Montana, those were some of the happiest days of my life. I want that all the time. I'm going to prioritize finding a partner who wants what I want and is ready to commit."

"Okay, then. Who is the lucky guy taking you out tonight?"

Aria's eyes glassed over at her sister's support. "Thank you for understanding."

"I'm your sister. I always have your back." Lyric clasped her hands together at her chest and her smile brightened. "You should wear that powder-blue dress that hugs your curves. You kill in that dress."

It was Nick's favorite. "That one is more a things-are-going-somewhere dress. I thought I'd wear the emerald-green one."

"That one makes your blue eyes stand out. Perfect. He won't know what hit him." Lyric caught herself. "Who are we talking about again?"

Aria's cheeks heated. "Mark Davis."

Lyric pressed her bottom lip against her top one. "Is he the guy who comes in here wearing a suit talking about investments?"

Aria nodded, a smile breaking out on her face. "He owns his own financial planning business. He's successful and looking to settle down."

Lyric still didn't seem excited for her.

"What is it?"

"Nothing. He's a nice guy. Says please and thank you. He's never rude. Doesn't give women lewd looks."

What Aria heard between those words was *boring*. "He is nice. And I'd like to get to know him better."

"Okay. But I'm just saying, Nick is...intense with an edge of dangerous. He's going to have to look at you the way Nick looks at you."

"How does Nick look at me?" She already knew. Like he wanted to strip her bare and worship her all night long.

Damn the man for reminding her that no one else compared.

Lyric echoed her thoughts. "Nick looks at you like you're everything he ever wanted and more."

"Well, maybe we don't all get our Mason." Like Jax found Layla. Like Melody reunited with Fox.

Maybe Nick just wasn't meant to be hers.

He was already married to his job and seemingly happy with his life just the way it was.

Maybe she needed to find a different kind of happy with someone else.

CHAPTER SEVEN

Aria met Mark downtown at the new American bistro that had opened a few months back. Melody and Fox had eaten there once and raved about the food. She parked her car, then walked a block to the restaurant and spotted Mark waiting for her outside.

He smiled the moment he saw her. He looked good in slacks and a white button-up shirt, the sleeves rolled up. He didn't have thick corded muscles in his arms like Nick. In fact he was a couple inches shorter than him, too.

Stop it, Aria.

His brown eyes swept up her, from her strappy black heels, up her bare legs, over her fit-and-flare dress, to her face. "You look fantastic." He leaned in and kissed her cheek.

Nick would have taken her in his arms and kissed her until she was panting and her panties were wet.

Not. Nick. Mark!

He took her hand and gently tugged her toward the door. "Shall we?"

She walked with him inside to the hostess stand, where Mark gave his name. The young woman led them to their table by a window and left them with their menus.

Mark's eyes sparkled. "I've been excited about this since you said yes."

"Me, too." She picked up her menu. "My sister loves this place. I've been too busy to try it."

Mark put his hand over hers on the table. "Well, I'm glad you took the time tonight. I had thought I'd never get the chance to take you out."

Aria had hoped Nick would be the last guy she dated.

"Hi, I'm Heather. I'll be taking care of you tonight. Can I get you something to drink?"

"Ladies first," Mark insisted, looking at her.

"I'll have a glass of the Moscato." She nodded for Mark to go ahead.

"The Moscow mule, please."

"Excellent. Are you ready to order, or do you need more time?"

Mark deferred to her.

"I'll have the chicken and dumplings." Comfort food sounded amazing right now.

Mark gave her an approving look. "I considered that myself, but finally decided on the meatloaf."

"Both good choices," Heather declared. "I'll be back with your drinks shortly."

Aria handed her menu to the waitress, then focused on Mark and getting to know him. "What do you like to do besides work?"

"I play online adventure games."

"Really. That sounds fun." She'd never played any kind of video game, but she always wondered what the hype was all about.

He looked a bit sheepish. "I love it. It's fun and challenging. Makes you think and strategize. We should play sometime." His goofy grin made her want to try.

"I'd like to, but I work most nights."

"I'm sure we can find a day to play."

Was she really throwing up obstacles already?

"What else?" she asked.

He grinned, like he really liked the next thing he was going to say. "I've recently started crockpot cooking. I love that you can dump a bunch of stuff in the pot in the morning and come home to a home-cooked meal. I make a really great pot roast."

"My mother loves her crockpot, too. In fact, she makes chicken and dumplings in hers a few times every winter."

"You'll have to get me her recipe. I could make it for you." That was two more dates he was hoping to have with her. Or maybe one if they did dinner and an online game.

Heather arrived with their drinks, then left to check on their order.

Mark held up his glass. "To finally saying yes and taking the time."

"I'll drink to that." Because that's what this was: her first step toward getting what she wanted. Not that Mark was *the guy*. But he could be. "I wish I could say I have a hobby, but I mostly like to spend my downtime watching TV and relaxing. I'm on my feet all the time, so sitting down and binge-watching a series or documentary gives me a chance to recharge. When I'm not at the bar, I spend a couple of days at my family ranch helping out. I love it out there, riding the horses and being outside, doing chores and feeling like I got something done. It's a good workout too."

Mark leaned back in his chair, completely relaxed and focused on her. "I run with a couple of buddies three days a week. And once a month I attend our family dinner, where my sister's six- and nine-year-old boys run me ragged, playing tag outside."

"Sounds fun." She smiled, enjoying herself and his company. She broached the next question cautiously. "So you like kids."

"I like handing those two rug rats back to my sister all wound up." His mischievous smile said he taunted his sibling the way all of hers did to each other, too.

Still, not exactly the answer she was hoping for.

Mark seemed to sense her unease. "Don't get me wrong, I love my nephews. They're great kids. I'm getting to the point where settling down makes sense. With the right woman. But I'd want to spend some time together, to be sure the foundation of the relationship is rock solid before adding kids to the mix."

Aria sighed in relief. "That makes sense."

He eyed her. "You just got out of something, I take it from the way you turned me down for months and have now changed your mind."

"I was involved with someone, yes. He lives in Montana and has a very demanding job."

Mark sipped his drink. "Long distance never works. They're living their life, you yours, and how can either of you know what's going on with the other when you're so far apart?"

"It was very difficult."

"Do you miss him?" Mark dropped that bomb just as Heather arrived with dinner.

Aria waited for her to leave them again and hoped Mark let it go, because the answer was simple. Yes. She missed Nick like she'd miss a limb. She wished he was sitting across from her.

Actually, if he were here, he'd have sat next to her, not wanting to be any farther away than right beside her.

"So. You miss him." Mark seemed to read whatever she'd let show on her face. "That's okay. Feelings don't just shut off right away, even when you know you want to move on. It's my job to make you forget about him."

She didn't think anyone could make her forget her sexy FBI agent. "We had different priorities."

"You are definitely one of mine."

She blushed. "Well, that's...nice."

But it wasn't like Nick didn't focus on her at all. When they were together, he spent every second making sure she knew he wanted and needed her. He made sure she felt every moment he was away by making sure she felt every minute they were together, too. That's why it felt so special. He cared. He really wanted to be with her, whether they were in bed or watching TV or eating together. It was so easy to be with him.

"How's the chicken and dumplings?"

She picked up her fork and took a bite, loving the thick gravy and tender chicken. "So good. How is yours?"

"Excellent."

They spent the next twenty minutes eating and talking about their families and his collection of shot glasses from all the places he'd visited, either for work or vacation. Which led them to talking about the places they'd been outside of Wyoming. She'd mostly stuck close to home. He thought it would be fun to take two weeks every summer for the rest of his life to go and explore someplace new.

"That sounds amazing. And what a great way to make memories as well as explore new things. Where do you want to go next?" Aria would love two weeks on a beach. Tropical drinks. Sun. Fun. Sex with the sound of the ocean right outside, the stars overhead. Her and Nick, tangled up in the sheets.

Wait. Shit. She was doing it again. Thinking about him.

"I was thinking ice fishing in Alaska for my next trip." He chuckled. "Not in summer, of course, but over winter."

That sounded cold and boring with the potential for polar bears. No thanks.

"I've got a bunch of brochures I'd love to show you. We could cuddle in a little shack and drink hot chocolate."

"You'd be more likely to find me back in the lodge by a roaring fire with a really good whiskey in my hand."

He smirked. "Seriously? Alaska doesn't sound amazing to you."

"Maybe in the summer when you can explore the beautiful landscape. But winter…" She shook her head. "Not really my thing. I get enough of the cold here."

"My buddies and I put down a deposit for this winter." He left it at that.

"I'm going to Boston soon. My sister is moving there. I can't wait to explore the city." Maybe she'd get on her app and find a date while she was there. Different town. Different sort of men. Maybe she'd find someone interesting.

And who still doesn't live near you!

Damn. Well, maybe it would be good practice. And a way to learn about someplace she'd never been.

Or you could ask Nick to take time off and go with you. His brother will be there with Lyric. It could be fun.

"Aria?"

She recognized the voice a split second before her gaze landed on him. *Damn it.*

Dan had lost a bit of weight, and his hair was a little longer. His gaze filled with awe as he stared down at her. "You look amazing. How are you?"

"Fine. You?" She wished he'd walked by without saying a thing.

"Uh, who's this?" Mark asked, his gaze bouncing between her and Dan.

"My ex." She left it at that, hoping Dan left her alone.

Dan didn't take his eyes off her. "I miss you. I didn't know how good I had it until you were gone."

Nope. She couldn't let him get away with saying that to her after what he'd done. "You lied and cheated and thought you could steal from me so you and that bitch who tried to ruin my cousin's life could run off together." But Dan didn't get a chance to screw her over, because she'd publicly humiliated him and his little home-wrecker in the bar, exposing both of their deceit, and kicked them both out.

His smile reversed into a deep frown. "When I saw you, I'd hoped you'd forgiven the past."

She eyed him. "It's not like I ever got an apology."

He leaned in close. "I'm sorry."

She shrugged. "I don't care. In fact, I've thought very little of you since I last saw you. I was too busy moving on with someone with integrity, who treated me like I was the best damn thing that ever happened to him."

Dan looked at Mark. "Lucky guy."

Crap! She'd done it again. Would she ever stop thinking about Nick?

"Goodbye, Dan."

Dan accepted her dismissal, left their table, and sat across the restaurant with a pretty brunette, who looked a few years younger than herself.

For a split second she thought about going over there and warning the woman that Dan was a treacherous asshole, but refrained because she had a captive audience of one in front of her.

Mark raised a brow. "Tell me how you really feel about your ex again."

"Sorry. He's the ex before the ex. Dan just pushes all my buttons."

"I can see that. And I get it. Cheating is the worst kind of betrayal."

"I agree." And it made Mark a little more attractive that he felt that way and put it out there so blatantly.

"But you didn't answer me."

"Mark..." She didn't know what to say. "You're here and he's not."

"Enough said. I hope I get to keep it that way."

Heather arrived at their table again. "Dessert?"

Mark raised a brow.

"Dinner was delicious. I'm kind of full."

"Want to split something?" Mark asked. "How about that double delight chocolate cake?"

"You're tempting me with chocolate. Not fair."

Mark grinned up at Heather. "One for the table, one for the lady to take home, too." He held her gaze. "So you'll have something sweet that will remind you of me tomorrow."

Well, damn, Mark had some game after all.

Nick was still awake looking at property listings in Blackrock Falls when he gave in to his curiosity and protective streak. He looked at the clock. 10:23 p.m.

She should be home. He hoped she was home alone and texted Aria.

NICK: I need to know you made it home okay and you're safe.

ARIA: Home and safe watching Schitt's Creek.

She loved that show and watched it whenever she wanted to relax.

ARIA: Would you rather ice fishing in Alaska or a tropical island beach?

Easy.

NICK: I'll take you in a bikini any day of the week, even in winter, with some part of me inside you.

NICK: I'd be just as happy to be in the same room with you just so I can look at you and feel the peace that comes over me when you're close.

ARIA: Why do you have to be so charming...UGH!

NICK: I take it you're home early because you were thinking about me the whole time you were on your date.

ARIA: You think you're so smart.

He knew he was right and he loved it.

NICK: You're all I think about too.

Until he'd read her texts, he'd been in a constant state of rage that some other guy was out with her, possibly touching her. He wanted to be the only one allowed to do that. He wanted to make her smile. He wanted to buy her dinner. He wanted to kiss her goodnight—right after he fucked her so good she screamed his name. More than once.

He adjusted his hard length in his boxer briefs and stared at the house listing on his screen that he thought would be perfect for them.

Did he bite the bullet and buy it?

Fuck, he wanted to right now. Especially since she'd texted him back after coming home alone after her date.

NICK: Nothing else to say? Then I'll just say good-night, sweetheart. Dream of me.

ARIA: You're infuriating.

A long ten seconds later, she texted again.

ARIA: I hate that I miss you so much.

NICK: I hate that you have to miss me, but I love it that you do, because I miss you. And I wish you were here. Or I was there.

He didn't get an answer and he finally understood why. Because if he wanted to be with her, he knew where she was and he should get in his fucking car and go be with her.

Saying it wasn't enough.

She wanted more. He wanted more.

He needed to show her he wanted a life with her.

Chapter Eight

It didn't take long for Nick to track down information on Javier Lopez and his recent illegal activity. After the raid that went wrong and Javier got away, Javier stayed under the radar for quite some time. Now it seemed he felt comfortable sticking his head out and doing business as usual.

And today could be the day he finally got what he needed to take Javier down for good.

"ASAC Gunn, this is Agent Hayward from Utah. I'm calling about the voicemail you left me about the case you worked on six years ago, involving Javier Lopez."

"Please tell me you have him in custody."

"Not yet. I've been picking up whispers over the past year. Sightings. Talk about parties he's throwing with very young party favors for very discreet and wealthy guests, who have particular tastes."

Yeah, Nick knew all about Javier's penchant for supplying underage girls and boys to the highest bidder and setting up dates in motel rooms. That's where he'd last seen Javier, at an upscale hotel where shit went bad. At least they saved six young girls, all of them between twelve and fourteen. It had been a virgin auction.

Just the thought of it made his stomach roll.

"Word is you had some contact with the sister." Hope sounded in Hayward's voice.

"Yeah. She wasn't a lot of help. They hadn't seen each other in a long time, according to her." But Nick had stayed in touch with her for weeks leading up to the attempt to arrest Javier.

"She's worked her way up in the world and is now managing the cleaning staff at a private ski, golf, mountain biking resort. When I say private, I mean exclusive. Gates with guards. A private airstrip. All the best amenities. They cater to celebrities, the overly wealthy, those with household name recognition, heads of businesses, and tech moguls. You know, the elite who think they're untouchable."

Sounded like a nice place for the rich to play. But he had a bad feeling about what else the resort could be offering to their very particular members.

"Julia Lopez was never tied to her brother's business." From what Nick remembered, she despised her brother.

"I'm not saying she is now. But it's really interesting that she's got access to a resort that isn't open to the public. Especially since we've raided two other members-only clubs here in Utah that we think have connections to Javier Lopez. Rumor is the Montana resort is on his circuit, too."

That was the thing with traffickers, they moved their product around. City to city. State to state in a circuit. Local police or even FBI would hear about something popping up, then they'd be gone before they could be raided.

Agent Hayward continued. "You've got a connection to her. You could ask some questions, feel her out. Check out this place. If they are working out of the private resort, it's the perfect setup. We could try to get someone inside. Someone close to her."

Nick shook his head, even though Agent Hayward couldn't see him. "It could take months for an undercover to get her to open up and reveal something. If she's anything like she used to be—afraid of her brother, suspicious of anyone asking about him—she'll be too guarded to let anything slip, let alone be willing to talk to someone about him. She made it clear she wanted nothing to do with him or his business. But let me feel her out. Maybe something has changed."

Agent Hayward let out a relieved sigh. "I was hoping you'd say that."

"I want Lopez in a cell for the rest of his life."

"You and me both. I also want to find out where he's keeping the kids, how many he has, and where. We know he's operating several groups, more than the two we've busted here in Utah. My guess is he's working Idaho and Montana right now, staying out of Utah until things cool down. I want him. This fucker deserves everything that's coming to him."

A cell would be too nice a punishment for someone like Javier Lopez. "I want to finally take him down. Send me whatever you have on him, including his sister's updated information. I'll look it over, then let you know when I can make contact." He rattled off his email address, then hung up.

And like he'd done every day since he left Aria's place, he pulled out his phone and called her.

Of course, she didn't answer. She never answered anymore, probably because the last time he communicated he'd ruined her date by simply reminding her how good they were together and no one else would make her feel the way he made her feel. Arrogant. Yes. But true. And he wasn't giving up.

"Hey, sweetheart, it's me. I miss the sound of your voice. I miss hearing about your day. I miss you so damn much. At this point, I'd settle for another text. Until then, I'm working on being closer to you. I have a meeting with my boss to talk about options. I'm not giving up on us. Have a good night at the bar, sweetheart." *I love you.* He never said it to her in his last four messages, because he'd never said it to her face. If you were going to say that to someone for the first time, it should be in person, while you looked them in the eyes. And he wanted the chance to make this right, to give her everything she wanted and deserved. Soon. He couldn't wait, because his impatience was growing and so was the number of days he'd been without her. Again.

One day, they'd spend more days together than apart. He couldn't wait for that day to finally come.

He clicked the meeting link on his laptop and waited for his boss to answer on the other end while he scrolled through pictures of Aria and him on his phone. He found a selfie of them and sent her a text.

NICK: By our third date I knew the distance thing was going to be a huge problem because all I wanted to do was be with you. I still feel that way.

NICK: Communicating more with you was step 1. Next up, moving closer to you.

He sent the picture of her sitting next to him in a restaurant. Just as he took the photo, she'd turned her face into his and kissed his cheek. He loved the picture. It was one of his favorites. That night, he'd taken her to bed and worshipped her for hours, because he couldn't get enough of her. Like every time they were together, he knew time was short and he needed to pack in as much as he could in the hours they had together.

The extended stays he had with her when she came to him, or he went to her, were filled with them just staying in, talking, eating, pretending they were binge-watching something when they spent the majority of their time making out on the couch. They'd make love late into the night. First thing in the morning when he got to wake up to her amazing blue eyes, gazing back at him, he'd kiss her like he'd never get the chance again and he'd dread them being apart again.

"Nick," his boss said by way of greeting. "Looks like you're deep into thinking about something."

More like someone. Her. "It's the reason I asked for the meeting."

His boss fell back deeper into his chair. "You're finally going to do it."

Nick raised a brow. "Do what?"

"Ask me for a transfer, so you can be closer to your brother." He said it like he'd been expecting it for a long time.

"Yes." But not just because of him, though he wasn't going to say that to his boss. It was one thing to want to be closer to his family, another to ask his boss to move him so he could be closer to his girlfriend. One who broke up with him six miserable days ago. "I want to know what options are available to me."

"I don't want to lose you, that's for damn sure. You're too valuable an asset."

Nick appreciated that. "I miss my brother. He and his wife are expecting. I want to be a part of their family in a real and present way." In more ways than one. "We've lost a lot of time with Mason undercover for so many years."

"I get it. With technology today, everyone is just a click, text, or call away, but that's not the same as holding your niece or nephew in your arms."

Nick pressed on. "I looked into some things the last few days. Mason's been helping out with cases in Blackrock Falls and the surrounding areas for a while now. Ever since he took down the Blackrock Falls PD lieutenant who was involved in the murder-for-hire operation being run out of that MC, the police have kept that position open because they can't find anyone qualified who wants to relocate there."

His boss leaned forward. "Are you thinking of taking that position?"

"Not necessarily." It wasn't ideal, but if it was the only thing available, he'd take it. But he had a better idea. "There's also been an uptick in federal cases coming our way in the state, so I've put some feelers out within the FBI and state law enforcement. Seems they'd like to have a bigger FBI presence in Wyoming."

His boss eyed him. "Is that so?"

"Yes. Mason is there. He could do more, but that would take away from him training our up-and-coming under-cover agents. And it seems more than one agent is needed in the region."

"What are you saying?" His boss sounded interested in the solution he'd come up with.

"Perhaps the bureau needs a new office in Blackrock Falls."

His boss leaned back in his chair again. "Interesting. I'm assuming you've gathered the information needed to support this request."

Nick clicked send on the email he'd already written. "It should be in your inbox any second."

His boss smirked. "You're very thorough."

Nick didn't comment. "The Blackrock Falls police department has some unused office space available in their building. The office will be central to all the major surrounding areas where we'll be needed."

His boss stared off into the distance for a moment, then turned back to Nick. "I'll look into this, evaluate your findings, and if I feel like it's warranted, I'll push it up the ladder."

"Thank you for the consideration."

"I'd hate to see you busted down to a lieutenant in a police department that wouldn't be able to use your considerable talents to the fullest extent of your abilities."

He shrugged. "I love my job. I just need to be there."

His boss nodded. "Understood. I'll get back to you soon."

"Thank you. I'll get back to the Javier Lopez case."

"I can't believe he's back."

He probably never went away, just stayed well hidden. But now he must feel like the heat was off and he could be a little more visible. And if he was operating out of that swanky private resort, he might feel brazen enough to poke his head out a bit more. All the better for Nick to chop it off and stop him for good.

"Agent Hayward out of Utah is hearing rumors and whispers about him operating here in Montana. I'm going to check in with Lopez's sister, see if I can stir anything up and make him come out of hiding." They'd have to put some surveillance in place surrounding the resort and see if they could spot Lopez, or anyone else connected to the operation.

"He killed an agent. That makes this a priority. Let's get him this time. Until then, keep me posted. And I'll get back to you about Wyoming."

"I'm on it." He ended the call and immediately sent Aria another text.

NICK: I think I found a way to come back to you. I wish I knew exactly how long it will take to finally be there with you, but now I know I'm on my way. Please be patient just a little while longer.

He needed to get back to work and finish this thing with Lopez so he could be with the only woman he'd ever loved. The only one he'd ever missed like this.

Chapter Nine

A ria pulled her phone out of her back pocket and checked the text alert. Nick. Again. This was the fourth one today.

NICK: I know you're at work. Just wanted to say goodnight. It's been a long, but really good, day. It would be even better if I got to talk to you.

How did he do this? Make her heart melt and miss him even more. Of course that was his goal. And it was working.

NICK: You know you can call me anytime. Day or night. Now works.

She was about to put her phone back in her pocket when it chimed again.

NICK: Ok. Fine. I wish I could kiss you goodnight. One day soon, I'll be able to do it all the time.

NICK: I can't wait for that day.

NICK: Goodnight, my love. I'll be dreaming of you.

What? My love? Dreaming of me?

That was kind of cheesy, but also romantic. He was trying really hard to get her attention.

He had it.

Nick had never said he loved her. Not once. Maybe if he had, she'd have given him more time.

No. That would only have strung things along, until it was even harder to leave him. He'd sent her that message about him possibly moving here, but he hadn't said anything about them taking the next step, like moving in together, getting married, or having a family.

He wanted to see her more. Great. But what did that really mean?

If you answered his calls or texts, maybe you'd find out.

Why hasn't he said what he wants? Besides me.

She'd made her needs clear.

He's really trying.

Yeah, now. But what about a month from now?

Great. She was back to arguing with herself.

She checked the time. Still three hours to closing. Then she'd walk upstairs to the tiny apartment she moved into after Lyric moved into a house with Mason. She'd sleep alone. Again. God she missed him.

And she did appreciate that he was sending her all these messages. At least once a day he left her a voicemail. And more often than not she got a text, too. Some days it was multiples of both, like today.

She'd learned more about what he did on the job over the last six days, since they broke up, than she had dating him for months. She liked the little glimpses into his world. She loved that he opened up in his voicemails, telling her he missed her. Hearing it in his voice was so much better than via text. And she guessed that's why he called every day, to remind her of how he sounded and how honest his words were when he spoke to her.

Needing to distract herself, she turned back to the bar patrons to see who needed another round and found Mason on the other side of the bar staring at her. "Was that him?"

She stuffed her phone in her pocket. "What can I get you?" she asked instead of answering his loaded question.

Mason leaned in closer. "He misses you. He wants to be with you. He loves you."

She pressed her lips tight. Mason found it so easy to tell her that, yet his own brother had never said those last three words. "I appreciate that you like the idea of me and your brother together."

"You're perfect for each other. I've seen it. Everyone sees it. I know this breakup isn't what you really want."

"I told him what I want. I made it perfectly clear what I can and can't do. And that's carrying on a relationship going nowhere, no matter how great we are together, no matter how much..." She choked up, tears gathering in her eyes. Apparently she couldn't say those three little words out loud either.

Mason rushed around the bar and took her in his arms. It felt almost like being in Nick's, though Mason was an inch taller and much bulkier than his older brother. He held her like a sister and not the love of his life. As it should be. But it also made it oh so clear that he wasn't Nick. "I'm sorry. I didn't mean to make you cry."

"What's going on?" Lyric came up behind her husband.

Mason gently set her away from him. "I was just talking to Aria about Nick."

Lyric took Mason's place hugging her.

"I'm sorry." Aria wiped away tears.

Mason shook his head. "It's my fault. Nick told me not to say anything."

Aria pulled away from her sister and stared at Mason's guilty-looking face. "Not to say anything about what?"

Lyric glared at her husband, though she wasn't ever really mad at him. "I told you to just wait and see."

"See what?" Aria asked, understanding that they knew something about Nick that she didn't. "Is he okay? Did something happen to him?" That was her worst fear. Something happening to him on the job. Where he carried a gun. Where he might have to use it. Where bad guys could be shooting at him—just like last week.

She broke out into a cold sweat just thinking about it.

"He's fine," Mason assured her. "He just wants you back so badly, he'll do anything to make it happen."

"As much as I appreciate the calls and texts, that's not enough to make a relationship work long-distance. We both have our jobs and our obligations." Nothing had really changed.

"Yeah, well, his have changed," Mason said under his breath, like he didn't want her to hear, but clearly he did because he said it from two feet away from her.

"What does that mean?" She glanced from him to her sister, hoping Lyric would clear things up.

Lyric shot Mason another glare, then turned her full attention on Aria. "Nick loves you. You know that, right?"

"Everyone keeps telling me that, except for him. So no. I don't know that he loves me. I do know that when I ended things, he said he wanted to fix it, but he had a helicopter to catch and a meeting that couldn't wait. Over the last six days, I get the calls and texts I wanted while we were dating, but really, how long is that going to last before he's too busy to remember that I exist?"

"It was never like that," Mason tried to defend his brother.

"I know. I'm being unfair. I get it. His job is important. Lives are on the line. I know. They *need* him." She choked up for the second time and rushed away before everyone saw her crying again. She made it all the way to the office and grabbed a wad of tissues before Lyric walked in behind her and closed the office door.

Lyric planted both hands on the desk and leaned forward. "Do you want to move to Montana to be with him?"

She raised a brow. "And leave the bar in Jax's hands while you and Layla have babies and your priorities shift."

Lyric stood back to her full height and stared back at her, completely serious. "If that's what will make you happy."

She rolled her eyes. Things weren't that simple. People depended on her. "I won't be happy leaving my family high and dry for a guy who hasn't even asked me to come up with a compromise that works for both of us. Instead, he left." And it still hurt.

"Not because he wanted to."

He never wanted to leave. She appreciated that, but it didn't stop him from leaving.

She didn't want to break things off, but it was the best course to save them both more heartache down the road.

"He's trying to show you that he wants to work this out."

"Lyric, what I want is what I see you and Jax and Melody have with your partners. There's so much love between you. I thought by now I'd be married with at least one little one. Instead, I'm watching you all marry and start families. My life feels so empty. I have the bar and you guys but otherwise, I'm alone. Waiting for him to show up when he could took everything out of me. The loneliness got so bad, I just couldn't find the joy in anything anymore. Every day just got harder and harder to get through."

Sympathy filled Lyric's eyes. Or was that pity? She hoped it wasn't that.

"What if you could have him back?"

Aria would love that but couldn't get her hopes up. "He said he was going to move here, but I don't see that happening. He'd have to quit his job. I wouldn't want that. He loves it. He's amazing at it. It's who he is as much as what he does. I understand that. This bar is as much a part of me as our family is. It's a piece of us. I love it here. I love being so close to all of you and seeing your lives change. I can't wait to be an aunt. I want to be here to see first steps and first birthdays and all the big and little things between and beyond."

Lyric didn't back down. "Is he the one?"

"I wanted him to be. You saw us. The second we met, something just clicked."

Lyric leaned in close, their eyes locked. "He loves you. I know it like I know Mason loves me."

Aria sighed and pulled out her phone. "Go home with your hunky husband. I've got a call to make."

Lyric's smile lit up the room. "I knew you loved him, too."

Yeah, maybe she should have told him that before she broke things off. Maybe it would have made a difference. Maybe not.

Lyric hugged her, then rushed out of the office door, closing it behind her and muffling the ruckus and music coming from the bar.

Aria hit the speed dial for Nick and listened to it ring. And ring. And ring, knowing he wasn't going to pick up.

"Leave a message." Short and sweet. But that voice was everything to her right now.

"Hey, Nick, it's me. You don't have to call me back. I need to get back behind the bar, and I'll probably miss the call anyway. I just wanted to say that I appreciate the calls and the texts and...yeah, I get it a little better now that you've opened this door to your world. And strangely, I feel a little closer to you, even though we're still so far apart. I hope you have sweet dreams tonight."

She hung up and stuffed the phone back in her pocket, took in a cleansing breath, and hoped she didn't regret leaving that message and the door open for her and Nick to get back together. She'd been disappointed too many times in the past. She couldn't take another six months of unfulfilled promises. She was tired of waiting for what she wanted.

But still, what did it really matter, because she didn't have the partner she wanted, so she couldn't fulfill her dreams of a family. Everything else in her life worked. Why couldn't she achieve this one thing?

She walked back into the chaos and noise and jumped right into things behind the bar. She got lost in filling orders and chatting up the customers, making sure everyone was having a good time. That was her job.

When the call came in, she couldn't help answering it, despite the noise and everyone singing along to Old Dominion's "I Was on a Boat That Day."

"Hello," she shouted, though he could probably hear her fine.

"Hey," he shouted back. "I was in the shower when you called."

Yeah, that sparked a really sexy fantasy and sent a wave of heat straight to her core.

"It made me so damn happy to see your number on my phone and to hear your voice. And I know you won't be going to bed anytime soon, but I wanted to say goodnight. I miss you. And I swear we will be together again soon." She could barely hear him, but his words sounded really sweet to her.

"Nick." She sighed out his name, hoping he understood everything it meant.

"I know. Me, too. I hate all the time we miss. I'm working on getting back to you. And I hope you'll be waiting when I do."

"I can't seem to help but spend every second of every day waiting for you."

"I feel like I should say I'm sorry, but I can't because that actually makes me really happy. I wish I could give you a specific day that I'll be there, but I've got a potential way to keep my job and be with you, plus a really important case. One I can't leave undone."

"I know." Because she knew him. He didn't leave things for others to do.

"Then know that I can't wait to see you. And when I do, I'm going to bury myself so deep inside you, you'll know you're mine and I'm yours and nothing will ever tear us apart."

Her heart melted at his words and how much he meant them. "I wish you were here," she whispered, knowing the sound of the crowd and music probably drowned out her words.

"I wish I was there. I don't feel whole when I'm away from you." He'd never been so open about his feelings.

"Do you mean that?"

"Yes. And if I was with you, I'd say what I really want to say but don't want to do over the phone. I should have said it that day we were together. I hope you felt it, the way I feel it every time you look at me, or touch me. It's in your words, on your face, the warmth of your touch. I know it. And if I haven't shown you enough, then I'm sorry. I won't make that mistake again. I promise." He loved her.

And she loved him. "I just want to be with you."

"I want to be with you. More than anything. Which is why I talked to my boss and why things are going to change. I just need a little more time." He really did want to be with her.

Her smile hurt her cheeks it was so big. "You know where to find me."

"Yes, I do. And I'm coming for you. You can count on it." The intent behind those words made her heart soar.

She believed him.

But her practical side said a lot could happen between now and whenever he decided to come. He could get another case he couldn't pass up. He could change his mind. He could get hurt on the job.

No. She didn't want to think about that. It was the one thing that scared her about his job.

Nick broke into her thoughts. "I hope to be there right after your trip to Boston."

How did he know about that? Mason, of course.

"Well, then I guess I'll see you when I see you."

"When you do, I'll tell you that thing I want to tell you."

She ended the call with a smile, hoping beyond hope that everything would come together and they'd finally get a chance to see if their relationship could go the distance when they were together all the time.

Chapter Ten

Nothing was ever simple. Nick spent the weekend going over his old case notes, regarding Javier Lopez. He spent two more days digging up everything he could on Javier's newest movements. He pulled one thread after the next from every whisper and associate even remotely connected to Lopez. He knew exactly what he'd known all along. Lopez was a piece of shit, who preyed on children.

Today he'd start hunting.

His phone rang as he drove out to the resort where Javier's sister Julia worked. He hit the button on the steering wheels to answer and said hello to his boss.

"Nick, I have good news. I looked into using the Blackrock Falls PD building to open a satellite FBI office."

"And?" Nick held his breath, hoping he got what he wanted. The lieutenant position would be okay, mostly supervisory, but not like what he did now.

"The uptick in cases we're overseeing in the area do warrant more attention and resources from the bureau. Mason's handled several cases already on his own and the other agents in the state are desperate for some help. I've signed off on setting up the new office and your transfer, as well as Mason's, if he wants it."

"Wait, are you saying you're going to partner me with Mason to run that territory?"

"And several other agents who are already in state. You'll head them all. How soon can you leave?"

Nick locked his jaw so he didn't gape, even as his heart pounded with excitement. This was what he wanted. He'd be working with Mason again and live closer to Aria. He could have a real shot at getting her back. She wanted to be a wife and mother. He wanted her and a family.

"I need time to bring in Javier Lopez." He hated that the guy was still on the streets, still hurting innocent children. He needed to be stopped.

"I'll let our group setting up Blackrock Falls know that you'll be joining them soon. Mason can oversee everything until you get there. I'd start looking for a place. Unless you plan on crashing at your brother's until you decide what you want."

I know exactly what I want and she's a five-foot-five spit-fire with dark hair and blue eyes, who has my heart—and my balls—in a vise at the moment, because she refuses to believe I'm coming for her.

"I'll start making plans." He'd already started.

"I'll contact Mason and make him the offer, though I'm sure he'll take it. I'll send the formal offer over to you as well, and we'll get the ball rolling on your transfer while you tie up this case with an arrest this time."

Nick didn't take any offense that his boss implied Javier's escape had been his fault. Helping his fellow agent, who'd been shot, took priority over arresting Javier. Still, Nick felt the pressure to stop Javier once and for all. "I'm on it. In fact, I'll be meeting his sister in about ten minutes."

"Good. I hope you get her to talk and we can get this guy once and for all. I'll have the team setting up the new office keep in contact with you about their progress. More soon." His boss hung up and Nick sat back, happy for the first time in a while that things were going his way.

He hit the speed dial for Aria on his phone and left her a message, because it was too early for her to be up yet. "Hey, sweetheart, it's me. I just got off the phone with my boss. He's transferring me to Wyoming. I already found a house I know you'll love. I'm going to buy it. For us. I don't know exactly when I'll be there, but soon. I promise. God, I miss you. I hope you think this news is as good as I think it is."

He hung up and tried to focus back on his case and what he needed to accomplish today.

Nick had Julia Lopez under surveillance, as well as the private resort where she worked.

Snowcap Resort was everything it claimed to be. The place to ski, mountain bike, fish, golf, and network with those who had risen to, or were born into, the upper echelons of society. The who's who of the small and big screen, the tech world, big business, even government, were members of the private resort. The surveillance team had gotten some great shots of the rich and famous enjoying the amenities.

Though there were a few children spotted, they were all carefully identified as children of the guests, or even school friends, tagging along on vacation.

They hadn't seen anything out of the ordinary.

Julia was seen entering and leaving the property each day that week, arriving on time and leaving within a relatively close time to her shift's end. Some days ran longer than others for her, but it seemed she kept to her schedule.

The only thing she did after work was stop by her mother's place to check on her.

Nick had learned that the elder Lopez had been frail for some time. Arthritis. Julia picked up groceries for her mother a couple times a week and stopped by to check on her every evening.

He found the Lopez place interesting. Aside from the main house, there were three small cabins on the property. All vacant.

He wanted to check them out but didn't have probable cause for a warrant. Yet.

But he wondered why Julia didn't rent out the cabins to earn some extra money.

Maybe she did from time to time, using some other means to advertise. Word of mouth even. But his mind went to something sinister, involving Javier, the dark web, and pedophiles. He'd have the cyber team look into it.

But first, he wanted to surprise Julia at work and see how she reacted and what she had to say about her brother.

Wednesday was a quieter time at the resort. Most people preferred to stay for a long weekend, while fewer stayed the whole week. He hoped to find Julia less busy and more willing to talk if she wasn't worried about catering to the elite guests.

He drove up to the guarded gate and flashed his badge. "Assistant Special Agent in Charge Nick Gunn. I'm here to speak to Julia Lopez."

"Do you have an appointment?"

"No. We're old acquaintances and this is official business. I'd prefer if you didn't tell her I was here and allowed me to meet her in her office, or somewhere private where I can talk to her."

The security guard picked up the phone to call someone, probably the manager, to find out if they should let him in. The last thing they wanted was a fed roaming the property. Their members expected privacy. This was a haven where they could relax and let their guard down.

The security guard hung up. "The hotel manager, Dennis Collins, will meet you in the lobby. Please park in the staff lot to the right of the resort." The guard handed him a pass to put on his dash.

Nick drove through the massive gates and down the tree-lined driveway toward the circular entry by the main doors. He pulled out of the loop to the right and followed a shorter road to the staff parking lot. It took him only a few minutes to traverse back to the main entrance and walk into the gorgeous lobby. Wood dominated the space. It was a mountain retreat, after all, but this one had huge crystal chandeliers overhead, forest-green upholstered chairs, and navy-blue sofas, accompanied by white marble-topped wood tables. To the right was the check-in desk in the same wood tone with a marble top. Two people manned the desk, while a third watched over the tall cabinet of keys to all the expensive cars parked outside.

"Agent Gunn?"

Nick turned to the gentleman in the black suit, white shirt, and green tie that matched the chairs behind him. "Mr. Collins."

"Dennis will do." He waved his arm out toward a more private area, away from their avid audience sitting at the check-in desk nearby.

Nick followed Dennis, still checking out the massive entryway. "This is a beautiful place." The fireplace in the adjoining room was big enough for Nick to stand in. Several guests occupied the seating area in front of it. The art on the walls was a mix of scenic views that matched the outside landscape and portraits of what he had to assume were prominent members.

"Our members expect the best. We give it to them. Now, I understand you wish to speak to Julia Lopez. May I ask what this is in regard to?"

Nick put the manager at ease that he wasn't here to arrest one of his guests, or disrupt the tranquil atmosphere. "It's a family matter. She's done nothing wrong. She's not in any trouble. I'm just following up with her about a matter we spoke of years ago."

Dennis relaxed. "Of course. This way. She'll most likely be in her office as she's already overseen the room attendants this morning." No maids here. "Midafternoon is usually quiet before guests are back in their rooms prior to dinner."

Nick kept his easy manner, letting Dennis know with his body language that all was well. He didn't want to tarnish Julia's name or job. As far as he knew, the only mark on her was being related to Javier. Not her fault. "I won't take up too much of her time."

Dennis led him through an Employees Only door and down a long hallway with several offices. No surprise that Julia's office was near the large laundry room, where several workers folded towels and sheets.

Dennis knocked on the doorframe as he stood in the doorway. "Julia. There's someone here to see you."

Dennis stepped back and let Nick take his place.

"Hello, Julia. It's been a long time. Do you remember me?"

"Of course. Agent..."

"Gunn. Nick Gunn. I'd like a few minutes of your time. I have some questions for you."

Julia's gaze shot to Dennis's rapt attention on them, then back to Nick. "I'd be happy to answer them for you. I have to check on something in one of the rooms upstairs; would you mind walking with me while we talk?"

Nick guessed she didn't want her boss standing outside the door while they talked about her brother's illegal activities. "Lead the way."

She stood and put her cell phone in her black slacks' pocket. She met Dennis's curious gaze. "This won't take long." She stood there, waiting for him to leave them alone.

"We don't have a problem, do we, Julia?" Dennis raised a brow, eyeing her.

She gave him an easy smile. "Everything is fine. This is a private, family matter." One she obviously didn't want to discuss with him.

Dennis held her gaze for another long moment, then turned to leave. As soon as Dennis walked back toward the lobby, Julia tilted her head toward the laundry room. "Let's go this way."

He followed her past the huge washers and dryers, toward another door that let them out into the end of a guest hallway with a service elevator in front of them. She used her key card. The sign beside this elevator designated it for staff, not guests. The sliding doors opened immediately. "Where are we going?"

"I like to check the suites after they've been cleaned and restocked to be sure everything is as it should be for guests."

He stepped into the elevator with her. "I imagine most of the rooms in this place are suites."

"On the upper floors, yes. But when I say suite, I mean the most expensive ones, reserved for special guests."

"What kind of special guests?"

"The kind with money and power, who expect the very best of everything. The ones we have to anticipate."

"I imagine you keep detailed files on guests' likes and dislikes."

"You are correct, Agent Gunn. I've worked very hard to rise from just a maid to managing the operation. It is a point of pride that complaints have dropped eighty percent since I took over."

They stepped out of the elevator into a long hallway. "That's quite impressive, considering your clientele. Those remaining complaints must be from those who simply can't be pleased no matter how hard you try."

They walked side by side down the hallway.

"Some think that nothing is ever good enough. Sometimes you can surprise them with something they never knew they wanted."

He wasn't here to talk about hard-to-please guests and changed the subject. "I heard your mother isn't doing well."

She stopped outside a set of double doors. "You heard?" She raised a brow, then opened the door with a master key card.

He walked in, taking in the opulence of the space.

She closed the door behind him.

The suite was everything he thought it would be and more. The entryway had slate tiles. The walls were the palest of blue. A huge arrangement of assorted pink, white, and yellow flowers stood on the entry table. Their sweet fragrance surrounded him. But the view through the floor-to-ceiling windows overlooking part of the world-class golf course and the mountain range that had some of the best skiing trails in the state...spectacular. He couldn't take his gaze away from the beauty of it all. Julia went about checking to be sure the fridge was stocked with expensive champagne and chilled vodka in the freezer. The bar held several types of top-shelf liquor. Cut crystal decanters were topped off and glasses stood ready to be used.

The living space boasted an elegant sectional, large-screen TV, a wood coffee table, and a couple of chairs. He could sit on that couch and stare at the view for hours as the clouds drifted past.

Julia clasped her hands in front of her. "So you want to ask about Javier? Go ahead. Ask your questions. But I don't know anything."

"When is the last time you saw him?"

She shrugged. "Maybe two, three years ago."

He narrowed his gaze. "Try again. I have a photo taken of you two together at a restaurant three months ago."

She pressed her lips tight. "It was my birthday. I was there with friends. He surprised me."

Yeah, and one of those friends posted the pics on social media and the FBI's face recognition software found the photo.

"Happy birthday."

"Thank you. He only stayed for a little while before he left again. I haven't seen him since he showed up out of the blue." She squeezed her fingers. "He knows I want nothing to do with him and his world. Although what he did for me was nice, he is not a nice man."

Nick knew that all too well. "Did he tell you where he's living? What he's doing?"

"I don't want to know, so I don't ask. He didn't say. He asked about me, our mother, if we needed anything. That sort of thing." Her gaze never met his. The words came out too smoothly, almost rehearsed. Like her brother told her exactly what to say.

"If you're scared of him...if he threatened you in any way...I can help."

She pressed her lips tight. "I don't need help. I have a good job. I make enough for what I need to take care of myself and my mother."

He made a show of looking around the opulent room again. "This is more than a few steps up from the motel I found you working at the last time."

Defensiveness filled her gaze. "I've worked hard to rise above my circumstances. I like it here. It's clean. The people are mostly nice. The ones who aren't I avoid if I can."

"Did one of the ones you couldn't avoid do that to your arm?" Nick gentled his voice, hoping she'd respond to his concern and open up to him about the bruises he had spotted the second he walked into her office.

She quickly covered the four bruises on the outside of her forearm. He bet he'd find one thumb imprint on the other side of her arm. Someone had grabbed her. Hard. And not let go. "Some men think they can put their hands on a woman because of their name or what they do and nothing will happen to them. But they learn different when it comes to me."

That was interesting. "Did you report him?"

She seemed to catch herself and waved that away. "It's not important. I dealt with it."

He wondered if she'd had Javier take care of it for her. Or if Javier was the one who marked her. "Do you have any information about your brother and where he might be?"

She straightened her spine. "Like I told you last time, he keeps his business, or whatever he's doing, away from us."

"This place has a lot of security." He'd noticed the camera in the elevator, several along the corridor outside the suites on this floor. He bet if he looked hard enough, he'd find one in the living space here. Hopefully not the bedrooms or bathrooms that split off this main space.

"The wealthy expect it along with their privacy."

He flipped open the room service menu on the bar. "You can get just about anything you want in a place like this." Yes, he was fishing to see if she took the bait and revealed anything.

Julia eyed him, probably guessing he suspected illicit things happened here all the time. "We pride ourselves on taking care of our members' needs."

He grinned, hoping to disarm her. "Anything and everything at their fingertips."

"We want them to enjoy the *experiences* this place has to offer." It sounded like there was a subtle hint of something in those words.

"What kind of experiences are you talking about?"

She actually smiled. "If a member wants to set up a special evening in his suite to celebrate a special occasion or romance his...partner..."

That pause made him wonder about the types of couples she'd seen here. He believed that love is love and everyone should be with the person who made them the best version of themselves. So long as they were of age and consenting.

Of course there were probably a lot of lovers meeting here undercover. Probably a lot of trysts with mistresses.

But was she hinting at something salacious or deviant just to taunt him? Or was he reading too much into her words because of this type of case?

"We are happy to set the scene and create the perfect ambiance for their experience. For our members, nothing is too big an ask, or out of the realm of possibility. Given enough time and money to pull it off, of course. We aim to please, even the most discerning members."

"Of course."

"Most of the guests are satisfied with the entertainment we provide in the club and community spaces. Many of our members are in the entertainment industry and like to perform for the guests at times. It's not uncommon to find a rock star or musician playing somewhere on the grounds and drawing a crowd."

"I bet that's something to see and hear when it's such a small gathering compared to a huge concert venue."

"I think that's why they like to do it, too. And here, they aren't swarmed by fans but appreciated by others who understand that here they are among people like them." She obviously loved her job and being here.

Who wouldn't? It seemed like an ideal place.

But was there something darker he was missing?

"Now, I have a lot of work left to do before my shift ends. If there's nothing else..." She shooed him toward the door.

He didn't push, not now, and pulled out his business card from his suit pocket. "If you hear from Javier, or he tells you anything about where he is or what he's doing, call me."

She took the card, but didn't even look at it.

He had a feeling it would end up in the trash the second he left the room.

She waved her hand out toward the door. "I'll see you out."

"Not necessary. You go ahead and finish checking the suite. I know you didn't just come up here to check the fridge and supply of booze. I can find my way out."

She nodded and crinkled his card in her hand as she fisted it at her side. "As you wish."

He wondered how often she said that phrase to members here. "I hope your mother feels better soon."

"Thank you, Agent Gunn." So formal. Another skill learned on the job here.

But he let it go and walked out of the suite. Instead of going to the elevator, he took the stairs down to the next floor. He wanted to check things out. Something about the way Julia spoke and acted set off a niggling in the back of his mind that not everything was as it seemed with her.

He expected her to be proud of working her way to the position she held now. But she seemed almost defiant about it. And also like the position gave her some sort of power over the people she was meant to serve.

It was strange.

The fourth floor was much like the fifth, with one extra door. He took the stairs down to the third floor and stared through the small window as Julia walked out of the elevator they'd used earlier and went to one of the guest room doors that had a sign on it. He couldn't read it from here. He opened the stairwell door just as the guest's room door opened and she rushed inside. The door closed immediately.

Odd.

He waited in the alcove, hoping no one discovered him lurking in the stairwell, peeking through the window.

He wondered whose room she'd gone into. Javier's?

In only a few minutes Julia came out of the room, pushing a rolling cart in front of her. It looked like one used for a coffee station.

Suddenly a man came into view, dressed in slacks and no shirt, his feet bare. Definitely not Javier. "Tell him I didn't mean to break it. It was an accident. I swear. You'll tell *him*, right." The man seemed almost panicked as he pulled a wad of cash out of his pocket and dropped it onto the cart. "That should be enough to make it right. If not, I'll pay more."

Several hundred-dollar bills fluttered to the floor.

Julia cursed, then knelt to pick them up. "You know he's not going to like this. You've been warned once already."

The guy grabbed Julia by her suit jacket lapels and hauled her up to her feet and close to his chest, their faces inches apart, his angry and defiant.

Nick couldn't stay hidden any longer. He rushed out of the stairwell and down the hallway. "Let her go."

Julia's head snapped toward him with a look of surprise and fear before she schooled her expression. "Agent Gunn, I'm fine."

He didn't miss the way she stressed his title, or the way the guy paled.

The guy let her go like she was on fire. His eyes rounded into saucers as he stared at her and started to sweat.

Nick looked from him to Julia and back again. "What seems to be the problem here?"

She turned to the guest. "I'll take care of everything. Please, go back inside and enjoy the rest of your stay."

The guy didn't even look at Nick again, just spun on his feet and rushed back into the room, slamming the door in her face.

He noted the sign on the door. Under Construction. "Why the sign? Isn't that guy a member?" Based on his tailored slacks, Nick would bet on it.

She pushed the cart to an unmarked door next to the room the guy had disappeared into and pulled out a different key card than she'd used on the room upstairs. She leaned in and dropped her voice. "He is a member. One who sometimes drinks too much and gets angry easily. I put the sign up so that if anyone hears him trashing his room again, they'll think it's just renovations or something."

Was she lying? To protect the member? To cover something up?

She held up the wad of bills. "As you can see, he thinks everything can be solved with money. But when the market is down, he takes it out on the things around him." She shrugged like it was no big deal. "Dennis will be angry that he's destroyed property and warn him again about letting his temper result in damages, but nothing else will happen, because he'll pay for it. An endless loop of no real consequences for the rich."

"I'm sorry he treated you the way he did. Are you all right?"

"I'm fine. I'll restock this coffee station and provide a new coffee maker and all will be as it should be."

"I can wait for you to restock it and go with you to the room to deliver it. I'd hate for him to take anything else out on you."

"I've dealt with him plenty. Better me than one of the other younger girls. He knows not to mess with me. I'll be fine." She cocked her head. "Shouldn't you have already gone by now?"

"Oh, I thought I'd take a tour of the floors. When am I ever going to get another chance to see a place as nice as this?"

She grinned, but it seemed forced. "Well, you should get going before Dennis gets even more nervous about an FBI agent skulking around the private members."

He bet she'd make sure he left as soon as possible. "You sure you'll be okay?"

"Yes." She shooed him away with her hands. "Now go before you get me in trouble for not doing my job."

"You should have one of the staff take care of this, but I get it, sometimes difficult customers will only deal with management."

She almost grinned. "It wasn't so long ago that I was one of the girls. It's nice to be in a higher position and making more money, but it comes with a lot more headaches."

"And assholes," he added. "Be careful."

This time he got a genuine smile. "Thank you, Agent Gunn."

"Thank me by calling me about your brother if you have any information. He's a wanted man. He killed an agent. We won't stop until we get him. You don't want him hunted down. Things could go really badly in that situation. Tell him to turn himself in. I'll meet him wherever he wants and we can do it peacefully."

"You know he will never do that. He's not meant for a cage."

"It's where he belongs for doing what he does."

Something seemed to suddenly shift inside the cart.

Julia stabilized it with her hands on both ends. "Everything must have shifted inside when he dumped it on its side."

He stared at her and the cart. He had no cause to make her open the cart or even ask her to do it, but he wanted to because this whole thing felt off. But he didn't want to spook her. Not if she could lead him to Javier.

And he'd be keeping a closer eye on her now.

"Have a good night." It was getting late. He'd been here longer than he intended. He didn't plan to leave just yet either.

This time he went to the elevator and took it down to the lobby, where he went to the reception desk and asked the twenty-something guy with dark hair behind it, "Mind opening the door to the offices? I'm meeting Dennis again." He pulled back his suit jacket to show them his badge."

He stood immediately, eager to help out. "Sure, sir. Is everything okay?"

"Yes. Just here asking some questions about membership."

He relaxed and grinned. "Oh. Well, I hope you sign up. We've got a lot to offer." The young man opened the door, then went back to his seat as Nick disappeared down the corridor.

He'd seen the sign on one of the doors marked Security and ducked inside, where he found another guy monitoring a dozen screens and live feeds from all the cameras around the property.

The dark-skinned man with cropped black hair and a bulky build abruptly stood. "Hey, you can't be in here."

Nick flashed his badge again. "Dennis knows I'm here." Technically, Dennis knew he was on the property, so he guessed that counted as the truth. "Can you pull up the third-floor camera by room 310?"

The security guard tapped a couple keys and the third-floor camera came up, showing Julia coming out of the door he'd left her in front of without the cart and going back to room 310.

"What is that room that Julia came out of?"

"Storage room. It's where they keep the cleaning carts, cleaning supplies, room supplies, like towels and shampoo and all that stuff. Anything that needs to be restocked is kept in there. Each floor has a room like that."

Julia knocked on the door.

A moment later, the same man with light brown hair opened the door, this time wearing a shirt buttoned up to mid chest and untucked. He immediately started talking, his posture rigid, his dark eyes narrowed on her.

She stepped into him, said something, and they both disappeared into the room.

"Can you print out a picture of the guy she's talking to and tell me who rented that room?"

The guard took a screenshot and printed it out, then turned to another computer and looked up the reservation information. "Huh. The room says it's closed for maintenance. No one is supposed to be in there."

"Does it say why it needs maintenance?"

The security guard put on a pair of readers. "The order says a leak in the bathroom. It's due to be repaired tomorrow."

"Then it's strange that someone put him in that room."

The security guard quirked an eyebrow. "What's going on?"

"That's what I want to know."

Julia had told him the guy had trashed the room, not that there was a leak, but the room was still serviceable for a guest. Odd. Suspicious as hell, too.

The guard offered a suggestion. "Maybe we were overbooked and they had to put him in that room anyway. The leak could be minor and they didn't want to turn away a member."

"Do you overbook often?"

He shrugged. "Don't know. Not my job."

"Okay. Thanks for this." Nick held up the printed photo of the guy. He'd figure out who the guy was some other way.

Before he left, he thought of something else. "Can you go back on the footage on that floor, that room, and see when the guy arrived?"

"Sure. It could take a few minutes, depending on how far back I need to go."

He was about to do it when Julia walked out of the room again. "Wait. I want to see what she does next."

Julia went back to the storage room, pulled the cart out, and pushed it to the elevator.

"Can you see where she goes with that cart?"

"Sure." The guard checked the elevator. "She's going down to the first floor." They caught her coming out into the hallway near the laundry room. "She's in the laundry area. We only have one camera back there. It's not a high-risk area."

Julia pushed the cart through the laundry room to a door at the back that was partially blocked by a tall rack of folded towels. She had to move it out of the way to get behind it, then she pushed it so that it blocked wherever she was going.

"What's back there?"

"Not sure."

"Do you mind coming with me to check it out?" He'd probably need a key card to gain access to some areas.

"Sure, but Dennis doesn't like it when I leave my post."

"I'll tell him I asked if he notices."

"Okay." The guard stood. "This way."

Nick followed the guard down the hallway, all the way to Julia's office at the end. They went through the laundry room to the back, where the rolling shelf of towels blocked access to another door.

The guard put his hand on the knob. "I don't think I've ever seen this door and I do rounds every other day. I wonder if the other guards know about it."

Nick bet they didn't. "Let's see where it leads."

They walked through the door and found another long hallway. "The golf shop is on the other side of this wall, I bet. And this probably dead-ends in the employee parking lot. That's probably why she went this way."

Sure enough, when they got to the end of the hallway, it turned right to an alcove where they found the cart and a metal door.

The guard opened the door and looked out. "Yep. Employee lot. But I don't think anyone uses this door. You'd need a key with this automatic lock." The guard let the door swing closed on the spring attached to it at the top. He turned to inspect the cart.

Nick stopped him with a hand on his shoulder. "Don't touch it. I'm going to have a team down here to check it out."

"For what?"

"I'm not sure yet, but I have some suspicions." Who knew exactly what Javier was into these days?

"Okay."

Nick focused on the guard. "How late do you work tonight?"

"Ten."

"Okay. I'm going to have my team ask for you at the gate. I'll have them park in the employee lot. Then I want you to let them in through this door. They'll do their thing with the cart. Then I want them to check out room 310."

"But there's a guest in there."

"I'm betting he's leaving soon or is already gone." Nick walked with the guard back to the security room. They checked the footage, and sure enough, while they'd gone on a fishing expedition to find out what Julia was doing with the cart, the guest had left.

The guard went back to the video, finding the moment the guest went into the room. Five minutes later, Julia delivered the cart. Without a coffee maker on top. It could be inside, but Nick had a feeling what was inside that cart had nothing to do with making or serving coffee.

"Can you make me a copy of the footage showing her taking the cart into the room and out?"

"Sure."

Nick handed him his card. "Email it to me." Nick took the piece of paper the guard had written his name and cell number on. "My guys will call you as soon as they get here. Thank you for your help and discretion."

"No problem. Should I notify Dennis about what's going on?"

"If I asked you to keep this quiet, would you?"

"I'll wait for your guys to show." The guard looked up at Nick with concern. "Do you think something bad happened in that room?"

"Yes, I do."

The guard shook his head, dismay in his eyes. "These people get away with all kinds of shit because they're rich and think they can do whatever the hell they want. You want to bust one of them for being a prick, be my guest, but tread carefully with Julia. She's a good employee, nice to everyone, and a hard worker. Don't mess things up for her."

Nick gripped the guard's shoulder. He couldn't promise anything right now. "Thank you for your help."

"Let me know if you need anything else." He turned back to his screens, then back around again. "Hey, you think Julia has something to do with that guy?"

"I'm not sure. It's just strange that he's in a room he shouldn't be in and she probably knows he's not supposed to be there."

"It could be as simple as her just trying to keep her job and not upsetting one of these assholes."

"Maybe." He didn't think so. He wanted to know why she took that cart all the way down to the employee parking lot. What had been in it? Drugs or...something. Maybe someone. A small someone.

Nick's gut soured. He hated to think about what that meant if it was true and he hadn't done anything to stop it.

"Thanks again." He left before the guard could ask more questions.

The second he stepped out of the hallway and into the lobby, Dennis spotted him from across the room. Nick dismissed him with a nod, then made his way to the young man who'd helped him into the back earlier. "Did you see a guy leave in the last ten minutes? Six feet, light brown hair, barrel-chested, wearing gray slacks and a white dress shirt."

"Mr. David just left."

"Is David his first name?"

He shook his head. "No. Gilbert David."

"What kind of car does he drive?"

The guy by the valet station perked up. "An Aston Martin Valkyrie. Sweet car. Rare. Dude doesn't appreciate it. There was what looked like chocolate stains on the passenger seat."

Nick hated that his thoughts turned dark and he thought of some kid in that car with that guy and his volatile temper.

But he didn't know if that was even true. Maybe a girlfriend or his wife was eating in the car and made the stain. Maybe it was his own kid.

Nick didn't know and it was eating him up, the things he was thinking and couldn't do anything about until he had some evidence to follow.

He turned to the reception desk people. "Thank you for your help." And just as Dennis was closing in on him, he walked out the front door and headed for his car. When he got to the employee lot, he looked around at all the cars and the empty space closest to the door.

What did she take out of the cabinet with her? He'd find out.

CHAPTER ELEVEN

Aria sat on the flannel blanket on the grass at the park downtown by Mark's office. He'd asked her to meet him for lunch, technically her breakfast. Their second date.

She felt guilty for not canceling because Nick was really trying to show her he wanted her back.

But she had a hard time disappointing Mark after she accepted this date at the end of their last one. Maybe they didn't have the kind of chemistry she and Nick shared, but she could at least give him a chance. Some relationships took time.

He'd packed lunch for both of them. A lovely charcuterie board with summer sausage, ham, salami, three kinds of cheeses, crackers, olives, and fresh strawberries and grapes. He'd even made them mimosas with some orange, peach, mango juice, and a mini bottle of champagne. For dessert, he'd brought a decadent New York cheesecake. The whole meal had been different but so yummy, and she was stuffed. They'd been enjoying the sunny day and each other's company. They talked a bit more about his job and family. She talked about the new suspense book she was reading and how she couldn't wait to be an aunt.

Mark put his hand over hers on the blanket. "And what about the bar? How's that going?"

She didn't mind the contact, but missed the zing she usually felt when Nick touched her. Like their connection was charged.

Stop thinking about him. Focus. "It's a party every night, so exhausting most of the time." She smiled, letting him know she was only partially serious. The bar had a vibe most nights that she loved. People out looking for a good time, laughing, talking, dancing, singing along to their favorite songs. She loved talking to her customers, most of whom she knew well after all these years. She loved being a part of their lives and hearing about what was going on in theirs.

Mark eyed her. "You don't mind working those late hours?"

She shrugged one shoulder. "I'm used to it."

"Yeah, but it makes it hard to date, I'd guess. And having a relationship with someone would be hard if you worked such different hours. Like we do." He seemed concerned they wouldn't have enough time together. Sweet or a precursor to him finding someone more available?

"You figured out a way to work out a date with me," she reminded him, not liking how he seemed to be putting obstacles in place all of a sudden.

"I like you. A lot."

"I like you, too." But she was feeling guilty about the date after Nick had been so good about communicating with her.

And just before she'd arrived, he'd left her a message telling her he was moving to Wyoming. He was really going to do it, change his whole life to be with her.

Definitely sweet.

"You said you were looking for serious." Mark squeezed her hand. "I could see us being close really fast. You're an amazing woman."

A blush warmed her cheeks. "Thanks. But serious takes time. This is just our second date."

He was moving a bit too fast. "I've planned more, because I'm confident that you'll see what I see."

"And what's that?"

"We're perfect together." That bold announcement came with him leaning in and kissing her cheek.

She leaned back and slipped her hand free from his. "Mark. We barely know anything about each other."

"We'll learn all the little details over time, of course. I'm just saying you're smart and beautiful and sexy, everything I'm looking for in a wife." He leaned in and nuzzled his nose into her hair. "I think about how good you and I could be in bed."

Wow. She had not pictured him naked, let alone in bed with her.

Because all you think about is Nick, his toned, sculpted body, and the way he makes you feel when he's deep inside you, making you come over and over again.

Her gaze quickly swept up Mark's body, noting the bulge at the front of his slacks.

Her cheeks heated when he caught her.

"See, you're thinking it, too."

She was actually thinking that Nick's muscles, added height, and bigger bulge made him a more appealing specimen. But she really loved Nick for always making her *feel* beautiful and smart and funny. He didn't just tell her.

And right now, Mark thought he was saying what she wanted to hear, but he didn't make her feel desired just because he was thinking about them in bed together. In fact, she was turned off by it because they didn't know each other well enough to be intimate.

And yet, you practically jumped into bed with Nick the first time you met.

Because there was something about him, between them, she couldn't deny. Something that was missing between her and Mark.

So why are you out with this guy and not getting back together with Nick?

"Mark, I'm not sure—"

He kissed her, cutting off her words. His tongue pressed along the seam of her lips and she planted her hand on his chest and pushed him back, breaking the kiss.

He cupped her cheek, his eyes narrowed. "Why'd you do that? Things were just getting good."

She took his wrist and pulled his hand away from her face. "I like you, Mark."

"Then say you'll be my girlfriend." His gaze swept over her, his eyes filled with want. "I know you went through a bad breakup. I'll make you forget all about him."

She didn't want to forget a single thing about Nick. She loved him.

And being here with Mark, who she thought was nice, but just not Nick, wasn't right.

"I'm sorry, Mark, but I need to go."

He grabbed her hand and tugged, making her lean over toward him. "We still have some time before I have to be back at the office."

"I'm sorry. I don't think we're going to work out."

He raised a brow. "You're joking."

She shook her head. "I enjoyed our time together. It's just that—"

"You're hung up on your ex." Resignation filled his words and eyes.

She shrugged, admitting the truth. "Yes, I am. And it's not fair of me to use you to get over him." Because she'd never be over him.

But can we be together?

She'd never know if she didn't try.

"Thank you for a lovely lunch. I really appreciate it, and I'm sorry it didn't work out." Not really, because she had someone who truly fit her.

Mark's genuinely confused face made her feel bad, but she knew this was best for both of them.

She walked to her car, feeling hopeful. She pulled out her phone and called Nick.

"Hey, I only have a minute." His deep voice made her belly tight and her blood heat.

"I got your message. I'm really excited that you'll be moving here."

"Me, too, sweetheart. Are you okay? You sound off."

"I'm sorry I broke up with you the way I did without first telling you that I was unhappy, so that we could discuss it and figure something out."

"Uh. This is a longer conversation than I can have right now. And I'm sorry about that. Can I call you later?"

"Anytime. And you don't have to really say anything. I just thought you deserved to know that I made a mistake and I'm sorry."

"You don't need to be sorry. I was taking us for granted. I'd given you no reason to think anything was going to change between us. And I have a lot more to say, but I really have to go and I'm sorry."

"Don't be. We'll talk later."

"Aria?"

"Yeah?"

"I really want to say that thing."

"I can't wait to hear it when I see you next." She hung up so he could do whatever he had to do, knowing she'd hear from him soon and that they were definitely going to figure out a way to be together again.

Chapter Twelve

"Morning, beautiful. I miss you." Nick's warm, rough voice woke Aria up in more ways than one.

Aria had worked late last night after she'd called him following her date with Mark. It was just past noon on Saturday and, like every day since she'd started accepting his calls again, his voice was the first thing she heard that day. "I miss you, too. What are you doing today?"

"I've got a surprise interview with someone connected to my case, then I'm going to work on packing up my place."

"Are you excited about your new house?" She still couldn't believe he was moving to Wyoming. She tried not to be too excited, but the anticipation grew each day. So did her need for him. She desperately wanted him in her arms and bed.

She restlessly pressed her thighs together and shifted, trying to ease the need building inside her.

"I'd be more excited if you were moving in with me." He sounded hesitant.

Are we ready to move in together?

"Don't get ahead of yourself." Was she saying that to him, or herself? Because she really wanted to dive into the deep end with him, but her cautious heart also told her to take it slow and see if they were compatible enough to live together.

"You love a good plan. This is mine for us. So tell me, did you like *our* house? Anything you want to change in it?"

Was he serious? "I don't know."

He'd obviously chosen the house because it was similar to the townhouse she used to rent and loved. "Come on. Play along. Tell me. I want you to be happy there."

She hesitated for a moment, then went for it. "I love that the house is on two acres of land. We should plant a garden. I love that we're not right up on a nosy neighbor, and that the kitchen has already been updated, and there's enough rooms that you can turn one into an office. I don't love the beige-y yellow they painted the interior."

"Me either. I think we should go with white walls, or maybe a really pale blue, like you had in your townhouse before you moved into the apartment above the bar. It's your favorite color."

"How do you know that?"

"You told me the first night we were together at your place."

"And you remember that?"

"I remember everything you tell me."

Her heart melted. "Nick."

"Stop saying my name like that. It gets my dick excited and I've been hard since the second you picked up the phone and I heard your sweet voice."

She giggled. "Sorry, not sorry."

"It's not funny. And I'm going to make you pay with lots of orgasms when I finally get to see you again."

"So you're going to punish me with a good time? I'm in." She laughed, smiling the whole time.

He growled. "Seriously, sweetheart, stop flirting with me. The situation is dire here."

"So take out that big cock and stroke it. Pretend it's my hand on you, fisting you hard, pumping up and down, my palm stroking the head the way you like it."

His breath went ragged and she knew he'd done exactly what she'd asked.

"That's it, baby, you like my hand on you. You love it when my hand is sliding up and down your shaft."

"Fuck, baby, yes."

"That's it. And I can feel how much you want me. While I'm jacking you off, you're kissing me like you can't get enough."

"I want more. Always wa-want more."

"Yeah, so your hand's in my panties and I'm so wet, I'm dripping down your fingers."

"Fuck, yes. And I pump two fingers deep inside that wet pussy."

She slipped her hand between her legs, rubbed her fingers over her wet seam, then sank two fingers deep. "Yes. You feel so good, baby. And I'm riding your hand."

"You better fucking be." His breaths picked up. He was close.

So was she. "You feel me. I'm right there with you, my walls clenching your fingers, trying to keep them inside me as my hand works up and down on your cock. I can feel the precum slippery over the head. You and me, we're so close," she panted out the words.

"Come," he ordered, and she heard him gasp and hold his breath as he came.

She pressed her palm to her aching clit, moaned out her release, and sank into the bed. Wrapped in the tangled sheets, completely relaxed but still wanting more. She hummed out her contentment. But as fun and satisfying as that was, it wasn't the same as having him touching her, him inside her. "I miss you more now."

"Fuck. So do I."

They stayed quiet for a few minutes. It was comfortable. Nice. They didn't have to say anything, they could just enjoy this moment of closeness as their bodies blissed out from their orgasms.

Nick recovered first. "What time are you leaving for Jax's wedding?"

"About two hours."

"Send me a picture of you in your dress. I want to see you all dolled up."

She wished he was going to be there, too. "I will. I should probably get up, have something to eat, and get ready."

Nick sighed, the sound full of his regret. "If I could be there, I would."

"I know." It didn't lessen the disappointment.

"It won't be long now. I know it doesn't feel that way without an exact date, but I swear I'm doing everything I can to close this case."

"I'm impatient because I want to be with you, but don't think I'm upset because you're doing your job. That's not it at all."

"It's as hard on me as it is you. I want to be there. I'm ready to be there."

That last part convinced her he really wanted this. "I know. I look forward to your calls every day. I'm thrilled when I get a text. I'll be the happiest woman on the planet when you're finally here and we can figure all this out."

"What's to figure out? We want to be together. So let's finally *be* together."

"Yes, well, you'll still be working like crazy. I work odd hours. We'll have to figure out when we can see each other and how often."

"If we lived together, it would make things easier."

"Or worse. What if you hate that I like everything in its place? And I'm nagging you about leaving the cereal box on the counter."

"If that's the worst thing that happens, I'm okay with it."

She sighed and stared at the ceiling. "You know what I mean."

"Then I'll just kiss you until you forgive me and we're tangled up around each other in bed, where I know you're not thinking about anything else."

She liked the sound of that, but there was more to a relationship than sex. "What if we simply still can't find the time for each other?"

Nick sighed. "Please, Aria, just give me a chance."

"I will. I just..."

"What?" His impatience came through loud and clear.

"I really want this to work out for us. I feel like it could be amazing if we could just get there."

"We will. Now, please, go and have a good time with your family. Send me pictures. I'll try to call you again later, so you can tell me all about the wedding."

"Do you actually want to hear all the details?"

"Yes. It's our family."

That *our* really melted her heart. "Nick."

"You're doing it again. Saying my name like that."

She giggled. "Have a good day. I'll be waiting for your call."

"Bye, baby."

Aria rolled to the side of the bed and sat up, smiling. She loved their chats. This one came with some sexy phone sex, too. And wasn't she lucky that he was trying to be so open and honest with her. Not that he wasn't before, he'd just pushed the door wide open now and let her in because he didn't want to lose her.

All they needed now was to spend some real time together, so they could blend their lives together.

He was coming.

He'd be here soon.

Chapter Thirteen

Nick parked behind Julia's car in her mother's driveway. He'd followed her here from her place. She'd stopped off at the market on the way to pick up groceries. He'd waited in the car while she shopped, then he waited for her to park at the house and go inside before he approached. He wanted to catch her by surprise.

Her apartment had too many people around. If she was going to meet with her brother, it would be here. This place was out of the way and backed up to a sparsely wooded area, the three cabins out back hidden among the trees.

He climbed out of his car and headed for the porch, hearing Julia call out to her mother, "If you want something to eat, you better keep quiet." The snap in Julia's voice made it clear she expected that order to be followed.

Nick frowned. That was no way to talk to your mother. Then again, he hadn't heard whatever the mother said before he got to the door.

Was she talking to someone else?

He'd find out. He knocked on the door.

Julia answered, her gaze shooting past him and searching for more agents, he guessed.

"It's just me. Can I come in? I have a few more questions to ask you."

She didn't move back from the door. "How did you know I was here?"

He didn't answer that. "I could ask your mom the questions instead of you, if you'd like."

She pressed her lips tight and held the door open wider for him to enter.

The living space was just a couch, two chairs, a TV atop a wood cabinet, and family photos on the wall that separated the kitchen and living room.

Julia walked back to the kitchen. "I have to finish putting away the groceries."

Nick walked to the entry between the living room and kitchen and stopped, staring down the hallway to the back bedroom, where he spotted Mrs. Lopez propped up in bed, dressed in a pair of joggers and a simple white T-shirt.

"Who are you?" she called out.

Julia went still, then called back, "He's with the FBI. Here about Javier."

Nick gave Mrs. Lopez an easy smile. "Have you seen your son recently?" It was a shot in the dark that she'd even answer, but worth a try.

Mrs. Lopez opened her mouth to say something, but Julia beat her to it. "Don't say anything. Let me handle this."

Mrs. Lopez crossed her arms over her chest. "I'm not a part of this."

Wondering what she meant, Nick turned and raised a brow at Julia.

She rolled her eyes. "She washed her hands of Javier years ago. She calls him a sinner."

"Well, I have to agree. Which is why I'm trying to find him. To hold him accountable for all his sins. To make sure he doesn't hurt anyone else." Nick stepped into the kitchen and noted the boxes of cereal, two gallons of milk, and frozen pizzas on the counter where Julia had unpacked them from the bags at her feet.

Mrs. Lopez had a sweet tooth with all the sugary cereal Julia had bought for her.

The giant box of taquitos probably didn't meet Mrs. Lopez's standards but they were fast and easy for someone who had trouble getting around. She probably couldn't stand over a stove for very long anymore with the arthritis in her knees.

"Good luck finding him." Julia put away the milk in the fridge.

He glanced at the counter and saw a brand-new bottle of a children's fever medication. "Why the kid's medicine?" His gut went tight.

"My mother doesn't tolerate pain meds very well anymore, so I give her the low dose stuff, which means I can give it to her more often during the day to manage her pain."

And yet when he'd looked down the hallway, he'd spotted several prescription meds on her bedside table. "Just to satisfy my curiosity, mind giving me a tour."

"He's not here."

Nick waited, hoping his silence and scrutiny would get him what he wanted, just so Julia didn't have to suffer his presence any longer.

"Fine." She waved him off. "Go look."

Well, that was even better. He made his way down the hall to the first room. It was set up with a sewing machine on a desk under the window with a twin bed opposite. The closet was closed. He took a peek inside. Stacks of fabric and tulle and sequin in an array of colors.

"My mother used to make quinceañera dresses before the arthritis made her hands ache too much to sew."

There was a beautiful aqua-colored gown hanging in the closet. "Yours?"

She nodded. "From another time."

"It's beautiful. Your mother did exceptional work."

Julia's eyes went soft. "And now she can barely hold a fork to eat."

"I'm sorry." He meant it.

"Come." She waved him to follow her with an exasperated expression. "Mama, the fed is going to check your room."

Nick did it quickly, trying not to stand in front of the TV or upset Mrs. Lopez further. "You have a lovely home. The dress you made Julia is gorgeous."

Mrs. Lopez nodded, then shooed him away with one hand, so she could finish watching the telenovela on TV.

He gave the bathroom a quick glance then walked back into the living room. "Would you mind showing me the cabins?"

She rolled her eyes again. "I need to make my mother dinner."

"Then we better get to it so you can get it started."

Julia flipped her long dark hair behind her back. "Ugh! Fine. Let's go." She went to the back door off the kitchen, grabbed a set of keys from the holder by the door, and walked out ahead of him.

When they reached the bottom of the steps, he noticed a cellar door that led under the house. It had a brand-new shiny lock.

"The old door rotted away. I had someone come and build a new one."

"What do you keep under there?"

"Until we got the new door, rats. Sometimes squirrels and larger animals. My mother is an old woman. She wants to live in peace with a roof over her head and no rodents keeping her up at night." Julia walked off toward the trees. "You coming?"

He didn't have much of a choice. If she didn't open up the cellar door, he couldn't get in without a warrant. She was accommodating him now. And he enjoyed the walk through the trees. The first cabin wasn't very far. He turned and looked back at the house, noting that he couldn't see the main house. And anyone at the main house couldn't see this cabin. Tire tracks led to the cabin as well. They weren't fresh, but they weren't grown over by weeds or obscured by falling leaves either.

He turned to her, noting her hands clasped in front of her, like she was nervous. She'd done it when he interviewed her at the resort as well. "Do you rent the cabins out?"

"Sometimes. It's extra money for my mother. Mostly in the summer. I'm too busy to keep up with it all year round." She walked up to the door and used her key to open it. The place wasn't that big. A bedroom and bath on one side, living space with a kitchen on the other. Neat. Simple. The fireplace would be a cozy comfort on cold nights and create a warm and inviting atmosphere to relax.

He walked to the bedroom and peered inside. He noted the bookcase and small toy chest. The bookcase held board books and chapter books, a few bestselling hardcovers.

Nothing out of the ordinary or suspicious about any of it, unless you knew that Javier trafficked kids. Then a single room with a queen bed with books and toys and no other bed for a child to sleep in made things feel a little creepier.

He didn't want to think about it, but it was his job.

"Let's go check out the other two."

Half an hour later, he found himself outside Mrs. Lopez's house with a creepy-crawly feeling dancing up and down his spine.

The other two cabins had been similar to the first one. One was a single bedroom like the first, though it actually had a set of bunk beds, the bottom bed bigger than the upper bed. The third cabin had two bedrooms, both with queen beds.

Again, on the surface it appeared that they were quaint little places to rent while you fished in the nearby river, or hiked the pristine countryside. But even the most mundane setting could be used to play out disturbing deeds.

"I assume you're satisfied." Julia stood beside him, trying to hide her nerves, but she kept rubbing her fingers together and clasping her hands in a nervous gesture she couldn't seem to stop since he got here.

"I'm satisfied Javier isn't here now. But I'm not satisfied that you haven't seen or spoken to him. I'd hate to see your mother here all alone with no one to help her if you're lying to me, or involved in some way and I have to arrest you as an accessory."

She squared her shoulders. "I've done nothing wrong. I showed you what you wanted to see. Next time, I'll ask for that warrant instead." With that, she stormed into the house, slamming the door.

Good. He wanted her off-balance. He wanted her scared. Then maybe she'd reach out to her brother.

He had a feeling the forensics team would find something in the hotel room or that cart she used to sneak something out of the hotel. He'd like to get them into those cabins to check things out, find things he couldn't see.

She was up to something.

He'd find out what it was and if it had anything to do with her brother, he'd use Julia to take Javier down.

Chapter Fourteen

Aria's eyes glassed over with tears as she stood with the other guests, watching her brother and Layla recite their vows to each other among their closest friends and family. The simple yet poignant ceremony really touched her and made her long for the same love and devotion Jax and Layla spoke of today. Nothing more was needed than to look at the beautiful bride smiling adoringly at her groom and him smiling back at her like he won the lottery.

Fox had, and he looked at her sister Melody like she was a million times better than any jackpot. The Wildes truly were lucky in love. Lyric and Mason were expecting their first child. Jax and Layla were getting married and ready to welcome their first child. Melody was about to move to Boston to be with Fox and start a whole new life. It wouldn't be long before Melody was married, too.

And Aria was still waiting for her love life to be more than just a handful of in-person days a month with nothing but calls and texts in between to save them from slipping away from each other.

"You may now kiss the bride."

Jax kissed Layla like she was the oxygen he breathed. The beautiful moment brought tears to Aria's eyes.

And Layla, she was a beautiful bride in her white gown with a fitted long-sleeve top that had a wide V-neck, with floral appliqués and a barely-there back. The chiffon skirt draped from her waist to the floor in a church-length train that puddled at the back of her feet, but wasn't long enough to hinder her during the reception. If you didn't know she was pregnant, you'd never tell in that dress. It was sexy and beautiful. Just like her brother's bride.

They looked so good together. A perfect match. The perfect couple.

She wondered if that would be her and Nick someday.

Jax dipped his bride right before he ended the kiss and pulled her even closer.

The officiant announced with exuberance, "I give you Mr. and Mrs. Wilde."

Everyone applauded.

She waited just long enough for Jax and Layla to head into the reception before she followed right along and headed for the bar.

She used to love weddings. They made her happy and hopeful. The room seemed to be filled with love and hope and anticipation for a wonderful future. For them. And while she was happy for her brother and Layla, she wished it was her.

Lyric sidled up to her. "What's that look?"

She pasted on a smile. "Nothing."

Lyric bumped her shoulder into Aria's. "Come on. Spill it."

It took her a minute to find the courage to say it out loud. "I wish it was me."

Lyric pulled her into a hug. "I know. And it will be."

She stepped back, but still held Lyric by the shoulders. "Do you think so? I feel like I pick men who don't pick me. Dan cheated. Mark was nice, but trying to move way too fast into a relationship. Nick is married to his job and lives in another state."

Lyric cupped her cheek. "Not for long. Mason said Nick is anxious to get here and be with you."

She released her sister and asked, "Has Mason said anything about this case Nick is working on? It sounds really dangerous."

"I imagine it is. The guy he's after killed another agent and took a shot at him. Other than that, I'm not sure. Why? Are you scared for him?"

"Yes. Aren't you when Mason is working?"

"Not so much now. He isn't undercover anymore and leads a lot of training. Though he still helps out on cases."

They watched Jax and Layla greet all their guests as they made their way through the room.

Aria kept her focus on Lyric. "How do you keep yourself from worrying to death?"

"I trust that he's trained and will do everything he can to keep himself safe. I believe that no matter what he faces, his end goal is to always come back to me. And I have faith that he will do everything he can to protect himself and others, while arresting those who deserve it. I don't let myself get mired in the what ifs. I focus on how proud I am of him for doing a really hard and dangerous job, because it's necessary and keeps us all safe." Lyric's mouth scrunched to one side. "Even though all that is true, I still worry. It's hard not to when I love him so much. So I know how you feel about Nick. It's especially hard when the hours stretch and you haven't heard anything."

She sighed. *Try days.* "I know he's good at his job. I trust him to be safe. I'm being ridiculous." And selfish. She was only thinking of herself, and not all the people Nick helped.

"No. You love him. He's lucky to have someone like you who cares and understands and still finds a way to let him do that job without holding him back. So instead of worrying about whatever he's doing today, let's celebrate with Jax and Layla. And maybe you could use a drink to help you relax and have some fun."

Sounded like a good plan to her.

So she immersed herself in the reception, giving one of the toasts, dancing with friends and family, enjoying the dinner and eating the decadent cake, and waving off Jax and Layla as they left for their honeymoon night.

But the thing that stuck with her as she drove home was the family picture they took. Mom and Dad, Lyric and Mason, Jax and Layla, Melody and Fox, ending with her standing without a partner. She'd sent Nick a text right after it.

ARIA: Just took family photo. All of us together with Mom and Dad. My siblings with their partners. It really hit me. You were missing.

NICK: I'm sorry. I wish I could have been there.

She unlocked the door to her place, still thinking about that text.

How many more texts would she get like that in the future? Was this what life with Nick would be like?

That future didn't seem as happy as the one she imagined.

Today hadn't been all it could have been if he'd been there.

Even if he moved here, he'd have the same job. Would she always be the one with the missing partner at events and in the photos?

Chapter Fifteen

Nick had texted Aria this morning asking about her plans for the day. She always had Monday and Tuesday off because the bar was closed. She'd spent the past weekend doing wedding stuff. Today she was at her family's ranch helping out and visiting her parents. As much as he wanted to take down Javier, he needed some new leads to follow. So he took today off work to come to Wyoming, check out the house he bought in person and see her. Hopefully she wanted to come with him. He wanted her to love the place and hoped they could talk about getting back together.

He had dinner plans for them, too, before he had to leave tonight.

Really all he wanted to do was spend time with her.

He parked outside the barn and made his way inside.

Aria was in a stall with a big bay horse, brushing him down. She looked amazing in tight, worn jeans, and a pink and dark blue plaid flannel, her dark hair pulled back in a ponytail.

"Hey, sweetheart. God, I've missed you."

Aria's head snapped up and her eyes went round with surprise. "Nick. What are you doing here?"

"I told you. I missed you." He opened the stall gate and caught her in his arms when she launched herself at him. He held her close and breathed her in. Leather, hay, and peaches from her body wash. He stared into her pretty blue eyes. "I'm sorry I couldn't make it over the weekend for the wedding. I've got until eight tonight, so I thought we could spend the day together before I have to get back to work tomorrow."

"You came all this way for like eight hours?"

"I wish it were more, but I'll take every second I can get with you. I should have done this more often in the past. I don't want to make the same mistakes I made before."

Her eyes went soft. "I really appreciate the effort and that you came all this way. But you could have asked me to come to you. I could have stayed until Wednesday morning."

"One, I wanted to surprise you. Two, I thought we could go see the new house. And three, I wanted you to know I'm putting in the effort because you matter to me."

Her smile brightened. "Yeah. You mentioned something about how much I mean to you."

"You mean everything to me. I love you." He finally kissed her, sinking into her mouth, his tongue caressing hers. He flattened his hands on her back, pulling her in closer. He slid his hands down over her ass and squeezed, letting her feel his rock-hard length pressed to her soft belly. She felt so good against him. He didn't want to let her go. He didn't want to leave here without her.

Aria pulled back and stared up at him, her eyes filled with lust and something more. "I love you, too."

His heart beat faster and expanded three sizes. He crushed his mouth to hers again.

Someone cleared their throat nearby.

Aria released the grip she had on his shirt and gently pushed back from him. "Uh, Dad. Look who's here."

Nick quickly removed his hands from Aria's ass and turned to her father. "Afternoon, Wade."

"I see you made it okay."

Nick nodded. "Thank you for finding someone to take over the chores for Aria so I can steal her away for the day."

"Looks like she was happy to see you."

Nick was more than relieved by how happy she seemed to be to see him. Especially since she'd gone on a couple dates while they were apart. While she told him about seeing some guy, she refused to give him any details about what happened. It couldn't have turned out well if she was jumping into his arms the way she did.

"Nick and I have some things to discuss." Aria untied the horse and took off his bridle, then collected the grooming tools and stepped out of the stall. "We're going to look at Nick's new place."

"I heard." Her father held out his hand.

Nick took it.

"It's good to see her smile like that again." Wade released him. "It's a big thing you're doing, moving here. You ready for that?"

"I am. I let work consume my life and I lost something I desperately need. I won't make that mistake again." Nick wanted Aria and her family to know he meant it.

He hated making Aria unhappy. He loved that his presence in her life mattered. After he'd nearly been gunned down in the street, he appreciated her love all the more and that he got this second chance.

"I'm ready to go if you are." Aria laced her fingers with his.

He squeezed her hand. "Let's go check out our place."

Wade raised a brow at the "our" but didn't comment. "Have fun."

Nick led Aria to his rental car and they both climbed in. He drove away from the ranch and out to the main road.

"I can't believe you just showed up." She was still smiling.

He headed to the new property, happy with his girl beside him. "I felt badly about missing the wedding, but I had some things to do on my case that couldn't wait. I did some packing, too. The house isn't mine for another week or so, but I wanted us to see it together."

Aria settled back in her seat. "I actually drove by it last week."

He turned to her. "You did?" He shifted his gaze back to the road.

"Yeah. I couldn't believe you actually bought it without seeing it in person. I wanted to check it out, just in case there was something you should know about."

"Even though we were broken up, you still checked out the place just in case there was something wrong, so you could tell me?"

"Is that so hard to believe? I didn't break up with you because I didn't care. I cared too much to keep going on the way we were." She sighed. "And I should have handled it better. I should have talked to you about what I needed to keep us together."

He rested his hand on her thigh. "I'm going as fast as I can with my case and getting here. Please, be patient a little while longer."

"I'll try."

"And no more dates?" he grumbled.

She grinned at him. "Except with you, right?"

He spotted the property up ahead and choked out the question that had been nagging him since he found out about her dates. "Did you sleep with him?"

Aria turned in her seat, took his hand, and faced him. "No. I did what you said I was going to do and thought about you the whole fucking time. I couldn't stop comparing him to you. You'll be happy to know, he didn't stack up at all. At first I thought he was nice. Charming. Attentive. We had dinner and talked, getting to know each other. The second date, he asked me on a picnic. I thought it was nice that he wanted to see me on his lunch break, because that was the only time I had to see him. It started off well, but then I came to a conclusion about why it felt off. He wasn't you."

Nick pulled into the driveway of what he hoped to be their new place. "You see that house?"

"Yes."

"I want it to be ours. I want you there with me because it's where you want to be. I want you to want to be my wife and partner. When we do this..." He notched his chin toward the house. "We do it together. And if things get out of balance again, then you come to me and tell me what you need, because I want you to be happy. I don't want to be the reason you're sad or frustrated or feeling alone." He brushed his fingers along the side of her beautiful face. "I'm sorry I made you feel that way. It won't happen again."

"I know you mean that, Nick, but I also understand that your job is demanding."

"It is. But things are going to be different with me living here. Just give me a chance to prove it."

She didn't say anything, just opened her car door and got out.

He met her at the front of the car. "What do you think?"

"The whole house is white. Maybe we can paint the trim with another color to add some detail."

He took her hand and brought it to his lips. "Okay. What color?"

"Hunter green. No. Navy blue."

"I like that idea. Let's go inside."

She turned to him. "I thought it hadn't closed yet."

"It hasn't, but the realtor gave me the combination to the lockbox so we can take a look inside."

Her smile took over her whole face. "I can't wait to see it. It looks different being here than just seeing it in the pictures you sent."

"Mason did a walk-through for me before I signed the papers. If I'd had the time, I would have done it with you, but once I decided I was moving, I wanted it done right away." He opened the lockbox on the door handle, retrieved the key, unlocked the house, opened the door, then waved his hand out for Aria to go in first.

They stepped into the foyer and open living room.

Aria walked into the spacious room. "I love the wood floors."

He did, too. "Let's check out the kitchen." He followed her into the dining area that led into the kitchen.

She stopped between the two spaces and stared at the newly updated kitchen.

He came up behind her, put his hands on her hips, and pressed his chin to the side of her head. "Can you see yourself in here with me?"

"Yes. And you're naked."

He chuckled. "If I am, you would be, too."

She turned to face him and her hands slid up his abs to his chest. "Want to christen your new place?"

He put his hands over hers. "I didn't come for that. I came to spend time with you and to show you our place."

One dark brow raised. "Are you saying you don't want to have sex with me on that quartz countertop?"

"It's not that I don't want to, it's that I don't want you to think that's the only reason I came."

"I never think that, Nick. Yes, maybe that's how we spend most of our time. I will never complain about that. It's just that I wanted there to be more between us."

"And I'm trying to give you that. I bought tickets for the movie you said you wanted to see, so we'll have to leave here soon. Then I have dinner planned."

"Great." She went up on her tiptoes. "Then we have time for this." She kissed him and he lost himself in her taste, her moans, her greedy hands moving over him.

He backed her up to the island and tugged her ponytail back, making her more open to the deep kiss he laid on her.

She dipped her hands up under his shirt and mapped his abs, chest, and shoulders before she got impatient and shoved his shirt up and out of her way.

He helped her get it off while her lips landed on his pec and she ran her tongue over his skin. He undid the button and fly on her jeans and slid his hands over her hips, down the back of her pants, inside her panties and over her lush ass.

He kissed his way down her neck. "You drive me fucking crazy."

Her hand slid down his chest and over his hard cock. She squeezed him through his pants and boxer briefs. He needed more.

He pushed her panties and jeans down her legs, then scooped her up and sat her ass on the counter.

She squealed. "That's cold."

"I'll warm you up in a sec." He pulled off her boots and dumped them on the floor at his feet. Then he took off her socks, pants, and panties all at once. It was nothing to pull her shirt over her head and toss it, then undo her bra and pull it down her arms to drop onto the floor.

He took the barest of seconds to admire her beautiful body before he dove in and took her tight pink nipple into his mouth.

Her fingers dug through his hair and she held on to him as he feasted on one breast and then the other.

"Nick. I need you, now."

He gripped her thighs and pulled her to the edge of the counter, then planted his hands on her thighs and pushed them wide. Her wet pussy made him salivate. He dipped his head and licked her from her opening to her clit.

"Oh. My. God."

"Just me, baby." He dove back in, licking her folds and sucking on her clit. He drove one finger, then two into her slick channel, pumping his fingers as he teased her clit with his tongue.

Her fingers contracted in his hair, pulling the strands. He didn't care. He wanted more of that mewling sound she made and her to combust on his tongue.

He drove her up high and higher, until she was wound so tight that when he sank a third finger deep and sucked her clit, she went off like a rocket. Her inner walls squeezed his fingers, milking them like she didn't want them to ever leave her body.

She came down from the climax slowly.

He kissed her with all the urgency he had moments ago to be inside her. His mouth latched onto hers and he lashed his tongue against hers, knowing she had to taste herself, too. She didn't back away. She kissed him back like he was the air she breathed.

He fumbled with his belt, then undid his jeans, pulled out his aching cock, and lined up the leaking head with her sweet pussy.

"Now, Nick. Please."

He thrust into her hard and fast, knowing she was wet and ready for him. "Fuck, baby. The things you do to me." He pumped into her again and again, loving the feel of her clamped around his girth, her tight channel taking all of him.

"More, Nick. It's been so long."

He gave her what she wanted. Harder. Faster. Unrelenting until he felt her clamp around his shaft as her head fell back and her body tried to squeeze the life out of him. He fell over the edge with her, thrusting into her once more and spilling everything he had into her.

He wrapped her in his arms and held her close. Chest to chest, he could feel the rapid beat of her heart and feel her heat against his skin. He waited for both of their breathing to calm. He cupped her face and stared into her blue eyes, seeing nothing but satisfaction and joy in their depths. "Every time it feels like the best ever."

She nodded. "I know. That's why I always want you so bad."

He'd been such an idiot to take her for granted. He'd seen how special she was, but he hadn't done anything to ensure their relationship became permanent.

He was glad he came today. He was even more excited about the changes he was making in his life. He couldn't wait to be with her all the time.

He pressed his forehead to her. "This is how we could be all the time. Here. In our home. Think about it. Please."

She bit the side of her bottom lip and nodded.

That's all he could ask of her. But he hoped for a lot more. Like for her to say yes and for them to start this next chapter. Together.

Chapter Sixteen

"Morning, sweetheart." Nick sat at his desk checking his emails while he called Aria.

"You know it's past noon, right?" She sounded off. Tired maybe. It had been a week since Jax and Layla's wedding and their Monday together. She'd loved the house, the movie, and dinner. Most of all, they both loved spending time together.

He hadn't pressured her about moving in. The house wasn't going to close for a few more days, so she had time to think about it. No matter what, he was getting ready to move to be with her, to have a more balanced life, and to enjoy being with someone he loved.

Aria was out of town for another family thing and he was still stuck in Montana. "It's morning for you. I figured you'd sleep in since you're in Boston for Melody's engagement. Have you been up long?"

"Yeah." She yawned. "I couldn't sleep, though the hotel Fox put us up in is lovely. Too much on my mind."

"Like what?" He hoped she wasn't upset that he hadn't gone with her, but he knew she wanted him there as much as he wanted to be there with her.

"Like closing the bar for the second Saturday in a row." Aria had left last night with the rest of her family to be in

Boston when Melody officially moved into her new home and Fox proposed to her with her whole family present today.

It was supposed to happen in a couple of hours, and Melody had no idea her family would be there to welcome her to her new home with Fox.

Nick had to give the guy credit, he'd gone all out to make Melody feel welcome at their place and to include her family in this very special occasion.

Nick needed to up his romance game. Maybe he couldn't afford to fly her whole family on a private plane, but he could do something meaningful for Aria. He needed to think about it and find something special to do for her.

"Melody has no idea Fox is going to propose, does she?"

Aria yawned. "I mean, they're on the plane right now. They've talked about getting married, so she knows a ring and proposal are coming, but not that we're here to celebrate it with them. It's really sweet Fox wants us to help her feel like this place is home, that we'll be coming to see her whenever she wants."

"She's going to love it. Especially if your sister and brother bring their babies for visits, too."

"She'll love that. All she wants is to be with him."

"I know the feeling well." He missed Aria every day. The calls and texts helped keep them close, but it wasn't the same as being with her.

"Me, too. Our day will come when we're finally in the same state and town together more than we're apart."

"I can't wait." He thought he'd be further along on his case by now. He should have gone with her to Boston. He'd have loved to be there with her to see her sister get engaged. Mason was there with Lyric. The four of them could have spent some time together, too. It had been a while since he and Mason saw each other in person, though they stayed connected because of work.

"Melody and Fox have so many plans for what they want to do together. Once she opens her restaurant, I bet they start working on a family."

He'd like to do the same with Aria. He wasn't getting any younger. Mason was younger than him and already married and expecting a child. If he didn't do something soon, he might find himself with a great performance record with the FBI and alone.

He wanted more in his life. He wanted Aria's love and attention and a million memories they shared.

His phone chimed with a text.

HAYWARD: Check your email. We caught a break in the case.

"Hey, babe, hold on a sec. I need to look at something."

"Sure. I'll just put on my makeup while you do that."

He pulled up the email forwarded by Agent Hayward from the lab. He stared at the results and took a double-take before he understood what he was looking at. The DNA found in room 310 at the resort matched that of an eight-year-old boy reported missing two years ago. Toby Simmons. Those results also matched DNA found in the cabinet Julia used to sneak something out of the hotel.

"Holy fuck! No. I was right fucking there!" Frustrated as hell, he dug his fingers into his hair, pulling it a bit. The pain barely registered beneath his rage.

He'd missed it. He should have figured it out. He should have asked more questions, or done something. Anything.

The kid was right there under his nose.

"What?" Aria sounded concerned. "What's wrong?"

"Baby, I'm sorry. I have to go. I just got a huge break in the case and if I'm lucky, I'll get to reunite a child with his family."

"Go. Call me and let me know how it goes. You've got this. Be safe."

"I will. Promise. Love you." He needed to save that kid.

And he had a good idea where to find him.

If she hadn't moved him already.

He picked up the phone and called Agent Hayward. "Tell me you got a warrant for the resort."

"I got it." Agent Hayward had come up from Utah a few days ago to help on the case.

"Good. Now get one for Mrs. Lopez's house, too. I think the kid is there. We'll send a team to search the resort just in case she's hiding any children there, but you and I will go to the Lopez house. I think she's got the kid in the cellar. She bought a ton of cereal and frozen pizzas, plus some children's fever reducer." He slammed his hand down on his desk. "Damnit, I knew something didn't feel right about her taking that rolling cabinet all the way down to the laundry and the side door." He didn't have time to berate himself. They needed to move on this quickly.

"I've got someone picking up Gilbert David." The guy who'd been in room 310. Julia had rolled the cart out of his room. He'd dumped all that cash on the cart, telling her he didn't mean to do it.

What had he done to the boy?

Nick's stomach turned. He didn't want to think about all the possibilities.

He focused on the case. "Is Gilbert David still in the state?"

"He never left. He has a place in Bozeman as well as the membership to the resort."

"Good. At least we don't have to hunt him down across state lines. How far away are you from the Lopez place?" Nick was ready to head out now. All he needed was his keys. He found them in the tray by his door and locked up and went to his car.

It sounded like a car door slammed on Hayward's side of the call. "I can be there in about twenty-five minutes."

"I'm about the same. Meet me there with the warrant and a team. I'll send agents to Julia Lopez's place to pick her up, too. Maybe we'll get lucky and we can use whatever we find to get Julia to give up her brother."

"Let's hope. See you there."

CHAPTER SEVENTEEN

Nick turned onto the road leading to Mrs. Lopez's place and spotted a white panel van in the driveway, the back swinging doors wide open. A man with tan skin, black hair, and tattoos on his neck, wearing a black T-shirt and jeans, pushed someone into the back of the van. Nick didn't have a great vantage point to see if it was an adult or child. But the second the guy spotted Nick closing in, he yelled something up to the house, closed the van up, ran to the driver's side door, jumped inside, and hauled ass out of there.

Nick called Agent Hayward.

"I'm five minutes out," he said when he picked up.

"White van headed east. Possible child abduction." He rattled off the license plate number.

"They're driving toward me. I won't miss them."

"Call for backup for me. I'm headed in to see who's still in the Lopez house. I've got Julia's car out front and a black Charger parked along the side yard. I might get lucky and find Javier here."

"Be careful."

Nick slammed on the breaks behind Julia's car, blocking it in. He jumped out and as he was headed for the open front door, he heard a male voice say, "Get down the fucking stairs."

He pulled his gun and announced himself. "FBI, come out with your hands up."

A child wailed.

Nick rushed to the kitchen, taking a second to glance down the hallway to Mrs. Lopez's room. She stared back at him, wide-eyed and scared.

That moment of distraction was all it took for him to miss Julia coming at him with a kitchen carving knife. She plunged the blade into his shoulder. He shoved her away and the blade tore out of him, making him grimace in pain. "Put the knife down."

What the hell! How could she come after him?

He held her at gunpoint and walked toward her, glancing into the kitchen, finding a young boy on the ground holding his arm, tears trailing down his cheeks. His arm looked swollen and bright red, probably broken. An ACE bandage and brace were on the counter right near Javier Lopez.

"Don't fucking move," he told Javier, who had a gun in his hand, pointed at the boy. "You don't want to do this, man. Not to that kid. Not in your mother's house in front of your sister." Nick kept his focus as his heart jackhammered in his chest and in his mind he prayed nothing happened to the small boy.

Javier sneered. "Let me go and no one gets hurt. Worse," he tacked on, looking at the blood spreading across Nick's shirt and chest.

"You're under arrest. Drop the gun and kick it to me."

Javier shook his head. "You drop it. I leave. You live to see another day, you asshole."

Julia stood in the corner, her back to the counter, her chest heaving. "Go, Javie. Please."

He glared at her with disdain. "I fucking told you to move the kids yesterday. Now look what's happened. What good are you to me if he arrests you for stabbing him?"

"I have things to do besides babysit your brats," she snapped.

The boy on the floor shook with fear, sweat dripping from his brow. He didn't look good. Pain etched lines into his forehead and made him pale.

Nick's fucking shoulder hurt like hell, but he kept his gun trained on the man he'd wanted in a cell for three long years.

Javier made a move toward the back door. The kid on the floor blocked it.

Nick shook his head. "Don't even think about it."

"I'm not letting you take me in. You don't get to be the hero after you betrayed me."

"There's no way out. More agents are on the way. My partner probably already has your man in the van in custody. You're going down."

Javier glanced at his sister.

Nick didn't take the bait. He kept his eyes glued to Javier.

"Javie," his sister pleaded. For what, Nick wasn't sure. To get her out of this. To take her with him. To turn himself in. She'd stabbed an FBI agent. She was going down with him.

Suddenly Mrs. Lopez shoved him from behind. "Get out of my house. All of you. I don't want any of you here!"

Chaos ensued.

Julia slashed out with the knife again, getting him across his back and arm as he tried to avoid being stabbed again. Mrs. Lopez kicked him in the leg, making him off-balance as he fell to his knee, then hip. Julia swung the knife down at him again. He shot her right in the chest.

She hadn't even dropped when a bullet hit him in the back. He spun and aimed at Javier just as he got off another shot, hitting Nick in the chest. He shoved himself backward and fired at Javier as Javier fired back at Nick again.

The bullet went through Nick's thigh. Nick's shot ripped across Javier's shoulder, near his neck, but didn't take him out of commission. Javier lunged for the kid. Mrs. Lopez was wailing about her dead daughter.

And Javier picked up the kid, using him as a shield, his face a mask of rage. "You killed my sister. I will fucking hunt you down and kill the one you love most, and then I'll kill you." He shoved the kid straight at Nick and ran out the back door.

The kid cried out in agony, then passed out in Nick's arms. Nick's blood soaked the floor beside him, but he managed to lay the kid down and turn to Mrs. Lopez. He barely made it to his feet without passing out himself, but he grabbed her around the waist, hauled her up to standing as she dropped her daughter's body to the floor. He cuffed her as she cussed him out and wailed, "You killed my daughter. You killed my daughter." She spit in his face.

He wiped it away with his shirt sleeve, noting the amount of blood still flowing out of the stab wound on his shoulder. Maybe it was from the cut on the back of his arm.

The Charger came to life outside with a growl of the engine, then tires squealing as Javier made a run for it. Nick hoped Agent Hayward or their backup got him before he escaped again.

Nick was in no condition to give chase. He was barely standing. And he had to keep the boy safe. No telling what Mrs. Lopez might do if she was willing to attack an FBI agent.

Fuck. Everything hurt.

Every breath made him remember the two bullets he took in the vest. And his leg was going numb and felt like it was on fire all at the same time. His vision went in and out as he fought passing out. He needed to stay alert and help the boy.

He pulled out his phone and texted his brother, Mason.

NICK: FUBAR

He didn't have much time before blood loss put him on his ass and he passed out. So he needed to act fast.

He bent over the kid and gently touched his cheek, hoping the kid would wake up.

"You can't lock me up," Mrs. Lopez ranted.

He shoved her into a chair at the table and ignored her, while he called Agent Hayward.

The agent got right to the point when he answered. "I got the guy in the van and one girl, age twelve, Emma Peters. She's from Maine. Taken from her brother's baseball game when she went to the bathroom."

Nick sighed with relief, sucked in a ragged breath, and gave his report, running on adrenaline. "I've been shot. One dead. One in custody. Javier got away in a black

Charger. I've got one boy, possibly more children in the cellar. I think he's Toby Simmons. The one we got the DNA match for. He's got a broken arm. I need help ASAP."

Hayward spoke fast. "I'm almost there. Ambulance is coming. Can you hang in there until help arrives?"

"Yes." Probably. Maybe. The blood loss was a serious issue. He grabbed the dish towel from the counter and wrapped it around his thigh, but it was too small for him to tie off and use to keep pressure on the wounds. He needed something else, but couldn't identify anything in the kitchen to use. "Just hurry the hell up." Nick hung up.

The boy started to come to and needed his attention.

Nick bent over the kid. "Hey, I'm with the FBI. Are you Toby?"

He nodded.

"Great. I've been looking for you. Are you okay?"

The boy held his injured arm to his chest and shook his head.

"Help is coming." Nick looked toward the back door, then back at the kid. "Are there any other kids here?"

It took Toby a second to work up the nerve to nod, then point to the open back door where Javier had escaped.

"I'm going to go get them. Stay here. I'll be right back. Don't move."

The boy raised himself up on his good arm and shook his head. He sat up and grabbed Nick's sleeve. "Don't go." His gaze shot to Julia, lying dead on the floor.

"She can't hurt you. Javier is gone." He kept his gun at the ready, just in case Mrs. Lopez got any ideas, or Javier decided to come back and finish him off. "I need to get the other kids. Do you want to come with me?"

He nodded.

Nick bobbed his head toward the door. "Okay. Let's go save them. You and me." Nick stood up to his full height, the room spinning a bit as he gained his feet. He could feel the blood running down his leg and soaking his sock.

He looked down at the boy. "Stay right behind me."

The boy nodded.

"Is there anyone else down there with them?"

Toby shook his head.

"Just the kids?"

The boy nodded again.

"How many are down there?"

He held up two fingers, then whimpered because he let go of his broken arm.

"Ambulance is coming. We'll get your arm fixed up and get you back to your family."

The haunted look in the boy's eyes intensified as they filled with fresh tears.

Nick went down the steps into the backyard, then turned back to the kid. He bent and looked the kid in the eye. "Whatever you did to survive was worth it. You survived. You were smart and brave and strong. You did what was *necessary* to stay alive. Look at you, you're still standing. You're still here. That is the most important thing. That's what will matter to your family. I'm so proud of you. I'm in awe of you." Two years this kid had been through what no one should have to endure and survived.

The boy's eyes went wide with surprise.

"Hello," a courageous girl called up from the cellar. "Help us."

"FBI," Nick called. "I'm going to get you out. Stand as far away from the door as you can. I'm going to shoot the lock open. On the count of three." He paused, giving the girl a chance to get herself and the other one back. "You clear?"

"Yes!"

"One." He aimed at the lock at an angle, so it would bust the lock and hopefully not send a bullet into the basement where the kids hid. "Two." He steadied his hand. "Three." He shot the lock, getting it on the first try. Thank fuck, because he felt woozy and off-balance from the blood loss. He needed to wrap something around his thigh and stifle the bleeding. But first...

He pulled off the damaged lock, tossed it, then opened the heavy door to the dark cellar. "Come on out."

The first girl he saw was dressed in a white nightgown that hit her mid-calf. Her feet were bare. Her bright blonde hair was a tangled mess around her shoulders. She looked about thirteen. Behind her a shorter, younger girl, maybe ten, peeked out from behind her. She had dark hair and big green eyes.

Nick held his gun at his thigh, out of sight of the girls. "My name is Nick. I'm with the FBI. You can come up. It's safe."

The oldest girl looked at the boy standing beside him, then at Nick. "They took another girl. Emma."

"My partner rescued her." He held his hand out to her. "Come on up. Are either of you hurt? Hungry? Thirsty? Need a bathroom?"

The second girl bounced from one bare foot to the other. "I gotta go."

"They only left us a bucket down there," the first girl said, her nose scrunched in disgust as she shivered.

Nick swore under his breath. "Come on." He used his good leg to pull himself up the steps. When he stepped into the kitchen, he spotted Julia dead on the floor.

Mrs. Lopez hadn't left her spot at the table and glared at the kids. "I told them not to bring them here anymore."

Yeah, he'd dive into that statement real soon. But right now, he needed to take care of the kids, so he ushered them out of the kitchen to the living room, trying to use his body to block the gruesome sight of Julia's lifeless body.

He turned and looked at all of them, staring up at him. "First door on the right is the bathroom."

The little brunette ran down the hall to the door, shut it, and locked it behind her.

He wondered if he'd need a negotiator to get her out again.

The oldest girl helped Toby sit on the couch and prop his arm on a pillow. Then she dashed back into the kitchen, grabbed three water bottles out of the fridge, and brought them back, offering Toby one after she uncapped it. She left one bottle on the table, then opened one for herself. She and Toby drank them down like they'd been in a desert for a week.

The little one came out of the bathroom, promptly sat down next to the oldest girl, and downed half a bottle of water in three seconds flat, too.

Nick was leaning heavily on his good leg and hoping the cavalry arrived soon. Until then, he headed to the bathroom, found a spare bath towel, and wrapped it around his leg, tying it tight. It hurt like a motherfucker, but staunched the flow of blood.

Just as he walked back into the living room, Agent Hayward walked in with a girl of about twelve, with curly honey-blonde hair, freckles over her nose, and haunted blue eyes. Emma.

"You didn't say anything about being shot in the shoulder," Hayward accused.

Nick winced when he moved the ripped piece of his shirt out of the way to check out the wound. "Oh, no, Julia stabbed me before Javier shot me three times."

The kids all looked at him, aghast.

Emma dropped her jaw, then said, "How are you still standing?"

"He's strong and brave and a survivor," Toby said, nearly making Nick cry, hearing him repeat his words back to him.

Instead he fist-bumped the kid. "Takes one to know one, right?" Nick looked at each of the kids. "Right?"

They all nodded.

"Now give Agent Hayward all your names so we can locate your parents and get you home." Suddenly the room began to tip on Nick. He fell into a chair as dark spots danced in his vision, and then everything went black.

He woke up some time later in the back of an ambulance, all the kids inside with him. The paramedic had braced and wrapped Toby's arm. He sat between Nick's legs. The other three were on the bench or floor.

The paramedic leaned over him. "They refused to be separated or transported without you."

Nick had enough brain cells firing to tell the kids, "I'm going to be fine."

"Promise?" Toby asked.

"It's a promise. My brother's on his way and he's bringing my girlfriend back to me, so I've got a lot to live for. Just like you guys did. Your families are going to be so happy to see you. Just like mine is to see me."

He noticed that the dark-haired little girl turned away and curled up on herself on the tiny bench. After all she'd been through, maybe she just couldn't hope to see the people she loved. She'd probably been told over and over they didn't want her. Poor kid.

Nick would make sure they all got back to their families.

The oldest girl held up his phone. "He called. I answered. I hope that's okay. I told him a little of what happened. He told me to tell you he and Aria love you and Fox and Hawk are flying them home."

Toby touched his bare knee. For the first time, Nick realized the paramedic must have cut off his pants leg to wrap his thigh.

"A fox and a hawk are going to fly them?" Toby looked confused.

"That's their names. Fox is marrying my girlfriend's sister. And Hawk is my cousin. He flies helicopters for a search and rescue team."

Toby nearly grinned. "That sounds awesome. I want to fly in a helicopter."

All the kids nodded that they'd like to do that, too.

"I can make it happen," Nick promised. "But I need you guys to do something. I need you all to talk to the FBI agents about what happened to you. I know it will be hard, but we want to make sure we get the people who hurt you."

Emma leaned forward. "We'll talk to you when you're better."

All the kids nodded.

Well, he'd earned their trust and he wouldn't break it.

Now all he had to do was get fixed up at the hospital and get some rest so he could do right by these kids.

And so he was well enough to kiss Aria's socks off the second she got here. Because damn he missed her, and this incident had been yet another really close call. Too close.

The thought of never seeing her again hurt his heart so much, he vowed he'd do anything to keep her.

Chapter Eighteen

J avier sped down the road, his hand covering the gash cutting across the meaty part of his shoulder near his neck. An inch separated the gash and certain death. If he'd been hit in the neck, he'd be dead.

Instead, he'd lost four kids, one of his men, and his sister. He worried about what they'd do with his mother, too.

He slammed the heel of his hand on the steering wheel, once, twice, three times. "Fuck!" Blood stained his shirt and seeped through his hand, but he'd managed to get away from his mother's house before other agents descended on the property and arrested him.

His sister's lifeless body flashed before his eyes. He wiped the back of his hand across his eyes and the tears that gathered there. He'd been shocked to see her go after the agent like that. He'd thought she'd let him handle it. He had a gun, after all.

She'd been fierce, but ultimately died for her recklessness.

You don't bring a knife to a gun fight.

Stupid woman.

But she was his sister and he loved her in his way.

When she'd gotten tired of living paycheck to paycheck and struggling to make ends meet, he'd come up with the plan to use the resort. He already had clients who were members. He even gave her the glowing recommendation that got her the job. The operation worked seamlessly. No one was the wiser until Agent Gunn started sniffing around. Now everything was fucked.

Well, Agent Gunn wouldn't get away with killing his sister, arresting his mother, or messing with his business.

He slammed his hand on the steering wheel again.

Retribution was coming.

But first, he pulled out his phone and called the doc.

"Pike, it's me. I need your help. Where you at?"

"I'm visiting family. Out of town." Like that mattered.

"I pay you well to take care of things like this and it can't wait. So give me an address. Better yet, send me a pin of where you want to meet, and it better be soon, I'm fucking bleeding everywhere."

"Oh. Uh. Let me see. I'll meet you halfway. But I don't have all my supplies. What's happened, so I know what I'll need?"

"I've been shot, but it's just a deep graze. Top of my shoulder. Near my neck."

"Oh. Okay. I can clean and stitch that. I'm sending you a location now. I'll meet you there."

Javier hung up and tapped the pin, then headed for the doctor. He'd get himself fixed up, then he'd get his business back on track and eliminate the FBI threat trying to take him down.

CHAPTER NINETEEN

Aria sprinted to the information desk in the hospital lobby, barely remembering Mason and Lyric were following behind her. "Which room is Nick Gunn in?" She didn't have time for pleasantries, or being polite. She just needed to see him.

"Are you family?"

"Yes." She held up her thumb and raised her arm to indicate behind her. "That's his brother and sister-in-law." She had no idea what she was to him. At the moment, labels didn't matter.

Well, actually, they kind of did, because being his fuck buddy or girlfriend wouldn't get her any information. It wouldn't get her into his room.

The older woman behind the desk looked past her to Mason and said, "Room 212."

Aria sprinted for the elevator to the left and hit the Call button like ten times in two seconds. She bounced from one foot to the other, impatient.

Mason put his huge hand on her shoulder. "Calm down. You go in there like a tornado and you'll upset him."

"He can be upset all he wants as long as he's okay."

"He's fine. You heard everything my mother said when she called. He's out of surgery. No major damage."

Except for two cracked ribs, extensive bruising across his chest and back, stitches for the two gashes he got when someone tried to stab him. And, oh yeah, a stab wound to his shoulder. That and the through-and-through gunshot wound to his thigh required surgery to clean up and repair. He'd be off that leg and using a crutch for a while. He'd need physical therapy.

The elevator doors opened. It was all she could do to wait for others to walk out before she dashed in and hit the button for the second floor. She should have taken the stairs. She could burn off some of the pent-up energy she'd stored up worrying through the long flight from Boston to here.

Lyric stepped in next to her and Mason filled the rest of the space.

Her sister hooked her arm around Aria's shoulders. "He's going to be okay."

They kept telling her that through the whole flight. She'd seen the look in Lyric's eyes when Mason got that text at the table while they were celebrating Melody and Fox's engagement. Mason had said something to her. Lyric's gaze had met his, and in her eyes, Aria could see the relief that it wasn't him. At the same time, lines of concern for Nick wrinkled her forehead.

Mason and Nick were so close. Brothers, yes, but it was more than that. What they'd both endured on the job and survived brought them even closer.

"My head knows he'll be okay. But...I need to see him." She couldn't explain it. Until she saw him with her own eyes, she couldn't take their word for it.

Nick was tough. Nothing ever really seemed to bother him. Well, except when someone he cared about got hurt or needed help. Then, he was there, ready to do anything and everything for them.

She wanted to be that person for him.

But he hadn't called her. He'd sent that text to Mason and gone silent.

She shouldn't feel like he'd picked Mason over her. Mason had explained they had a system in place for when things went to shit. As they often did in their line of work. So when Mason got the text, he'd called his parents to let them know Nick was in trouble, most likely hurt, then he'd called in to the FBI office to get an update. Mason had shared very few details from that ten-minute call.

All Aria knew was that Nick had gotten close to capturing a very dangerous man. Their suspect shot him three times. Thank fucking God for his vest, or he'd be dead. The guy's sister stabbed Nick, while Nick tried to save some children.

Heroic stuff.

That was her Nick.

There to help everyone. To right wrongs. To take down the bad guys. To rescue children taken from their families.

But Aria wanted to be Nick's first call.

The elevator doors opened and she nearly ran into his parents. "Oh. Sorry."

Nick's mom, Adeline, took her by the shoulders. "He's going to be so happy to see you." She pulled Aria into a hug, holding her close for a few seconds before stepping back.

"Where are you going?" She stared at both Adeline and her husband, Noah, who she'd met several times when they came down to Wyoming to visit Mason and get to know Lyric.

Noah gave her a quick hug, then looked from her to Mason and back again. "Nick is asleep. We've been here all night. We're just going home to freshen up, have a good meal, some sleep, then come back later. They'll discharge him and the children tomorrow."

"Are their families here?" Mason asked.

Adeline shook her head. "Not yet. They've notified the parents and helped them get flights, but they won't start arriving until tomorrow afternoon. The FBI will want to interview the kids before they send them home. From what I understand, the kids refused to be separated from Nick. They're all in there with him. They won't talk to anyone, just among themselves."

Aria still hadn't been told about the children and their situation. "Are they okay?"

"One has a badly broken arm. The others seem to be fine, though how can they be when they've been kidnapped and trafficked." Noah's disgust for the people who did that to them rang in his words, along with his sorrow for the children.

"I'm sorry. I need to see him." She rushed past Adeline and Noah and straight to room 212, where two agents stopped her.

Mason came up behind her. "Aria is Nick's girlfriend."

They gave the nod and she burst through the door and found Nick straight ahead, lying in a bed, dead asleep.

"Ssh."

She turned to the other four beds packed in the room and found a young boy with a broken arm and three girls. The group looked to be somewhere between seven and twelve years old.

The boy's eyes went wide when Mason walked in behind her. At six-three and solid muscle, he looked intimidating to most people.

Aria wanted to put the kids at ease. "This is Nick's brother, Mason. I'm Aria, Nick's girlfriend." She pointed to her sister. "And that's my sister Lyric. She's married to Mason."

"Nick said you were coming." The oldest girl whispered like Aria had done to keep from waking Nick.

Still, he mumbled from the bed, "Ari."

She went to him and brushed her fingers through his hair. "Sleep. I'll be here when you wake up." She kissed his forehead, then pressed her head to his and inhaled a full breath for the first time in hours. "I love you."

He leaned his head to hers for just a moment, then she felt him relax back into sleep. She stood next to the bed and for the first time really looked at him. His left shoulder was wrapped in bandages. The other side of his chest was bare, except for a mottled bruise blooming on his pec and barely seen over the sheet. She carefully lifted it and hissed at the massive bruising.

Mason moved to the other side of the bed and checked it out with a wince. "Thank God he had his vest on," he whispered, then met her gaze. "He's okay."

She knew that, but looking at him only brought home how close she'd come to losing him.

Lyric put her arm around Aria's back, her hand on Aria's hip. "It looks bad, but you know he's going to be up and ready to go in a couple of days. Nothing keeps a Gunn down for long."

"That's for damn sure," Mason agreed, then turned to Hawk, who had walked into the room after taking care of the helicopter he brought them here in. "Gunns don't quit. We never give up."

Lyric yawned. The pregnancy was making her exceptionally tired, and it had been a long day.

Mason jumped to it and went around the bed to pull her close. "He's asleep. Let's go to the cabin and get some rest. We can come back in a few hours."

Lyric looked to Aria. "Come with us."

She shook her head. "I'm staying with him." She settled into the chair beside the bed and laced her fingers through Nick's. She wanted him to know she was here. If he woke up, she wanted to be the first thing he saw.

"I'll hang out a bit, too." Hawk pulled up the chair across from her and sat down.

Lyric gave Hawk a hug, then left with Mason.

Hawk stared across Nick at her. "Rumor is you two broke up."

"I ended it, because he seemed to care more about work than me. Then he told me we weren't over. We started really talking to each other. He convinced the FBI to set up an office where I live and bought a house. I'm so damn happy he refused to let go." She picked up his hand and kissed the back of it.

Nick didn't wake, but he turned his head toward her.

"So you're back together?" Hawk's sharp gaze studied her.

"He is everything I want and more. But I know he loves his job. I'd never ask him to give it up. The way he'd never ask me to leave my family and the business we've built. It seemed we couldn't overcome the distance."

"But Nick found a way." Hawk glanced at his cousin, then back to Aria.

"That's what Nick does. Right? He's moving to Wyoming to be with me." Saying it out loud made it seem all the more real. It made her love him all the more because he was changing his life to be a part of hers.

"So, you're all in now."

"He has my whole heart. He always did. But I couldn't stand to be the last thing on his mind, or the thing he put off for something else. I'm hoping things change once he's in Blackrock Falls."

Hawk nodded, a frown on his face, though he never really smiled. "That had to be hard."

"I want a life with him." She stared at Nick's gorgeous face. "I almost lost him twice before we could make our dreams a reality."

"He's tough. It's going to take more than a couple of bullets and some psycho with a knife to take him down."

Aria looked over her shoulder at the kids. "Since he goes up against people willing to try to kill him all the time, it's not that reassuring."

Hawk acknowledged that with a tilted frown and nod. "He's going to be really happy to see you."

"I've missed him so much. I hope this case is over and we can finally be together."

"It won't be over until Nick has his man in custody."

Aria sighed, knowing Hawk was right. She briefly glanced at the four kids trying to be quiet while they whispered between them. "I just hope those kids are safe now."

She wondered if the reason they weren't asleep was because they were too afraid to let their guard down.

Hawk narrowed his gaze on all of them. "They've probably been through more than their fair share of misery."

"I'm bored," one of the girls whined. "Can we watch TV?"

The oldest girl shook her head. "Agent Nick needs his rest."

Hawk stood, drawing the attention of every child. "I'll go see if they've got something in the gift shop downstairs for you to do."

Aria picked up her bag and pulled out some cash. "Raid the snack machine for them, too."

Hawk stared at the stack of bills. "That's a lot of ones."

"Tips from the bar," she whispered back with a smirk.

Hawk approached the kids to ask for their candy order, then he walked out.

The room remained quiet until he returned with a pack of cards, a checkers set, and enough candy to fill a Halloween bucket. The kids were all smiles, making her wonder how, after everything they'd been through—being taken from their home and family, being at the mercy of monsters—they still trusted a stranger, who handed them candy and sat down to play a game with them.

Resilience. Courage. Strength. Heart.

Those were the things monsters couldn't touch or take or crush, because a hero found them and restored their faith that good people do good things, and they recognized the difference between a good man and a monster.

They recognized anyone associated with Nick was a good guy.

"What are your names?" Hawk asked, keeping his distance, letting the kids get used to him.

The oldest spoke for all of them. "I'm Nicole. That's Emma and Stacy." She notched her chin up toward the boy with the cast on his arm. "Toby can't wait for Nick to wake up."

Aria smiled at the little boy. "Me, too." She wanted to ask how he'd broken his arm, but was afraid of the answer and reminding him of what he'd gone through.

"Is there really an agent outside the door?" Toby asked. "Is it because Agent Nick thinks *he's* coming back to get us?"

Hawk stood and left little Emma's bed and headed over to Toby. He stood at the end of the bed and looked the little boy in the face. "There are two agents outside that door. They will protect you with their lives. But they aren't there because the FBI thinks someone is coming for you. They're there to make *you* feel safe until your family comes to pick you up."

Stacy's bottom lip trembled. "What's going to happen when we go home and there are no agents?"

Hawk turned to her. "Nick and every agent on his team are going to find the people who hurt you and they're going to lock them up and never let them out again." Hawk took a couple of steps closer to Stacy, then sat on the edge of her bed. "I know you're scared. I would be, too, if I was you. I was in the military. I fought in the war overseas. I know what it feels like to be really scared. And when you go home, you may feel that way a lot. But you'll have people there who care about you, who will help you learn to feel safe again. It will take time. But one day you'll catch yourself laughing or smiling or just having fun. And it will feel weird, because you've been through what no one else has been through exactly the way you've been through it. You might even think you don't deserve to be happy. Or you'll think, finally, you do get to be happy. Whatever you feel, however you feel, just keep telling yourself you do deserve to be happy."

Aria appreciated that Hawk spoke plain and didn't make promises that everything would magically be better. He simply told the kids the truth.

She wondered what Hawk's long-sleeve shirt was hiding. What was beneath his skin? What lingered in his mind? What tormented his sleep? What was he holding on to that kept him quiet and on the fringe of the family?

Because the haunted look in his eyes matched the one in these children's eyes.

Aria wanted to see them laugh and smile and feel carefree. She hoped that hadn't been permanently stolen from them like their childhoods.

Nick would want them to find that again. It's why he worked so hard to save them. Why he put his life in jeopardy.

Why he'd never quit.

She'd accepted that. Now she had to find a way to live with it, and be the person in his life who helped him through the hard times and enjoyed the good times they'd have together by his side.

Chapter Twenty

Nick woke up holding Aria's hand and seeing her sweet smile. The TV was on low and the kids were watching a *Futurama* rerun. They all looked relaxed.

Aria squeezed his hand. "They just finished dinner. Hawk went out and got them all ice cream. They finished the whole tub. Mason and Lyric will be back soon."

He smiled for the first time since he'd last seen her. "You made a new friend."

Stacy was sound asleep on Aria's lap. Aria held the ten-year-old, her arms wrapped protectively around her, Stacy's head tucked under Aria's chin.

"She had a bad dream. I offered her a hug. Told her I could use one, too. She went right back to sleep, though I think it had more to do with a full belly and her trying to stay awake and on guard."

He couldn't fault the child for that after all she'd been through. "I want you in my arms so badly right now," he whispered, not wanting the kids to overhear him. Not caring that Aria heard the desperation in his plea.

"I want that, too. How are you? Are you in pain? Do you need me to get the doctor?"

He shook his head, setting off a wave of pain through his shoulder and chest. "The nurse probably knows I woke up. She'll be here soon."

"That didn't answer my questions."

"I'm fine. It's nothing."

Her eyes narrowed and her nose scrunched. "Getting shot three times and stabbed is not nothing," she whisper-yelled at him. "Why the hell did you go into that place alone?"

He answered her by looking at the kids in the room.

She huffed out a frustrated breath. "You could have died."

It had been another close call. Closer than he'd really like to think about. "Are you really mad? Is this too much for you?"

"What? No. I'm not mad at you. You saved these kids' lives. I was scared to death I'd lose you. I'll take you any way I can get you, but you better try to stay in one damn piece."

His grin grew into a full-blown smile. "I'll do my best."

The nurse knocked gently, then walked into the room. The two girls at the other end of the room went on alert until they realized it was just the nurse they'd had last night. Nick had asked that they limit the number of new faces that came into the room, so the kids weren't in a constant state of fight or flight.

"It's just me, Carly, kids. You all good?"

The girls nodded. Toby barely managed to open his eyes before closing them again, thanks to the meds the nurse gave him earlier for his broken arm.

"You push that button if you need anything. Right now, I'm going to check out your superhero."

Nick rolled his eyes.

Carly did her usual routine, checking his blood pressure, heart rate, oxygen level. "One to ten, what's your pain level right now?"

"About a six."

"Have you hit that button for the morphine since you woke up?" She checked the monitor and his IV line.

"No. I wanted to be lucid while I stared at my gorgeous girlfriend holding a little girl like she's her favorite thing in the world, besides me."

Aria chuckled. "She is a good snuggler."

"She needs them." Nick was so glad to see Stacy reaching out to someone for affection after what she'd been through. Kids in her situation lost their trust in others.

But Nick got why Stacy ended up in Aria's arms. Who could resist her warmth and understanding?

"But soon, it's going to be my turn." He held her beautiful blue gaze.

"You took ten years off my life, Nick. You owe me some affection."

"I will deliver." He winked at her.

Carly narrowed her gaze. "Not in your condition, honey. You can't even raise your arm."

Nick shrugged his good shoulder. "I guarantee I can manage with one arm."

Carly rolled her eyes. "You just take some time to heal first."

Nick stared at Aria. "She's the best medicine I could get."

Aria blushed, but she never stopped smiling. "I think he's definitely on the mend."

Yeah. And he had work to do to protect these kids from the bastard who tried to kill him. "Has Agent Hayward been by?"

Aria glared at him. "Yes. I sent him away. You need your rest. You need to take some time to let what happened to you settle."

"I'm fine, Aria."

"Are you? Because I wouldn't be if someone tried to kill me." Tears gathered in her eyes and one spilled over her lashes, killing him.

"Baby, please don't cry. Not when I can't get out of this bed and hold you."

The girls scrambled off the bed across the way and immediately went to Aria, wrapping their arms around her.

Nick stared in astonishment.

"It's okay." Emma patted Aria's head.

Nicole squeezed Aria's hand. "They were going to move us that afternoon. If he hadn't shown up, who knows if anyone would have ever found us?"

Nick stored away that little bit of information.

Emma petted Aria's hair again and again. "They were trying to find someone to fix Toby's arm, but the guy didn't answer his phone. Some doctor named Pick."

"Pike," Nicole corrected.

Stacy woke up in Aria's arms. "What's going on?" She looked at the two girls. "Is everything okay?"

"Agent Nick's awake."

Stacy sat up with a grin. "You slept a long time."

"I needed it, like you."

Nurse Carly went to Stacy. "I think Miss Aria would like to give Agent Nick a big ol' hug. Let's get you settled back in your bed. If you're ready."

Stacy glanced up at Aria. "Thanks."

"Anytime, my friend. Would you like me to help you get snuggled under the covers?"

Stacy's cheeks pinked, but she nodded despite the embarrassment.

"You got it." Aria rose and hugged Stacy to her chest.

He hadn't thought much about having a family. With his demanding schedule, he didn't know how he'd fit it in. But now, things were changing. Because of her. All Nick could think was that one day she'd carry their child in her arms and put them to bed just like that. And just like Stacy, they'd look into Aria's eyes and feel her love and know that they were safe and loved.

That's how she made him feel, too.

Now, having kids didn't seem so challenging. He wanted to see Aria as the mother of their kids. He wanted that happy, chaotic family life he remembered from his childhood.

Aria settled Stacy and turned off the light over her bed. The other two girls crawled back into their beds and did the same.

Nurse Carly pressed the button on Nick's pain meds for him. He glared at her.

"You need them, use them. At least for tonight. The more sleep you get, the better you'll feel, and the more you can be with her."

Aria came to his side. "I'm not going anywhere, so take her advice and get some sleep."

Nick held up his good arm even though it hurt his chest and cracked rib. Aria gently leaned over him, kissed him softly, and held him close. Her familiar peach scent filled his nose and eased him. She smelled like summer and sunshine. She smelled and felt like home.

He buried his face in her neck and didn't want to ever let her go. "I'm sorry I ruined your trip to Boston. I know you wanted to check out the city."

"Nick, it's okay. I'd rather be here with you anyway."

She'd been looking forward to the trip. She didn't often get to travel. The bar and her family took up all her time. "I'll take you there. We'll go together and explore everything. You can visit your sister."

She pulled back and looked him in the eye. "You don't have to make anything up to me. As long as you're okay, I'm happy."

"I want to make you happy."

"You do." She kissed him again and all he wanted to do was pull her into the bed with him and kiss her over and over again until neither of them were thinking about anything but each other.

But they had an audience and every jostle of his body hurt like hell.

Aria sensed him tensing in her arms and immediately released him and stood up. "Just rest, Nick. You'll be out of here soon and we'll figure the rest out."

Mason and Lyric walked in slowly, giving the kids a chance to see them, before they headed for Nick.

"How you doing, man?" Mason put his hand on Nick's shoulder and gave him a gentle squeeze.

"Waking up to her is heaven every time."

Aria smiled at him. "He's feeling guilty because we cut our trip to Boston short."

Lyric waved that away. "Melody is marrying a multi-millionaire. Fox offered to fly us in any time we want."

Nick reached for his phone on the table beside his bed, but Aria snatched it away first, then turned to Mason and whispered, "Nick is sidelined, so you're up, big guy. Emma said that they were going to get a Dr. Pike to fix Toby's arm but he's out of town visiting a sick relative. From the story Nick gave you about what went down, Javier is hurt and can't exactly go to a hospital with a gunshot wound. I bet Dr. Pike has already heard from him."

Nick stared at Aria.

"What?" She raised a brow.

"You'd make a good agent."

She shook her head. "I'll leave that to you. After you get some more rest." She brushed her hand over his head and kept running her fingers through his hair, soothing him. The drugs were starting to kick in and make him sleepy.

"I'm on this." Mason walked out of the room, probably to call Agent Hayward, who was heading up the investigation while Nick was out of commission.

Aria tugged Lyric closer. "We could go out later and get the kids a few things they'll need before they see their parents again."

Lyric's eyes lit up. "Yes. Absolutely." They kept their voices low so the kids didn't hear, but Nick heard and loved Aria even more for thinking of them and what they'd need for the next couple days.

Aria squeezed his hand. "If you give me your keys, I'll go by your place and pick up some clothes for you."

He barely had enough energy to smile at her. "Mom and Dad are going to bring my stuff tomorrow."

"Okay."

He worried about her leaving. "You don't have a car."

Lyric sat in Aria's vacant seat. "Hawk and his brothers came by Mason's place while we were there and left us his Land Rover."

Aria leaned over him just before he fell asleep. "You have nothing to worry about. The kids are fine. Mason is getting someone to track down the doctor. I'm not going anywhere. Sleep."

The last thing he remembered was he wanted to tell her he loved her and the taste of her sweet lips against his before everything went blank.

Chapter Twenty-One

Nick woke up with four kids staring at him in the morning. He knew it was easier for his fellow agents to guard them like this, but it still would have been nice if Aria could have stayed with him. All he'd wanted last night was for her to crawl in the bed beside him, so he could hold her close and sleep knowing she was right there.

The kids hadn't wanted to be separated from him since he found them. He understood they needed some sort of assurance that they were safe. He loved that they trusted him. It would make things easier when they had to question the kids about what they'd been through and with who. If they even knew any names to begin with.

He hated the idea of making them relive their worst nightmares.

All he could think about right now was that Aria was here, in Montana—not in his room where he wanted her at the moment, but close. He wondered how long she planned to stay.

And when she'd get back here.

"Someone looks really grumpy this morning." His mom walked in with his dad.

Dad smirked at him. "There's a blue-eyed brunette missing from his side." His dad pulled his mom into the crook of his arm and kissed her on the head.

Nick wished Aria were here right now.

He certainly wasn't jealous, but he did envy his parents' close and long-lasting relationship. It's what he wanted with Aria. He lost her because of the distance between them. Then he'd nearly been killed again the day before yesterday. Today, all he wanted was for her to be here with him.

Just when his heart rate started spiking on the machine beside him, the door opened again and Aria walked in ahead of her sister Lyric, both of them holding up backpacks in each hand. Their bright smiles saturated the room with their excitement.

The kids all perked up and smiled.

He couldn't help the swell of love that went through him seeing Aria so joyously present a dark blue backpack to Toby and a deep purple one to Stacy, the quietest of the girls. Lyric handed a light green one to Nicole and a forest-green one to Emma.

Squeals and smiles and even a few tears from the girls as they opened their gifts filled the room. Each of them got two new outfits, including a pack of underwear and socks and a pair of tennis shoes. The girls each got a nail polish in a bright, happy color, a bottle of fruity-scented lotion, some candy, a bag of double-chocolate cookies, a word search book, a journal with a pen, and a travel-size game. Yahtzee, Uno, and Sorry!

Toby gaped at the new clothes and shoes. When he found the small dump truck and race car, he smiled so big his cheeks puffed out. He also got Go Fish and War cards, plus some crayons and two coloring books to go with his new stash of candy and cookies.

They all looked so happy as they showed off their stuff to each other.

Aria and Lyric stood back, watching them, smiles on their faces, their hearts on display for everyone to see.

"My boys got lucky with those Wilde girls." Mom squeezed his shoulder and smiled down at him as Mason walked in the room.

"We did." Nick choked up a bit because he was so damn proud to call Aria his, but also because he was still trying to figure out how to keep her. The job in Blackrock Falls would be less demanding, since he'd have fewer agents to oversee. The cases would be more local. He wouldn't have to travel so much. Which meant he'd be home more, but still be helping people and taking criminals off the streets. And if he trusted his guys more, let loose the reins on them, allowed himself to not have to control everything, he wouldn't have to be in the field so much.

He'd work on that, so he could spend more time with Aria.

And if he couldn't let go enough to have a life, he'd talk to the FBI's counseling team about it. Because the last thing he wanted to do was ever make Aria feel like he cared more about his job than her.

She turned to him and held up a shopping bag he hadn't seen until now. "I hope you didn't think I forgot about you."

He didn't need anything but her. "I have everything I need standing in front of me."

She leaned in and kissed him. It was soft and tame and nowhere near enough, but he'd take it for now. "Don't you want to see what I brought you?" She set the bag between his legs.

He peeked inside and grinned at a dozen of his favorite chocolate croissants from the bakery he loved beneath an oval metal key chain that held a picture of him and Aria kissing. A selfie she snapped when they were on their first official date.

"I have a matching one. We belong together. So when you finally move, we'll have matching keys to *our* place."

Their place. Finally she agreed to move in with him. *Yes!*

The joy he felt in that moment was quickly eclipsed by the threat Javier spewed at him in that kitchen before he left Nick bleeding all over the floor. *I will fucking hunt you down and kill the one you love most, and then I'll kill you.*

Nick couldn't take the chance that Javier went after Aria. More than likely he'd go after his brother, Mason. An eye for an eye and all that. His brother could protect himself and Lyric. But Nick was in no shape to protect Aria. The only way he could do that was to stay away from her until Javier was in custody. Dead would be better, because Javier had a far reach, people who owed him. People who would do anything for him to keep their secrets safe.

Fuck.

He couldn't tell her he wasn't coming home anytime soon.

"Nick?" Her worried gaze searched his.

He'd waited too long to say something and now he had her worried that moving in with her wasn't what he wanted more than anything. He pulled out the key chain and held it in his fisted hand. "You have no idea what this means to me."

"It means everything you want it to mean. Everything we talked about. You and me and a life together." She bashfully glanced at his parents, then back to him. "Right?"

He held her gaze. "That's exactly what I want."

"Then that's what we'll have." She pressed her lips tight and her gaze shied away from him.

"What is it?"

She turned back and shook her head. "I don't want to spoil this."

He wanted her to be able to tell him anything. "Aria, talk to me."

She huffed out a frustrated breath. "I can't stay." She was needed at home. At the bar. "Mason wants to stay and help you with the case; Lyric is of course staying with him. They'll discharge you in a couple of hours, and though you're supposed to go home and rest, I know you're going to take these kids to be reunited with their parents. As much as I'd like to stay and help you with that..."

His heart deflated. "I understand. You have to go."

"I don't want to." The anguish in her eyes hurt his heart.

"I know you don't. Just promise me you'll be careful. Stay alert. If you're tied to me, you could be a target."

"I can take care of myself." She took his hand and squeezed it. "I'll be fine. You're the one who needs to watch your back."

"It's just...if something happened to you...I couldn't take it."

She kissed him, her lips soft and warm against his. "I don't want to lose you either."

"How are you getting home?"

She pressed the back of his hand to her belly as she held it. "Hawk is flying me back."

That made him feel better. She wouldn't be traveling alone.

He squeezed her hand. "You know I'd rather go with you."

"I know. But they need you." She turned and smiled at the kids.

Nicole and Emma were painting their nails. Stacy was coloring with Toby. They were all relaxed. Happy.

All too soon, he'd take them to their parents and the reality of their past would come back to haunt them.

He squeezed her hand. "Thank you for doing this for them. For giving them a little piece of normal before they have to face their past."

"They're kids. They're resilient. And we'll keep in touch with them, make sure they're safe and okay."

He stared up at her, amazed by her big heart. "Why would you do that?"

"Because you saved them. And they deserve to have good people in their lives who stick. Mason told me on the plane, there are a lot of people you help that you're still in touch with."

He felt humbled. "What else did he tell you?"

"Nothing I didn't already know. You love your job, because you help people. You care. And that's why I love you."

"I love you, too."

She brushed her fingers through his hair. "I know."

"I hope you'll still love me when my caring so much means I spend way too much time away from you."

She leaned in, her gaze right on him. "Even then." She kissed him again.

His mom sighed next to him.

Nick could feel his father's pride and happiness that Nick had someone like Aria by his side. On his side. "I don't deserve you."

"I bet those kids would say you deserve everything good that comes your way."

"You're the best thing that ever happened to me."

"I want to be." She brushed her fingers through his hair. "Now, eat before you have to get ready to go. Can I get you a coffee?"

"No. Just stay right here. I don't want to miss a minute before you leave again."

She helped him hand out croissants to everyone in the room, then sat beside him while he ate two himself. Mom and Dad caught up with Mason and Lyric. They talked a lot about the baby Lyric was carrying and made plans for a baby shower and visiting them as soon as the baby was born.

Aria chimed in with ideas for the baby shower and made a list of things they'd need for the baby. She seemed really into it, but he saw the hint of envy in her eyes that it was her sister and not her.

He couldn't wait to have a family with her. But first he'd like to get them under the same roof. And in the same bed every night.

Soon.

Well, as soon as he could get Javier Lopez locked up where he belonged.

Chapter Twenty-Two

Nick watched the reunion at the FBI offices between the parents and children. Everyone looked hesitant, excited, worried, and a bit wary. He couldn't imagine not knowing where his child was, or if they were dead or alive.

Nicole hesitated. She didn't get too close to her parents until her mom broke down crying and said, "I love you so much. I've missed you so much." Nicole rushed into her mother's arms and held her like she'd never let go. Nicole had been missing fourteen long months. All that time, abused and wishing to go home but told no one wanted her back.

It was a tactic used to dehumanize and disillusion victims. Make them feel like they're not wanted. Make them feel like there was nowhere for them to go.

He hated seeing that look in someone's eyes, like they weren't worth saving.

Everyone was worth saving.

Everyone deserved a safe and happy life.

And Javier Lopez deserved life in a cage for making Nicole hesitate for those few seconds, for making her believe that maybe they didn't want her back with every fiber of their being.

It sickened him.

But their reunion made him believe that good won over evil.

He wished Aria could be here to see this.

Emma's dad didn't hesitate to scoop her into his arms, hold her close, and cry, even as he smiled into her face and said, "Thank God," over and over and over again as his wife buried her face in Emma's side and Emma held a fistful of her mother's hair. Emma had been taken from her brother's baseball game nine months ago. Mom and Dad had been right there, waiting for her to return from the restroom.

The panic they must have felt when they realized she was gone. The guilt and second-guessing they must have done, thinking if only one of them had accompanied her, kept her safe.

But it wasn't their fault. They thought their daughter would be safe in their town, with so many good people nearby to help if needed. They'd probably let her go to the restroom dozens of times before and everything turned out fine.

You couldn't live your life expecting the worst. That was no way to live.

It would be harder for them to live carefree now. To not set boundaries that stifled Emma.

They'd find a balance. Someday. Right now, all they wanted was Emma close.

Toby shook like a leaf when his parents approached him. Tears cascaded down his face. "I'm sorry," he whispered, his head bent, eyes on the ground. He'd been taken two years and one month ago, when someone walked off with him from the mall when his mother turned to pick out a new shirt for him and he wandered away from her.

His parents both kneeled on the floor in front of him. They both said the same thing. "You didn't do anything wrong. We're so happy to have you back." Toby didn't fall into their arms. He stayed three feet away. He was the youngest, taken when he was just six years old. So easy for someone so young to forget what life was like at home with his family. Especially when he'd been abused, mentally and physically, groomed by countless men.

Nick wished he could wash it all away for him. For all of them.

Toby's mother took a step toward him and crouched low.

Toby took a step back.

The heartbreak in his mother's eyes didn't dim the smile on her face.

All the parents had been warned by a psychologist that the kids might not want to be touched. They would be overwhelmed, unsure, and scared.

Toby's parents took it in stride and tried to coax him to talk more with them. "What do you have in your hand?" his father asked.

Toby held up the Pontiac Firebird Aria had given him.

The dad looked impressed. "That's a really cool car. Where did you get it?"

Toby looked up at Nick, then back to his parents. "Aria gave it to me."

Nick couldn't kneel like the parents due to the crutch he was using to keep himself steady and upright while he kept his weight off his injured leg. "My girlfriend and her sister bought the kids the backpacks and clothes and toys, so they'd have something of their own to take home."

"Agent Nick," Stacy called out, backing away from her father and grandmother, panic in her voice. Apparently her mother wasn't in the picture anymore, hadn't been for years. Stacy had been reported missing twenty months ago by the grandmother, though the story didn't quite add up, because Karl said he'd been at work since Stacy left for school that morning and had no idea when Stacy went missing. He thought maybe she'd stayed at a friend's house for the night.

Who doesn't know where their ten-year-old is? Especially when they aren't home after school, or by dinner?

The grandmother, Donna, went to pick up Stacy at school the next day, like she always did on Tuesday, but Stacy never came out to the car in the pickup line. The grandmother went to the classroom and spoke to the teacher, only to discover Stacy hadn't been to class in two days.

Nick excused himself from Toby and his parents, then turned to Stacy.

Karl took a quick step toward her when she called to Nick again. Karl grabbed her arm and yanked her toward him, whispering something in her ear. Stacy's hands trembled at her sides and suddenly the lavender-colored leggings she was wearing turned a darker shade of purple between her thighs. It took Nick a second to realize she'd peed her pants.

Donna gasped. "Stacy. You should have said you needed to go."

Karl glared at her and held her arm tighter. "You stupid girl."

Nick fumed at the derogatory reprimand. "Let her go." His order made everyone in the room stop and stare. He didn't want to frighten the children, but he needed to get Stacy away from Karl.

Who reprimanded and scared their kid so badly they peed after what Stacy had been through?

Karl seemed to catch himself and released Stacy, then stood, looking nervous, sweat glistening on his brow. "She's fine. Aren't you, girl."

Girl. Not honey. Sweetheart. Some other nickname that meant something special. Stacy was his daughter. She'd been missing for nearly two years, and this was how he treated her.

Stacy wrapped her scrawny arms around her middle, her whole body trembling.

The kids had all warmed up to Nick, since he found them and spent a day and half with them in the hospital. So he took a chance that he didn't make things worse for Stacy, leaned over, so his mouth was right next to her ear, and asked, "What can I do for you?"

She turned her big, watery, green eyes on him, then whispered in his ear, "Save me again?"

His heart broke in half right before the rage hit him. He hooked his right arm around her hips, picked her up, and used the left crutch to keep the weight off his bad leg, and carried her right out of there, despite how much it hurt his injuries. Holding her was definitely not helping his stab wound or bruised ribs, but he'd muscle through the pain to protect her.

"Hey. Where are you going?" Donna called.

Stacy kept a death grip with both her arms locked around his neck as he took her out of the conference room and through the office. He ducked into the first empty room he found and slammed the door.

Stacy trembled in his arms.

He hoped she wasn't afraid of him. "You're okay, sweetheart." He leaned against the desk, released the crutch, and rubbed her back, just holding her, hoping she said something more about why she needed to be saved again, so he'd know what to do.

"I-is A-Aria coming back s-soon?"

The quake in her words hurt his heart.

"Do you want to talk to her?" Maybe that's exactly what she needed. A woman. Someone she knew. Someone who'd been kind to her. Someone she trusted. "I can call her right now and you can talk to her."

Stacy leaned back, her bottom lip quivering. "If I tell her the secret, she can t-tell you, and you'll s-save me."

His heart bled even more for her. "You can tell me. I *will* save you."

She bit her bottom lip. "Can we still call her?"

Choked up and trying not to lose it as this little girl broke his heart with her big, sad eyes and her quaking body, her whole face telling him she had something really bad to tell him, he could only nod.

He hated to bring Aria into this, but if the kid trusted her and him, then she'd get both of them. "Let's call her."

Aria wouldn't disappoint her. She'd never disappointed him.

He pulled out his phone as he held Stacy against his chest, her arm still hooked around his neck.

Nick put the call on speaker after he hit the speed dial for Aria. The phone rang once and Aria answered. "Hey, you. I miss you already." Her cheerful voice did a lot to ease his anxiety.

"I miss you, too. And so does someone else." He held the phone closer to Stacy.

"Aria," Stacy called out, then used her free hand to hold the phone closer to her.

"Stacy? Is that my sweet girl?"

Not stupid girl. Not just a girl. Aria's sweet girl.

Stacy almost smiled. "Yes. It's me."

"How are you doing, sweetheart?"

Nick answered for her, because he wanted to try to give Aria some kind of warning. "Stacy's upset. The families are here. Stacy got a little scared and overwhelmed. She needed to hear your voice."

"Well, I'm glad you called. I was worried about you, honey. You didn't want to talk about your dad in the hospital. I get it. It can be hard to be away from someone for a long time. You're not sure how they'll be when you see them again. Is that it, honey?"

Nick was so damn proud of Aria for trying to connect with this scared, traumatized little girl.

Stacy shook her head, though only he could see that. "No. Maybe. It's just…"

Nick took over, since the little one didn't know what to say. "Aria, Stacy asked me to save her again."

"Of course you will." Not a second of hesitation before that declaration.

He loved her even more for having such faith in him.

"But why, Stacy? What's wrong?"

Nick looked into Stacy's troubled eyes. "Stacy has a secret she wants to tell us."

"You can tell us anything, sweetheart. It won't change how we feel about you. You're so special, sweetheart. Whatever it is, we will help you."

Stacy met his gaze. "Promise?"

"I promise," Nick and Aria said at the same time.

"Go ahead, sweetheart," Aria coaxed. "You are brave and strong. I know you can do this,"

Nick stopped breathing, waiting for her to say whatever she needed to say, hoping it was something inconsequential like she still wet the bed at night. But he knew before she even spoke it was going to be something worse.

She leaned in and whispered, "My dad gave me to the man who gave me to the other bad man who shot you."

Aria gasped. "Oh, honey, I'm so sorry he did that to you."

Nick reined in his fury and kept his gaze on Stacy. "The man he gave you to...was it someone he knew?"

Stacy nodded, her eyes watery with tears. "He owed him money. But he didn't have any to give him, so he gave him me, because the man wanted me real bad. But I didn't like him. He acted real nice but his eyes were...strange. He looked at me so...hard. And then he...hurt me. Made me do stuff."

Nick didn't want to push, but he needed more information to keep her safe. "Do you know his name?"

"Perry. He owned the big company in town. Daddy played poker with him. And lost. A lot. He'd get really mad and say if he didn't have to feed me he wouldn't need so much money."

That fucker blamed his child for his gambling. Nick fumed, but tried not to show it.

"It is not your fault, sweetheart. Your dad was supposed to take care of you, not gamble away all the money. He should have protected you." Aria's leashed anger still permeated her words, and maybe that's exactly what Stacy needed to hear and know, that someone was furious about what her father did to her.

Nick still needed more. "How long did you stay with Perry?"

She shrugged, but her eyes filled with tears and her lips pressed tight. "A while. He wouldn't let me go to school. He kept me locked in a room in the basement. And he did...bad things. It hurt. Then he dressed me up and took me to a fancy place. It had pretty things and a big bed and big windows. I could see a big pool and lots of trees. I wanted to run away but he never let go of me, or let me outside. Then the other man showed up. Javier. He said I looked nice. Sweet." Her gaze dropped to the floor. "He said the others would like me." Those whispered words gutted him.

"Why did Perry want to give you to Javier?" Maybe this question was too broad for her to answer.

Stacy shrugged again. "Perry said he had to mend him, or something. Perry kept saying sorry to Javier, but he just looked mean at Perry."

Mend him? Mend? Perry was sorry. Maybe... "Did he say make amends?"

Stacy nodded, then shrugged. "That sounds right. Maybe. I was trying really hard to be good and be quiet so I didn't get punished."

"Was Javier mean to you?"

"Not really. Not like Perry. He wasn't around much. There were others like Julia who kept us." Not took care of them. Kept them. What a distinction she'd made at such a young age.

Nick tried to get a little more from her. "Were you with Javier for a long time?"

She nodded. "I was there for a few days, and then Emma arrived and they kept us together."

That would help him figure out a timeline, once he pieced the other kidnappings together and put it all into one complete story.

"Did Javier ever hurt you like Perry did?"

She shook her head. "He came around sometimes, but mostly Julia kept us in the cellar and took me to the bad men in the cabins or at the big place."

"The resort."

She nodded.

He didn't want to get into what happened to her in the cabins and at the resort. They'd have a child psychologist ask those questions in a way that wouldn't cause more damage. He was not qualified for that. "Is there anything else you want to tell us?"

"Nicole told me to ask them their names, so we could tell the police."

"Do you remember some of the names?"

She nodded again. "All of them. She made us remember. We'd say them, so we never forgot who hurt us, so we could hurt them."

Nick hugged her tighter. "You are amazing. I will make sure that you get to hurt them." He'd arrest every single one and ruin their lives the way they ruined this little girl's childhood. And it would be Stacy who ultimately won by living the rest of her life free, while those bastards rotted in a cell, having lost everything.

Aria sniffed back tears. "Sweetheart, you are the bravest, strongest, most fantastic person I've ever known. You will get your chance to make them pay for hurting you. And then you are going to do big, bold things with your life. I know it."

"Can I come live with you?" The desperate plea hit Nick like a sledgehammer to the heart. "I don't want to go back with him." Her eyes begged him. "Please. Don't make me go back."

"Nick? What happens next?" Aria asked.

"I'm going to save Stacy. She will not go back with her father." The man didn't deserve that name. "I'll call you when I'm done."

"Sweetheart, it's going to be hard to get through this." Aria reassured Stacy. "But you are going to be okay. You will be safe. And I promise you, you will see me soon. Okay?"

"Okay."

"Now you do what Nick says and he will keep you safe, even if you have to be with someone else for a little while. Nick will make sure it's someone good."

Nick nodded at Stacy. "Would you feel safe with your grandmother?"

Tears fell over her cheeks. "I want Aria."

A knock sounded on the door. "Nick, it's me. Everything okay?" Agent Hayward asked.

"Wait right there, but give me a sec." He kept his focus on Stacy. "Why don't you want to go with your grandmother?"

"She hates me more than she hates my dad. She says he's a deadbeat dad and she didn't want another brat to take care of."

Well that was unexpected. "Okay. Well, I can't get you to Aria right now. She's in another state and we need you here while we work on this case. So you'll have to be placed in protective custody with agents until we catch Javier. I promise the agents will be nice. They won't hurt you. Okay?"

Aria asked, "Nick, you'll give me the agent's name so I can check on her, right?"

"No. It's not safe to give out the name or location. I'm sorry. But I'll be able to get updates on Stacy and fill you in."

Aria wouldn't abandon Stacy.

Nick knew Aria's big heart wouldn't let her rest until Stacy was with people who would love her. "Say goodbye to Aria. And let's go get one of the bad guys who hurt you."

Stacy nodded, then looked down. "I need to change my clothes." Her cheeks turned pink with embarrassment.

Nick had forgotten she'd wet her pants when her father touched her. "We'll get you all cleaned up. Promise." He held the phone close to her again.

"Bye, Aria. Thanks again for all my stuff."

"You're welcome, honey. And I'll call you as soon as Agent Nick can make that happen, okay?"

She held the phone tighter. "Don't forget."

"I won't. You can count on it."

Nick turned the phone toward him. "Thank you for your help. I'll call you later."

"Stay off that leg. I love you." Of course she was worried about him.

"Love you, too." Nick hung up.

Stacy looked at him. "When can I see her again?"

"Soon as I can make it happen. But first, you understand that there's a lot we need to do to get all the bad guys."

She nodded, her bottom lip trembling. "Okay."

Nick unlocked the door and found Agent Hayward staring back at him, a look of impatience on his face.

Agent Hayward planted his hands on his hips. "Stacy's family is anxious to speak to her and take her home."

Nick glared. "Yeah, that's not happening."

Agent Hayward raised a brow. "Why?"

"Because Agent Nick is going to arrest the bad guy." Stacy gave the other agent a firm nod.

Agent Hayward glanced back to Nick, a question in his eyes.

Nick answered. "Her father used her to pay off a gambling debt."

Agent Hayward opened his mouth, probably to swear, then looked at Stacy and closed it with a click of his molars. "Well, then, let's go arrest the bad guy."

Nick grabbed the other agent's arm to stop him from leaving. "Stacy and the other kids know the names of all the bad guys who hurt them, too."

Agent Hayward gaped at Stacy. "You do?"

She nodded.

Agent Hayward grinned at her, pride in his eyes. "Maybe you four will grow up to be kick-ass agents."

"Maybe." Stacy held on to Nick's neck, looking very proud of herself now.

Nick let Agent Hayward lead the way back to the conference room. Stacy was getting heavy in his arm, the pain in his chest intensifying, but he refused to put her down. She trusted him. And he wanted her to have the perfect view of her father being arrested for what he did to her.

Agent Hayward stepped into the room just as Stacy's dad stood and rushed forward. "You can't keep her from me."

Nick stopped next to the table and stood Stacy in the chair in front of him as he kept a protective arm around her middle. "You will never see her again."

Karl's eyes narrowed. "What? You can't do that."

Nick caught the grandmother's gaze fall to the floor and a look of shame come over her face. "You know what happened," he accused.

Her gaze shot up to his and her face fell in remorse. "He gave a drunken confession three days after she went missing. He tried to get her back but that asshole Perry Whitehouse refused and threatened to kill her if Karl or I went to the police."

Agent Hayward pulled out his cuffs and headed for Karl and Donna, though his gaze held Stacy's. "Lucky you, sweetheart, you get two bad guys arrested today. And we'll get Perry Whitehouse next."

Agent Hayward cuffed Stacy's father and called in another agent to take her grandmother into custody. Karl walked out with his head down, no words for his little girl. No remorse. Not even a half-assed apology.

Donna stopped by the door and looked back at Stacy. "I'm sorry," she said. "I-I didn't know what to do." She walked out, head down.

She should have done the right thing and called the police. She could have saved Stacy nearly two years of abuse and trauma.

The other families watched it all play out. The other kids had tears in their eyes and stared at Stacy.

She turned and buried her face in Nick's chest and cried so hard her whole body shook.

Nick wrapped her in his arms and held her. "You cry all you want. That was a terrible thing they did to you. You're safe now."

Those words made him think of Perry Whitehouse out there somewhere. And Javier Lopez with his threat of retribution.

He needed to warn Aria and find both those monsters and make them pay for everything they'd done.

Chapter Twenty-Three

"Good morning, sweetheart." Nick's deep voice rumbled over the line and shot right through Aria's system, settling like a ball of heat between her legs.

"Mmm, you sound so good." His deep, rough voice always electrified her body and made her a puddle of lust.

Nick chuckled. "I hope that means you were dreaming about me."

"I am now. And I can almost feel your lips and tongue and hands all over me."

Nick growled into the phone.

That set off another wave of heat, rushing through her veins. Aria grinned. Good. Now she wasn't the only one thinking about his tongue bringing her to climax. "How are you?"

"Hard. Desperate. All the blood rushed to my dick the second you painted that little picture."

She didn't feel bad about that at all. "Maybe it will get you here faster if I keep you in a constant state of wanting me."

"I feel that way all the time, sweetheart. And I'm desperate to be with you, especially since I hardly got to spend any time alone with you before you left. I really need my Aria fix. Now."

She needed him just as much. "Well, come and get it."

"I wish I could, but I've got some bad guys to talk to today to help wrap up this case."

That quickly dissipated her desire and raised her hackles. "It's not over though until you find that asshole who trafficked those poor sweet kids. How are they?"

"I spent the morning getting all their statements. Or at least as much as they were willing to share right now. It included all the names of the people who hurt them."

"Oh, Nick, that must have been really hard for them. And you."

"There were so many names."

"And you'll get them all."

"Already on it. We've got agents picking up the people the kids knew first and last names for. They were often given drugs to make them more compliant, so a lot of times they only could remember the first name. But we'll get them. The resort likes to name-drop who stays there, so we'll link names to dates stayed there to any video surveillance we have of Julia delivering the kids in her fucking cart. Julia had an encrypted computer. Tech guys are trying to crack it now. We think she kept records. And possibly video to blackmail anyone who threatened their business."

"You've been busy." Aria was impressed.

He'd barely slept. "There's so much to do. This case is so big. Javier didn't just have these four kids. There were more. There *are* more. He's got others working for him, doing this shit in multiple states. If we get him, maybe we can get the rest of them."

"You will. Are the kids happy to be back with their parents?"

"It seems so. But they've got a long road to recovery. I found a therapist who will reach out to the families. I think it would be good for the kids to stay in touch with each other. She thinks a group session with all of them will help them open up about their experiences because they all looked out for each other and experienced the same trauma."

"That was very thoughtful. What about Stacy? Is she settled into the safe house?"

"Two agents took her last night." He sighed. "I hate leaving her with new strangers. She really connected with you and me. I connected with her."

She understood his apprehension. "Stacy's been through a lot. I'm not sure how to help her with the trauma she's suffered. That's what a therapist will do for her. But she needs more than therapy. She needs someone to love and take care of her, to give her a safe place."

"I want her to have that," Nick admitted. "But the only place she's going to end up after the case is closed is in foster care."

"Focus on one thing at a time, and that's putting the bad guys behind bars. She's safe right now. Go do good things. Make those assholes pay for what they did to those kids."

"I will."

She knew he would, because protecting people, taking down bad guys, that's what Nick did best. But what she knew he needed, what she knew he wanted, was some balance in his life. He wanted a wife and family, like his brother, Mason, had with her sister Lyric. He wanted some happiness, stability, and connection to balance out the darkness he saw at work all the time.

She wanted to be the light and joy in his life. She wanted them to join their two lives, so they could stop wishing to be with each other and actually build a life together.

Soon.

CHAPTER TWENTY-FOUR

Mason walked into Nick's office with two cups of coffee and a white bakery bag. He and Lyric were staying in Montana a little while longer. Mason had helped Nick and Agent Hayward conduct the interviews with the kids yesterday, going over how they were kidnapped and what had happened to them after. Each of the kids astounded them with their ability to recall the names of the people who'd hurt them and what had been done to them in basic terms. They didn't have first and last names for all of their abusers, but that's where the investigation into Javier and his contacts and customers would fill in the blanks.

Today, though, he and Mason would concentrate on Stacy's case and trying to get Mrs. Lopez to tell them where her son, Javier, was hiding.

"How's the leg and shoulder?" Mason asked, handing over a coffee cup and the bag.

Nick peeked inside and found a chocolate croissant and a glazed donut. "Thanks. The leg aches and the shoulder sucks. The meds help." Though both injuries still throbbed and his ribs reminded him that he'd been shot with every breath.

"Sounds about right. Lyric and I are planning on heading home tomorrow, unless you need me to stay."

Nick shook his head. "I've got my interview end of day with IA about the shooting, then I'm on leave."

"Aria will be happy to hear that. You two can spend some quality time together and get things back on track."

Nick wished he could just go to Aria. But... "You forget that I have a death threat looming."

"Fuck." Mason took a sip of his coffee and eyed him. "So what are you going to do?"

"I'm going to Wyoming. I contacted the realtor and confirmed I closed on the house. I'm going to move in and lie low while Agent Hayward and the team go after Javier. He shot a fed; that means he's our number one most wanted at the moment. There's nowhere he can go that we won't be looking for him." And with all the resources the FBI was using to find Javier, he'd be in custody soon.

"Good. I want that motherfucker, too."

Nick appreciated his brother's enthusiasm for justice. Nick wanted to make sure Javier didn't hurt anyone else either. He polished off his food, feeling better for it and the caffeine kick. "You ready?"

"Let's do this. Who's up first?"

"Mrs. Lopez." Nick remembered how feisty she was going after him.

Mason rubbed his hands together. "Moms know everything. Let's get her to talk."

Nick doubted Mrs. Lopez would cooperate with him after he shot and killed her daughter. But he did have some leverage with her.

They walked down the hall to the room where Mrs. Lopez had been brought after spending another night in a cell.

Nick opened the door and stepped in. Mason followed but crossed the room and took up an intimidating position closer to Mrs. Lopez's seat. Her lawyer didn't seem fazed, but Mrs. Lopez eyed his bulky brother with the tattoos and death glare like she was facing her executioner.

He tried for a businesslike tone, even though he wanted to rage at her for keeping those kids in her cellar. "Good morning, Mrs. Lopez. I suspect you had a miserable night on a cot in a cell with your arthritis. I hope you were given your meds this morning and you're feeling better."

She rolled her eyes and folded her arms over her chest. "Like you care."

"I do care. That's why I saved the children being held hostage and used as sex slaves by your children."

"Those accusations are unfounded." Daniel, her lawyer, defended her.

"I have statements from the four children, who were regularly abused, physically and emotionally."

Daniel interjected again. "Mrs. Lopez certainly didn't touch or even interact with the children."

"They all saw Mrs. Lopez at one time or another while they were locked in her cellar. More importantly, she saw them, too. She knew they were there and did nothing about it. I found the kids stashed in a dark, dank, cold cellar with no blankets, food, or water. They were inadequately dressed for the temperatures, which got as low as forty-five degrees at night, making the kids have to huddle together to share body heat to keep warm. Mrs. Lopez showed no good will toward the children at all. She didn't attempt to rescue them, let alone provide a blanket. She was as heartless as her own children." Nick glared across the table at her.

Mrs. Lopez finally lifted her gaze to his. "I couldn't."

"Because your son is a monster? He wasn't there most of the time. He only checked on his product a few times a month, whereas your daughter was in charge of feeding them and pimping them out to her and Javier's clients." He hated talking about the kids in those terms, but that was basically what happened and it made his stomach turn. "Toby had a spiral fracture to his upper arm. You know how that happens? Someone twisted his arm until it snapped. The boy...eight years old...was in excruciating pain. All he got was some mild over-the-counter pain reliever that did next to nothing to help. He needed a doctor. A hospital. Instead, he wailed all night, crying in those little girls' arms as they held him and pleaded at the top of their lungs for someone to come help them. All you did was turn the TV up to drown out their cries." His hands fisted on the table. All he wanted to do was wrap them around her neck and shake her.

Mrs. Lopez showed no remorse. "If I did something, he would be very mad."

"Do you think he cares if you end up in a cell for the rest of your life? Because that's what's going to happen. You are an accessory to his crimes."

Daniel leaned forward. "I'm sure there's a deal to be made here."

"Why?" Mason asked, staring down Mrs. Lopez. "We have her dead to rights on this. And she doesn't seem apologetic, let alone ready to help stop her son."

She locked her arms around herself more tightly. "I don't know anything."

"All your family knows how to do is lie and destroy other people's lives," Mason spat out. "You deserve a cold cell and the loneliness of knowing he's not going to do a damn thing to save you."

Her head snapped up and her sharp gaze met Mason's. "He won't let anything happen to me."

Nick laughed, though it held no humor. "He was there. He could have taken you with him. Instead, he left and saved himself. He knew you'd be arrested and he didn't care."

"He's going to come after you for killing my Julia."

"You think that means he cares. All that is, is a way for him to save his reputation. To show everyone that he's a cold-blooded bastard, who will take out anyone who comes for him. So if you know what's good for you, tell us where he is and maybe we'll go easy on you."

"We want an actual deal. In writing," Daniel added.

Nick stared across the table at Mrs. Lopez. "What will it be? Save yourself, like he'd do if he was in your seat? Or save him?"

"I don't know anything." Not a single ounce of conviction tinged her words.

Nick seethed. "Then enjoy your new accommodations."

Daniel turned to his client. "Let's talk before you lose any chance to bargain."

She shook her head.

Nick stood. "I can appreciate the fact that you want to protect your son. I have a mom just like that. But in this case, you're letting a monster roam free to keep hurting children. That's not noble. That's not being a good mother. A good mother would want her child to own up to his crimes and suffer the consequences so he never hurts anyone else again. Instead you're allowing him to roam free and profit off the children he hurts. You're letting him feed pedophiles' deviant needs. You are making yourself as bad and complicit as him. So either you help me stop him, or you suffer the consequences of his actions." Nick didn't know how else to get through to her.

"Listen to what he's saying," her attorney pleaded with her. "You don't want to spend the rest of your life in prison. Not for this. The other inmates will not look kindly on you for hurting children."

Even Nick hadn't thought to play that card, but the lawyer was right. Mrs. Lopez would be a target once she was transferred from her holding cell to prison.

She looked across the table at him. "He moves around a lot. I never know where he'll be. I don't know all the places he'd go. But he owns a bar and a motel. He has a cell phone that he keeps on all the time in case I need him."

Mason pulled out a notebook from his back pocket and a pen. "Write it down. If it pans out, it'll go a long way to reducing your charges."

Daniel tapped his finger next to the notebook. "I want her charges reduced to misdemeanors."

Nick shook his head. "Only if her information specifically leads to his arrest. If not, we'll reduce some charges, but not all."

Daniel nodded for Mrs. Lopez to go ahead. "That's fair."

And better than Mrs. Lopez deserved after neglecting those children and saving her ass and her son's over helping those poor innocent souls.

He thought of Stacy and how she had no one to go home to. She didn't deserve what her father and grandmother did to her, let alone the bastards who assaulted her.

This whole case made his stomach turn and his heart bleed.

Mrs. Lopez scratched out the name of the bar, motel, and one other place her son owned, along with the cell phone number. She slid the paper across the table to him. "I will never forgive you for killing my daughter."

"She tried to kill me. You want to blame someone for that, look to your son. This is all because of him." Nick stood and headed for the door. He was done with Mrs. Lopez and the guilt she wanted to lay at his feet. He mentally kicked it away. He hadn't wanted to kill Julia. He'd thought she was holding out on her brother's location. He never suspected her of helping her brother, until she used that cart to sneak something out of the resort.

Now he knew Toby had been hidden inside. With a broken arm. In agony.

Time to talk to the bastard who hurt him.

CHAPTER TWENTY-FIVE

Nick and Mason left Mrs. Lopez and her attorney and walked into the room next door. The vibe in this room was a lot different. It was hard to tell which of the two confident men were the lawyer and suspect, given they were both smug and smiling in their designer suits.

But Nick had already seen the bastard on the left, bare chested in his slacks, tossing money at Julia like it solved everything. He'd find out soon enough, money didn't buy your way out of everything.

Nick gave Mason a subtle side-eye to go over and intimidate the asshole with a star stamp on the back of his hand. The stamp reminded him of the paper covered in heart and flower stamps hanging in Agent Hayward's office that his little girl made for him.

It made Nick sick to think how he got that stamp on his hand and if he used the stamp to reward the children he abused.

Nick wiped that ugly, disgusting thought out of his head and faced off with fucking Gilbert David.

Before Gilbert said anything, his lawyer placed his forearms on the table and clasped his hands. "My client is an upstanding citizen with no record, not even a speeding ticket. He's been detained on charges that are not just preposterous, but inflammatory."

Nick glanced at Mason. "I guess we've been put in our place. I mean, all that evidence we have against this up-standing citizen is absolutely going to prove he's a child predator, who should be locked up for the rest of his life. But we must be wrong." Nick scoffed at the idea and glared at the two men across from him.

Gilbert squirmed in his seat. "I haven't done anything wrong."

"Maybe in your sick fucking mind you think that. But according to the law, and decency in general, you've sex-ually and physically assaulted a minor." Probably a lot of minors.

The lawyer scoffed. "These charges are baseless."

Nick turned to Gilbert. "You know they aren't. You saw me at the resort when you put your hands on Julia Lopez. Toby was inside that fucking cart, arm broken, probably terrified if he cried out or made a sound, you'd kill him. Or Javier would. Right?"

Gilbert's eyes went wide with fear.

"We found Toby's DNA in the cart and in that room right after you left. Scurried away is more accurate. You were afraid I'd arrest you right then and there. I'm sorry I didn't ask more questions and find Toby in that cart. I'll have to live with that. But you, you'll have to live with the consequences of what you did to him. Because we both know you're not sorry. You were more concerned about what Javier would do to you for breaking his product. You were frantic, throwing hundred-dollar bills onto the cart, telling her you hadn't meant to break *it*." Nick glared at Gilbert. "*It*. He's a boy. A child. Not an *it* you can use and abuse and toss out when you break him, like it means nothing. Like you're not responsible for tearing that kid's world apart."

"I didn't mean—"

"I don't give a fuck what you meant, or how you feel about that boy. No doubt your excuse will be some twisted version of how you care for him." Nick took a deep breath. "Back to the evidence. At the time we met, I thought you'd broken a coffee maker or something. You said it was an accident, but you twisted that little boy's arm so severely it snapped. And you panicked and called Julia to fix your mess. You told her the money should be enough to make it right. That kid's arm is going to take surgery and months to heal. It will take him years to work through his trauma. Who knows if he'll ever get over what you did to him in that room. And I'm guessing he's not the only one you hurt."

Gilbert pounded on the desk with both hands. "I didn't mean to hurt him."

His lawyer immediately put his hand on Gilbert's arm and squeezed. "Don't say another word."

Nick didn't relent. "You did hurt him. You traumatized him. And it wasn't the first time."

Gilbert quickly glanced at his lawyer.

"You were at that resort every day for a week. I have the surveillance footage of you going into the room marked "under construction." The room Julia let you into after she rolled her cart in and left you alone with what you'd ordered." Nick sat back in his seat. "Not exactly a room service item. But you knew just what to do to get your special delivery."

"And now you're going to tell us." Mason's tone made it clear it was a non-negotiable order.

Gilbert almost looked relieved they were giving him something he could do to make this better for him. "If I give you that, will you drop the charges?"

"You are facing multiple counts. And we're sure this isn't your first offense. What will we find when we go through your phone records, your laptop at home and at work, and start talking to your contacts? We've just begun."

"You don't know that Mr. David ever saw the child who was hurt."

Mason growled under his breath. "The child identified him in a photo lineup. He's prepared to do it again in person if your client requests it."

"Will I get to see him?" Gilbert's too anxious and excited question made Nick want to punch him in the face.

"No," he and Mason snapped at the same time.

"But I want to talk to him. To explain why we can't see each other anymore."

It took everything Nick had not to pull his gun and shoot the fucker. Instead of talking to the dickhead, he turned to the lawyer. "Advise your client that when he says shit like that, I feel less inclined to take things off the table and not just throw the book at him."

"Toby is special." Gilbert, at six feet, one hundred and seventy pounds, almost looked like a child himself when he said that. But he was an adult, talking about a child he'd abused over and over again.

Nick slammed his hand on the table. "Don't ever say his name again."

The lawyer turned to his client. "You're just helping them convict you."

Gilbert finally seemed to be coming to terms with what he faced. "It's over. I'm ruined." He looked to Nick. "You're not going to tell my wife, are you?"

"I think she's going to find out when you don't come home tonight and you're in prison."

Tears welled in his eyes. "She'll never let me see my kids again."

"I'd worry more about the damage this is going to do to your kids when the FBI interviews them about what you did to them."

His back hit the chair as he scoffed. "I would never hurt my kids. I love them."

"So it's just other people's kids you want to ruin and harm and steal their childhoods from." Nick sneered, disgusted by this so-called man.

"I cared for them. I loved them."

Not just Toby, but *them*.

"Gilbert, please, stop talking." The lawyer looked stricken that his client had just copped to hurting more than just Toby. There were more.

Them.

How many?

He hoped they all came forward once Gilbert David was outed as a pedophile.

Nick stood and stared down at the lawyer. "Get your client to cooperate and write down what he knows. Because it is over. We aren't going to stop until we find every single one of his victims."

Gilbert laid his head on his arms on the table and broke down crying.

Nick had zero sympathy.

Mason even less it seemed as he spat out, "You're a pathetic excuse for a man, let alone a father."

Nick walked out of the room, hoping he'd done enough to get Gilbert to cooperate so that he didn't have to bring in Toby to ID the guy in person. He didn't want to put the little guy through that. Toby deserved to put this whole thing behind him. But Nick knew it was going to be a long road to get justice for him and the girls.

Chapter Twenty-Six

Nick clicked the video call through to Aria and waited for her to pick up. The second he saw her face, he smiled.

"Did you talk to her?"

He smirked. "Hi to you, too, love."

Her shoulders slumped but her smile didn't dim. "Hi. How are you?"

"Good. Feeling better. Leg still hurts like hell, but I'm getting by using the crutch."

"Don't overdo it."

"I won't. And yes, I talked to Stacy. She's doing well. Playing a lot of board games with the agents protecting her and watching TV. She's obsessed with a show called *SciGirls*. It's a show based on STEM. Each episode there's a question that the tween characters have to solve, I think. She seemed really excited about it."

"She's missed a lot of school. Wherever she goes next, she'll have a lot to make up. I'm glad she's found something interesting to take her mind off everything that happened to her and is still going on." Aria pressed her lips tight. "What did the agents say about her?"

"She's quiet. Does what she's told. But she has nightmares and doesn't sleep well. They say she asks about us and when she can see us." Nick wished he could go see her, but he didn't want to compromise the case or jeopardize Stacy's location.

Aria put her hand to her chest. "I miss her. I can't wait to be able to talk to her again."

Nick nodded. "Hopefully, that will be soon. Toby, Nicole, and Emma are doing as well as can be expected at home."

"I'm so glad, even though they still have a way to go." Aria held her phone and walked into her kitchen. "Mason told me you're officially on leave." Hope filled her gaze.

"I am."

"Does that mean you're moving here?"

"Soon. We still need to figure out a few things between us. Plus, this case isn't over. In fact, there's something I didn't tell you."

"What?" She sucked in a breath. "You're not changing your mind, are you?"

He tightened his grip on the phone. "No. Not about you, or moving to Wyoming. This is about the case."

She sighed out her relief. "Okay. Well, what is it?" Anxiety rolled off her words and shone in her eyes.

"Javier Lopez threatened me."

Aria huffed. "I'm sure that happens a lot with the people you go after."

He shook his head. "This wasn't an idle threat. I killed his sister. He threatened revenge and that he'd take the person I love most, too."

"Oh." Her face paled.

"I couldn't handle it if something happened to you."

"Nothing is going to happen to me because you're going to catch him."

He appreciated her confidence in him. "I need you to be safe. I don't know what I'd do without you. You make me smile. You're the one I want to spend every morning kissing and every night wrapped up with. I love you, Ari. You're my everything. And if he ever hurt you...please tell me that you'll take the threat seriously. Javier Lopez is dangerous. Who knows what he'll do if he gets his hands on you." Nick couldn't let his mind go there. He'd end up locking Aria in a room and never letting her out until Javier was behind bars or dead.

"Well, he'll find it hard to do anything to me when I'm usually in a bar full of people. Plus, you know I know how to take care of myself."

He did know that.

And her sass and confidence helped ease his mind.

Plus the extra security Mason and Jax had set up at the bar and at Aria's apartment when Lyric had lived there and had a stalker would help keep her safe.

He wanted her cautious, not scared. "Just be careful. Keep an eye out. Don't go anywhere alone. Call or text me throughout the day, so I know you're okay."

"Will you do the same?" It sounded like he better.

"I have been for weeks." He immediately regretted how he'd said it. "I'm doing everything I can to make you a part of my life."

"I know. We're so close to having what we want. I appreciate the effort you're putting in and that you're coming here to be with me. It means everything to me that you'd make that sacrifice."

He wanted to touch her, to reassure her. "It's not a sacrifice if I want to do it. I'll still have my job." Though he planned to work a lot less.

"Not the one you earned. I know the one you're taking here will be less risk and probably more responsibility without so much traveling."

Thank God. "Which is what I want so that I can have a life outside of work. So I can spend more time with you." He'd have some balance and happiness in his life.

"I just don't want you to regret these choices." She was so sweet.

"I don't. And I won't. Not ever. Not when I have you."

Aria paused for a moment. "Do you mean that?"

He didn't hesitate at all. "Yes. You're mine. And I can't wait for us to be under the same roof. When this case is over and it's safe, will you move in with me?"

She sat up straighter and grinned, so big her cheeks pinked. "Yes. I can't wait either."

He smiled back at her. "Good. Something to look forward to."

Aria leaned into the camera and studied him. "Are you okay? You know, after having to protect yourself and shooting that woman?"

He hadn't had a lot of time to dwell on it. "It's never easy, no matter the circumstances."

Julia had given him no choice but to defend himself.

"You're a good man, Nick. Never forget that." Her words and how much she meant them hit him right in the heart.

"As long as I have you to share all of this with and to brighten my day, I'm good. I'll also be talking to the FBI counselor about the shooting. You don't need to worry about me."

"I do. I always will. I love you, Nick. Hurry home to me."

She was his home.

He would make sure nothing happened to her because of him.

CHAPTER TWENTY-SEVEN

Maybe it was her, but it felt like there were a few new faces in the bar tonight. It wasn't like Aria knew everyone by name. Mostly she did. Small town and all that. Of course there were always a few faces she didn't recognize at all. People who drove in for a fun night from neighboring towns. People just stopping by while they passed through, that kind of thing.

But tonight there seemed to be a couple of strangers watching everything. Including her.

Maybe you're just paranoid after talking to Nick yesterday about the criminal they were hunting. That monster should be locked up behind bars for the rest of his life.

And now she was angry all over again about what he did to Stacy and the others, the threat he posed to Nick. Mason. Her.

How did he get off threatening Nick for something his sister instigated? She had gone after Nick. If she'd just surrendered, she'd still be alive and the real person responsible for doing harm would be behind bars.

How could she work for her brother doing that?

Aria didn't know how anyone could harm an innocent child.

Ugh! She tried to shake off the rage and focus on her job, the bar. The customers were here for a good time and usually she aimed to please.

Nick had sent a picture of Javier Lopez, so she'd recognize him if he showed up.

She'd never seen him before. Of course she hadn't. Because she didn't associate with human trafficking assholes. And if Javier Lopez came into her bar, she'd make damn sure he left in cuffs. And at least with a black eye for what he did to Stacy.

Tonight was one of their slow nights. Still, the bar was more than half full with regulars. She preferred it when the bar was packed and they couldn't keep up with orders. The craziness of it, the no-time-to-think, made the hours go by quickly. Another day done. Another day closer to Nick finally moving here.

She hoped he was taking care of himself and not overdoing it. She didn't want him to overtax his body and suffer just to get here faster.

She grabbed the full trash bag behind the bar and headed through the kitchen and out to the dumpster. She tossed the bag in the huge container and turned back to the bar, but stopped short when she spotted someone lurking on the other side of the building, watching her.

"Can I help you?" she asked across the distance, putting a hand on the knife she used to open cases of beer in her back pocket. "You're not supposed to be back here."

"Just having a smoke and getting some air," he called back, turning to walk around the building back to the front parking area. No one was allowed to go through the kitchen. Safety hazard, and all that.

She shrugged it off, until she walked into the bar and spotted the guy saying something to a woman at a two-top table on the edge of the room. She was dressed in jeans and a white button-down shirt, the sleeves rolled up, and wearing flats.

He was in black denim, a white shirt, sleeves rolled up, too, and wearing work boots.

Something about them tripped her radar. She pulled out her phone and called Nick.

He picked up on the first ring. "Hey, sweetheart, I was just about to call you. How's your night going?"

"Good, so far, but...I went out back to take out the trash and some guy was back there watching me. Then I came into the bar and he's whispering to some woman. I've never seen them before, and you said to be careful. So, could they be part of Javier's crew?" She really hoped not and didn't want to cry wolf every time someone in the bar made her uneasy.

"Send me a picture of them."

She took the pic and texted it to him.

"Don't be mad."

That made her back go straight. "Why?"

"They're FBI. Your protection detail. I handpicked them."

Well, that was sweet. If frustrating. "Then why didn't you tell me about it?"

"I want you to be alert, but not make it obvious you know you're being watched. And you did a damn fine job of it tonight, spotting them as suspicious. I'm even more impressed and grateful you called me to make sure everything was okay."

She appreciated the praise and assessed the agents again. They weren't exactly in the suits she expected of FBI agents. But their dressing down needed some work. Especially for a place like this where denim and plaid ruled.

"Please tell me this means there are agents watching your back, too. Because the way I see it, you are the target."

Nick sighed and she felt it all the way through the line. "He wants to make me pay for what I did to his sister."

"She tried to kill you! You defended yourself. And I hope you know that it wasn't your fault. You had no choice."

"I don't want to talk about it." The short, deep, clipped words backed up what he said.

She understood it was hard for him. "Okay. It sounds like you're having trouble sleeping because of it." He sounded so tired.

She wished she could be with him to help him through this.

"I miss you, okay? I worry about you. A threat has been made against me and mine. Everyone is being protected. Just in case. So please, don't be mad."

"I'm not. I appreciate that you're trying to keep me safe. Mason has been in a lot, too, watching out for Lyric. And me."

"I asked him to keep an eye on you." Sounded like Nick wanted to be the one doing it. "I miss you like crazy. Especially now that I don't have work to distract me."

She stepped behind the bar, caught the first customer holding up an empty beer bottle asking for another and bent to the fridge to grab one. "What have you been doing today?"

"Physical therapy before lunch, then my cousins came over and helped me pack up the last of my stuff."

She handed her customer his beer, turned and added it to his tab, then turned back to the bar and poured another customer a whiskey straight. "Does that mean you'll be here soon?"

"I have my interview at work about the shooting day after next and some other things to tie up here, like saying goodbye to my family."

"I bet you're really going to miss them." She closed out a customer's bar tab at the register and handed him the receipt.

"I will. But I'm sure we'll be seeing a lot more of my parents once Lyric and Mason have their baby. I wouldn't be surprised if they got a place nearby out there so they can see their grandchild as often as they like."

"That would be amazing. I love your mom and dad."

"Well, it's mutual." A smile filled those words. "I talked to my mom yesterday and she told me that after the shooting I should really prioritize my life better and put you and our family first."

She poured a glass of wine, then mixed a margarita. "Nick, I understand that your job is important to you. Things are going to change when you move and work here."

"I'll still need to travel sometimes." He didn't sound thrilled about that, but it was part of the job, given they were out in the sticks.

She tried to cheer him up. "But you'll be coming home to me, right? That's the plan?"

"Yes. That's exactly what I want. But I can't come back yet."

At least they were on the same page now. She'd just need to be patient a little longer. "I feel your frustration."

"It's because I want to be with you so much." His eagerness filled every word and made her smile.

"I feel the same way. And we're getting there." She sent the waitress off with the two drinks. The other end of the bar was getting restless and her brother was about to go off shift. "I wish I could talk longer, but I have to get back to work."

"I love you. I'll be there soon. And please, pretend there aren't agents watching you. They're just doing their job."

"What agents?" She grinned, even if he couldn't see it.

"Smart-ass."

She smirked. "You love my ass."

"I'd like to be biting it right now."

"Sounds dirty. I'm in."

The lady sitting in front of her lifted her glass in salute.

Nick groaned. "You're killing me."

Yeah, she didn't want to get both of them all hot and bothered and restless for the other. "I have drinks to pour."

"I have a cold shower to take," he teased back.

"Not for long, Nick. I'll see you soon." They both needed the reminder that this wasn't forever and the day when they were together all the time was coming.

If only they didn't have Javier Lopez and his threat hanging over their heads.

Chapter Twenty-Eight

Javier sat outside the sprawling, white, single-story, four-bedroom, three-bath ranch house, sitting on three acres of land, according to the online real estate ad he'd looked up after seeing the For Sale sign out front. He watched Nick and his brother, Mason, along with the two guys who'd driven the moving truck, unload from the spot where he'd hidden his truck amongst the trees.

He'd had a couple of his men on Nick since the bastard killed his sister. His mother was still behind bars for assaulting a federal agent and being an accessory to kidnapping and child trafficking. Those bullshit charges should have been dropped. She was an old lady with crippling arthritis. She was no threat. But he knew they kept her, hoping she'd rat him out.

She was too smart and too helpless to go against him. Sure, she gave up his legit businesses. He expected that. But the feds wouldn't find anything there. He'd made sure of it.

And he'd take care of his mother in time. A couple of bribes to the right people and the charges would go away. She just had to be patient. She didn't know anything that would lead them to him. He had people and places she knew nothing about. Oh, the feds raided a couple of places he'd used in the past. They'd even come close to finding one of his locations in Idaho, but he'd had everyone move after that shit went down at his mother's house.

Seemed Agent Gunn and his brother were relocating, too.

All he had to do was follow the brother and take him out. Let that fucker feel the way he felt seeing his sister gunned down. She didn't deserve that. She was only following his orders. She knew what would happen if she didn't. And she made him good money.

Rich assholes loved depraved shit. And those who wanted kids, they'd go to extremes and pay any price to get their hands on what they craved. Especially when they could simply walk into a room, explore their every desire, and leave without the fear of being caught. Or the kid talking.

He gave them what they wanted and they paid him dearly for his services. Especially when he brought their deepest desires right to them.

But this fucking agent stabbed him in the back, making him look like the fool. Then he'd killed Javier's sister, the one person who made it possible to do business under the radar. She was more than family, she was an asset.

And he'd taken the kids.

Oh, he had more. Lots more. He kept things spread out. Because there were sick fucks all over the country who would pay to get what they wanted.

And he would get what he wanted when he took out the person Nick loved most, and then killed the asshole for all his transgressions against Javier and his family. He'd do it for his sister. For his mother, even though she'd rather spit on him than love him anymore.

That didn't stop her from taking his money when she needed it.

The lawyer trying to get her out of federal custody was bought and paid for by him. He'd do his job or suffer the consequences.

He lit up a joint and tried to cool his ire, but the hatred he felt burned inside him. He shouldn't be running from one place to the next, looking over his shoulder.

He should be taking care of business.

Finally, two hours after the move-in began, the moving truck pulled out. The brother was probably going to leave soon, too. Javier knew he was an agent. A big fucking dude, who looked like he'd seen some shit.

Javier didn't care. Whatever it took, he was going to get his revenge. Now would be a good time to make his move. But the front of the house was too open. He needed to take them by surprise.

Maybe he could recon the house, choose a spot to pick them off one at a time.

Just when he was about to exit his truck and use the cover of the trees to walk the perimeter of the place, the brother came out of the house.

Nick stood in the doorway, watching from the wrap-around porch as his brother climbed behind the wheel of his car and pulled out. Nick had lost the crutch. He even helped with some of the lighter boxes, but Javier could tell his shoulder and leg were still fucked up. Good. He wanted him in pain. He wanted him to hurt. Fucking traitor.

Fed. Always mucking up his business.

Javier rubbed the scar next to his neck where he'd been grazed by a bullet. Such a close call. Next time he faced off with Nick, that fucker was going down. For good.

He waited until Nick closed the door before pulling out of his hiding spot and following Mason down the long road. He didn't want to get too close. The agent would catch a tail. And out here, it would be easy with so little traffic.

That's why Javier had bought a secondhand truck to blend in.

He followed the guy all the way back to civilization and the bar that seemed to be the place to go in this small town. He parked in the lot, opposite where the agent parked near the back.

Since the bar was packed and he'd changed his appearance by cutting his hair and changing out his slick suits for faded jeans, a button-up cowboy shirt, and worn boots so he could blend in, he went inside and lost himself in the crowd. He checked out the woman in the kitchen the big guy had his arms wrapped around as he kissed her.

She had her fingers dug into his hair and the flash of her diamond proclaimed her his wife. When they pulled apart, Javier saw the baby bump right before the big guy put his hand over it and smiled at her.

Javier narrowed his gaze. "Well, I guess you've got a lot to lose." Which meant the big guy would fight to stay alive.

Javier didn't have someone like that in his life. Oh, he satisfied his needs with one woman after another, but commitment wasn't an option in his line of work. A woman would be a liability. Anyone he cared for was a potential target for the feds, his competitors, even those who worked for him, who wanted to take what he'd built. Caring about others made him weak, so he simply didn't bother to care at all. Except for his sister. They didn't always get along. They disagreed a lot. But she was family and he tried with her in his way. She told him the truth, even when he didn't want to hear it. She loved him even when she hated him.

And now she was dead, leaving his life cold.

The only comfort he had left came from the money he made and the power he wielded.

Though it was little comfort when he got sentimental and saw the way Mason's woman looked at him.

That warm, sweet, cushy life wasn't for him. Not now, anyway. Maybe someday, when he was old and tired of the game.

Mason hooked his arm around the woman's shoulders and led her out through the back door. That's when a guy sitting in a booth that faced the kitchen stood up and followed. He was in jeans, a long-sleeve thermal, and boots. Still, his actions and presence made it clear he was here watching her.

FBI.

Fuck.

That meant Nick had taken his threat seriously and his brother had, too, if he had an agent watching his wife at work.

It wasn't going to be so easy taking out the brother then. No matter. He'd find a way.

Nick would pay. Soon.

Chapter Twenty-Nine

Nick stared out the window of his new place and his heart ached for Aria. She should be here with him. They should be together. But he couldn't risk Javier finding out about her and going after her. It had to be this way for now.

If Aria found out he'd moved into the house three days ago without even telling her he was in town, she'd kill him.

Worse, she'd feel betrayed, like he didn't want to be with her. Except he desperately wanted to see her.

But he couldn't paint a target on her back. It was bad enough he was stuck in the house, keeping a low profile after the move. The only thing that comforted him was that Javier probably had no idea he loved her, and that kept her safe. Along with the FBI agents watching her.

She already loved the house, since it was similar to the old townhouse she used to rent. She loved that place. He'd moved in a few things. They'd need more furniture and stuff for the kitchen. Most of all, the house wouldn't feel like home until she lived here and put her stamp on the place.

Missing her like crazy, he called her.

"Hey, you. Did you finish packing yet?"

"I'm ready to see you, sweetheart." He didn't answer her question. He hated to lie to her, so he said how he really felt. He was in fact surrounded by boxes of all his stuff.

"It won't be long now." She sounded so hopeful.

"Are you doing what I asked and staying vigilant? I couldn't take it if something happened to you." He walked back down the hall to the living space. He needed to set up the TV and get hooked up to the satellite service.

"Nothing is going to happen to me. I'm being watched. I'm sticking close to the bar. I don't go anywhere alone."

He plugged in the power strip behind the TV stand and then plugged in the TV. "Good. And I know it's a pain in the ass, but the threat is real."

"I know. I just hope they catch him soon." She sounded weary of the whole thing.

"Me, too." His guilt weighed on him and it was getting harder and harder not to beg her to come to him, or for him to go to her. "Are you ready to move in with me?"

"I can't wait."

He felt he same way. "If I had you in my arms right now, I wouldn't let you go for days."

"Yeah. You ready to make up for some lost time?" That sultry tone really did it for him.

"I'd get on my knees and beg if I had to." It would hurt his thigh, but he'd take the pain for even a minute of pleasure with her.

"Well, I do like what you do to me when you're on your knees, but we can simply use a nice, soft bed, so I can have my wicked way with you and you won't hurt."

"Don't worry about me. I'm good to go." He'd been working on his physical therapy and getting more range of motion in his shoulder and strength back in his thigh.

"I've gotta go. Big delivery at the bar. Love you."

"Love you." He hung up and stared at the mostly empty space around him in the house he wanted to make a home with her.

Fucking Javier had to go and mess this up for him.

He needed to get his strength back, because if that bastard didn't come at him soon, he'd have to go on the hunt for him.

Chapter Thirty

Aria was tending bar, minding her own business when Mason came in, dropped off a bag of cookies to his pregnant wife with a kiss, then sat down at the bar, phone to his ear. She held up a bottle of the local IPA he liked and he shook his head. Instead, she got him a soda and set it in front of him as she made her way down the bar, refilling drinks and taking orders. By the time she got back to his section of the bar, she overheard him say, "Be there soon." That was all. But something in the way he purposely kept his gaze averted and his voice low tripped her radar.

Was he talking to Nick?

"I'll call you back when I'm on the road. Yes, I picked up the stuff."

If Lyric wasn't in the back working the grill, Aria would swear he was talking to her. But she did know better and wondered why Mason was being so coy about talking to his brother.

Of course, she could be wrong. But she had this feeling the last couple of days that Mason was uncomfortable around her, when he was normally friendly and like another brother to her.

He ended the call and put his phone away, taking a sip of his drink like he didn't know what to say to her.

She raised a brow and stared right at him. "Everything okay?"

"Yeah. Good. Just have to run an errand. Will you tell Lyric I'll be back in an hour?" He stood and started walking away.

"Sure. No problem. But aren't you going to kiss her goodbye?" The man never missed an opportunity to get his hands on her sister.

Mason turned, gave her one long look, then headed back to the kitchen to get his Lyric fix, because the man was addicted to his wife.

Nick feels that way about me. He loves me. He promised he'd be here soon.

Except it had been another three days of him telling her that something else came up and he couldn't leave Montana just yet.

And now Mason was acting weird.

Well, she'd had enough. She walked over to Jax. "Can you handle the bar for a little while? I need to go do something."

Jax punched in another order on the register. "Sure. No problem. Where are you going?"

"I'm not sure yet." But she pulled off her apron, ignored her brother's curious stare, and walked around the bar toward the back office, knowing her FBI shadows were watching. At the end of the hall, instead of going into the office, she turned left toward the restroom, knowing anyone behind her would think she went through that door, but instead she unlocked the back door just past it and snuck out. She closed and locked the door behind her, then went to her car and climbed behind the wheel. Mason was just pulling out of the lot and headed, not to town, but toward his home and her family ranch.

Maybe she was wrong. Maybe he was going home to finish some work.

Still her gut told her to follow. So she did. At a very discreet distance. He was FBI; he'd spot a tail. And if he did, she'd simply demand some answers.

Nick opened the door the second he spotted Mason pull into the drive.

Mason went to the back of his car and pulled out two bags of groceries and a small cooler. He looked up as Nick met him and took the bags. "You're screwed and you better think of something to say before she gets here."

"What are you talking about?"

"She followed me."

"So you led her straight here?" Nick panicked. He never panicked. But Aria meant more to him than anything and she was not going to be happy that he'd been lying to her for a week and a half. "Fuck."

"Keeping her in the dark isn't helping anything. Staying here and missing her is making you a cranky asshole. I get that you want to protect her, but leaving her alone every night is not the way to do that."

"She's not alone. There are two agents watching her every move, even when she's up in her apartment."

"Yeah, and if that asshole Lopez gets past them and you're not by her side protecting her, you're going to blame yourself for whatever happens after that."

True.

Fuck.

Sure enough, Aria's Bronco came around the corner and she stopped for a second, then hit the gas and came in hot, tires skidding as she hit the brakes, killed the engine, and jumped out of the vehicle, her gaze blazing at him.

Mason took the bags back from him and headed toward the porch. "I didn't want to keep it a secret from you," he yelled to Aria.

She didn't halt or say anything to his brother, she just jumped into Nick's arms, wrapped her legs around his waist, and kissed him like her life depended on it. His initial shock turned to molten heat as he fisted his hand in her hair and took the kiss deeper.

She pulled back and looked him in the eyes, hers still inflamed with anger. "You're *here*. I am so mad at you for lying to me. But you're here." She kissed him again.

Okay, if she wanted to be mad at him like this, he could deal with it.

She leaned back again. "You are going to explain everything, then you're going to grovel like you've never groveled before, and after that, you're going to make this up to me." She kissed him again.

Make-up sex. No problem.

"I'd do what she says." Mason shoved Nick off his car. He'd been leaning against it trying to keep his weight plus Aria's off his bad leg. "Take it inside," he ordered, then got into his car.

Aria kissed him one last time, then hopped off him and headed for the front door, leaving him standing there, dumbstruck.

"Go get her," Mason yelled as he backed up down the drive.

Nick headed for the house to do some major groveling. Oh, who was he kidding, he'd start by making it up to her first.

Aria looked around the living space at the TV set up in front of Nick's black leather sofa. An empty beer bottle, paper plate with half a sandwich, and a bag of chips sat on the coffee table. Nick had been in the middle of lunch. The empty grocery bags were folded on the counter in the kitchen. She went in and opened the fridge, which was mostly stocked with lunch meat, cheese, vegetables, a few apples, milk, condiments, and some leftovers from the bar.

The freezer had a couple of pizzas, pot pies, and ice cream, including her favorite: coffee, fudge, and almond swirl. She slammed the door shut.

Nick came up behind her, spun her around, and dropped to his knees, taking her hips in his hands and laying his forehead to her belly. "I know you're mad."

"Damn right." She still slid her fingers through his soft, golden hair.

He stared up at her, his hazel eyes so earnest. "I did it to protect you."

She gripped his hair tight enough to get his attention, but not actually hurt him. "That's not what I need."

He slid his hand up her jeans skirt, hooked his fingers in her panties, and pulled them down her legs, over her boots, and right off her feet. Then he pulled one boot, and then the other off, dropping each of them on the floor with a thunk.

She brushed her fingers through his silky hair. "What are you doing?"

"Make-up sex." He stared up at her as he kissed her thigh. "I know you want it as much as I do, because those panties are soaking wet."

"Get off the floor, Nick, you're going to hurt your leg." She'd seen him wince twice already.

"I've hurt you a lot more and I want to make it up to you. I will. Starting with this." He shoved her skirt up to her waist and stared at her bare pussy. "Spread your legs."

She did it without any real thought. She was beyond that, because everything in her just wanted him so badly to touch her.

He slid one finger down her seam, coating the digit with her juices. He kissed her thigh just above her knee. "I'm sorry." He slid his finger deep inside her in one long, slow push. He kissed her thigh a bit higher as he pulled out. "I'm sorry." He pushed two fingers inside her wet channel, filling her even more. He kissed her thigh up higher. "I'm sorry."

She kept her grip on his hair, hoping that he'd finally reach her clit and give her what she desperately needed, but all he did was kiss her mound as he sank those two fingers deep, once, twice, a third time in fast pumps that took her even higher toward that edge. But not close enough.

He started on her other leg, kissing her thigh above her knee, saying, "I'm sorry," before he moved higher and added a third finger as he fucked her and kissed her and apologized over and over again.

"Okay, Nick. I believe you. I've missed you so much."

His free hand squeezed her ass cheek. "I've missed you. I'm never leaving you again." He hooked her leg over his shoulder, opening her to him, then dove in and latched his lips over her clit, sucking her hard and pumping those fingers into her core as he licked and laved her clit. The orgasm gathered strength.

Nick had to know she was close as she mewled incoherently, thrusting her hips out as she rode his face and fingers, looking for that friction.

He looked up at her as he tongued her clit. "Give it to me. Now." He sucked her clit again and fucked her harder and faster with his fingers, hitting her G-spot and detonating an explosion of rippling pleasure through her as she yelled his name and leaned back on the island for support.

Nick kissed her pussy one more time, then slid his hands up under her shirt and cupped her breasts, tweaking her aching nipples. "I'm not done with you yet. I've only just begun to make things up to you. For your patience." He kissed her belly. "For giving me a second chance." He kissed her between her breasts as he stood, pulling her shirt up and over her head, letting it sail to the floor. "For loving me, even when I make it hard." He kissed her lips, tasting herself and him and loving the combination they made.

She slid her hand over the thick length of him against the fly of his jeans. "It doesn't seem like I've made it that hard for you to stay away. Maybe I need to show you how happy I am to see you, even if you should have told me you were already here." He'd unpacked most of his stuff and settled in.

He kissed her forehead. One cheek, and then the other. "Move in with me. Let's build a life and a family here."

"We need to work on our communication and how you find it so easy to lie to me." Her orgasm buzz was seriously fading.

"I thought it best that I stayed away from you. More than likely Lopez doesn't know you're mine. If he finds out, he'll go after you. I don't want him near you. Ever."

She gripped his sides and stared up at him. "Am I ever going to be your partner?"

A pained look came over him. "You are. You're mine. And I'm yours."

"It doesn't feel like it when you make these decisions without me. You could have told me you wanted me to stay away because of him. I wouldn't have liked it, but I would have done it because you asked. Either you trust me or you don't."

"I do. A thousand percent." He brushed his thumb across her cheek. "I'm sorry. I just need to protect you. If something happened because of me...I couldn't live with that."

"I get that, but all you're doing is driving a bigger wedge between us. I know your work is dangerous. I know this guy is out to get you. But maybe if we stick together, we can protect each other and not ruin what we are trying to build here."

Nick put one big hand on her chest, over her heart. "I want you to be safe."

"And I want to be with you," she snapped. "What if he never comes? What if he's in hiding and all this time apart is just time wasted?"

"He's not going to let this go."

She took his wrists and pulled his big hands away from her body. "Yeah, well, neither am I. Either you're here to take our relationship to the next level, or your job is more important than us. Which is it?"

"That's not fair."

She knew she was making more out of this unique circumstance than she should. But damnit, he needed to let her in.

Nick brushed his hands up and down her arms. "You know I want to be with you more than anything. And yes, my job is important and takes me away from you, but it is not more important than you. I love you."

"Then love me by trusting that I can take care of myself. I am capable of following directions and not going anywhere without my trusty babysitters."

He held up both of his fisted hands. "You're here without them."

She pressed her lips into a tight frown. "I snuck out to follow your brother. The FBI agent. If anything happened, he would have helped me."

"I can't believe he led you here."

"Doesn't it tell you something that even he thinks we're better off together than waiting this out alone and separately? Doesn't it tell you something that I'm willing to take the risk of being with you now, despite the danger we face?"

"I just... It's..." He raked his fingers through his hair. "If something happened to you, I'd never forgive myself." He ran his hand over his head again, fisting it in the back of his hair. "Fuck. Why do you have to be so smart and stubborn?"

She grinned. "I'm a Wilde. We're made that way."

He chuckled and shook his head. "And I love you that way because you love me, even though I've given you a million reasons to walk away, including a murdering, child-peddling asshole bent on revenge, who is after me, and probably you because you mean so much to me." He palmed her cheek and kissed her softly.

She pressed her nearly naked body to his, feeling how much he wanted her in the hard press of his cock to her soft belly. "Take me to bed, Nick. Show me how much you missed me and love me."

He hooked his hand around her hips and nudged her to walk past him. "Wait for me in our bedroom at the end of the hall. I'll text the agents who are supposed to be watching you that you're with me, then lock up and be right there."

She gathered up her discarded clothes and headed for the bedroom, looking into the spare rooms as she went. She'd seen the pictures online and done a quick walk-through when Nick brought her here to see it. The house was open and spacious and perfect for them.

The primary bedroom had windows on two walls. The bathroom off the third wall. Another bedroom on the other side of the fourth. It was big. The king-size bed dominated the room. Nick had made it up this morning. She pulled the charcoal-gray comforter, white blanket, and light gray top sheet down the bed. Nick had good taste in the color scheme and the softness of the blankets. He didn't skimp on cheap sheets. She loved that he splurged on something. He deserved a nice, soft, comfortable bed after working the long hours he did more often than not.

She hoped that changed now that he'd moved here to take on a new role.

And she'd make it worth his while to be home. To prove that, she dropped her clothes at the end of the bed, peeled off her skirt and bra, then crawled up the middle of the bed and lay down on the pillow. She pulled her knees up and slid her hand between her legs. He wouldn't miss what she was doing as he walked down the hall.

A moment later, he came into view and there was a distinct hitch in his step when he spotted her with her fingers dipping in and out of her slick folds.

He peeled off his shirt just as he came through the door. The mottled bruising on his chest was fading. She wondered how long his stitches had been out. He pulled the gun from behind his back and set it on the dresser behind him.

She hadn't realized he was armed. He probably didn't want her to know, to remind her that someone wanted to hurt him, then kill him.

"It's just you and me here," he reminded her. He undid the button on his jeans and her mouth watered and her sex clenched around her fingers. He slid them down slowly, revealing his long, thick length. His thigh looked better. Just a raised pink scar, no stitches.

He lost the rest of his clothes and shoes as he watched her work her pussy.

She made it nice and wet and ready for him. "Do you like what you see?"

"I love it."

"Then come and get it."

Nick crawled up the bed, just like she'd done, only he crawled over her, his hard cock bobbing as he leaned over her and took her hard nipple into his mouth. He sucked, then laved it, drawing it into his mouth again and again and teasing it with his tongue.

He gave her other breast the same attention; all the while she kept stroking her clit with one hand and fisting his cock in the other, stroking him up and down. No one could say she wasn't a good multitasker.

But Nick grew impatient and brushed her hand away as he settled between her thighs, notching the head of his cock at her entrance. She gripped his sides and pulled him into her as he thrust forward, burying himself deep inside her.

"Fuck. If you keep clenching me like that, I'm not going to last."

She hummed out her appreciation for him. "You feel so good. And I'm so close." She'd worked herself up to another orgasm.

Nick pulled out, then thrust deep again and again. She hit the crest and rode out her second orgasm. Nick gritted his teeth above her, then distracted himself by leaning down and teasing her breast with his tongue again.

She hooked her legs around his waist and pulled him in deeper.

He groaned, then rolled her with him across the bed. She ended up straddling him, his hands on her hips. "Ride me, baby. I need to feel you come again on my cock."

She rose up and sank down on him in a slow glide.

"Faster, baby. Fuck me like you mean it."

She rode him hard and fast.

He slipped one hand around her hip to her ass and squeezed it tight. His other hand went to where they were joined and he played with her clit, circling it with his thumb as she bounced up and down on top of him, one hand braced on his chest on the opposite side of the scar where he got stabbed.

"Nick." The worried tone in her words caught his attention.

"I'm fine. Don't stop." His head pushed back into the pillow. "You feel so fucking good."

She kept up her pace and reached back below her ass and caressed his balls. Nick went off like dynamite, his cock pulsing inside of her as he pressed his thumb to her clit and she clenched around him, milking every last drop from him.

Cautious of his injury, she gently laid herself down, keeping most of her weight on his right side and away from his hurt shoulder.

He wrapped his arms around her. "You're not hurting me."

"I didn't think at first, I just wanted you so much."

"I'm fine." His big hands rubbed up and down her back and over her ass. "God, the things you do to me."

"It's mutual. I'm so glad you're here." She hugged him closer. "I can't believe you're here. Finally." The last was said with so much relief he felt her body expel it on a sigh.

He held her close and kissed her forehead. "I'm exactly where I want to be."

"I love the house. It's got so much of what I love. The kitchen...those counters...the island. I can't wait to cook and eat with you in there."

"I knew you'd love that and the freestanding tub in the bathroom. You can soak in there after a long shift on your feet." Nick nuzzled her neck with his nose.

She raised her head from his shoulder. "You should turn the bedroom by the front door into your office. We could close up the hallway door and put in some glass French doors, or sliding doors, into the entry. That way if you're working from home and have someone over for a meeting, the office is right there. Private enough, but also open to the rest of the house."

Nick stared up at her. "That's a great idea."

"That leaves the two other rooms that share a bathroom for the kids."

The grin spread across his face, brightening his eyes. "When are we starting on these kids?"

"I thought maybe in a year."

"That will give us time to settle in together." He rubbed his hand up and down her back. "When are you moving in?"

"I just need to pack up the last of my stuff in the apartment. Most of it is still in boxes from my last move."

"Then it won't take long." He brushed her hair back on both sides of her face and held her cheeks. "I promise, things are going to be different now."

"Good. Because that's all I want, for us to really start our lives together."

Nick pulled her back down to his chest and held her tighter. "Hey, aren't you supposed to be at work?"

"Yes. Jax should have it covered for another hour, then I'll have to go back and help with the rush."

"So you're saying I have about forty minutes to make you orgasm again before we go back to the bar and I pack up your stuff while you finish your shift."

She raised her head and stared down at him. "Really. You want to move me in tonight."

He grinned up at her. "Never letting you go, remember?" Nick palmed the back of her head and brought her in for another scorching kiss. From there, things just got hotter and he had her coming on his face, then his cock again.

This part of their relationship had always worked for them. They were compatible in every way in bed. But out of it, they spent too much time apart. It would change now. And she hoped it would add to the intimacy they shared. Because they lived so far apart, it was hard to really feel like she knew everything going on in his life. They caught each other up on their days over the phone, but that wasn't the same as sharing space and time and being there with them when they spoke about their day and the emotions showed in their eyes and on their face.

Now they'd have all of that and more. She couldn't wait.

Once they rid themselves of the threat Lopez posed, because they couldn't really move on with their lives until he was behind bars.

Soon, this place would be a home. Their home. And no one was going to take that from them.

Chapter Thirty-One

J avier watched the agent kiss the beautiful brunette before he helped her into her car. The kiss they shared was filled with leashed passion. They'd spent a good amount of time fucking in the house. He'd had a front-row seat from the tree line, looking right into their bedroom window. The agent fucked like a champ and she rode him like a porn star.

The way they touched, the way they looked at each other, there was history there. She wasn't some new fling.

She mattered.

Nick Gunn had someone special in his life. Someone he'd obviously kept at a distance, until now.

Did he think Javier wouldn't follow through on his threat? No. Nick knew him far too well to think he'd get away with his double-crossing and killing his sister.

The brother was a harder target to take out. He'd be an eye for an eye. But the woman...Nick would lose his mind if he lost her.

Javier couldn't wait to make Nick pay.

Chapter Thirty-Two

Nick placed the last box in his SUV, then headed back into the bar. He'd packed up her clothes, bathroom stuff, and bedding. She also had a stack of boxes of her things from her townhouse. All in all, she didn't own a lot. Her last place had come furnished, so she had no furniture to move. Thank God. His thigh couldn't take much more of the stairs that led up to the second-story apartment she'd been using above the bar.

It used to be Lyric's place before Aria moved in after Mason and Lyric bought a house and got married.

Like he and Aria were doing now.

Lyric handed him an order of carnitas street tacos the second he walked into the kitchen. "Try these. Tell me what you think. I might add them to the menu."

He took a bite of one and groaned. "So good. But more of the cheese stuff." He only knew the crumbled white stuff was cheese based on the taste, but didn't know what it was called.

"Okay, but otherwise?"

"It's simple and yummy. What more do you want?"

She chuckled. "Okay. Thanks."

He left with his two tacos and found a seat at the bar.

Aria came over immediately and checked out his food. "Where'd you get that?"

He cocked his head toward the kitchen. "Your sister made it for me."

"Can I have a bite?"

He picked up the taco and held it to her mouth.

She took a big bite, and said around it, "I'm starving."

"Take a break and eat with me. I've got everything packed and in my SUV. I'll take it home and unload before you get there. Anything you need right away?"

"You."

He grinned. "You have me. And now you can have me anytime you want."

She pointed to herself. "Lucky girl."

"Lucky me," he shot back and handed the other taco over to her. "Eat that so you're up for later." He wasn't done making things up to her just yet. They had a lot of lost time and ground to cover to make this relationship into what they wanted it to be.

Aria finished off half the taco, then hesitated. "I texted my mom a little while ago to let her know you were in town and that I'm moving in with you."

Nick stopped chewing and stared at her. "What did she say?"

"About damn time." Aria smirked.

He laughed, because that sounded like Robin. Though Aria's parents both liked him, they didn't like that his and Aria's relationship had been complicated from the get-go. Or that the relationship appeared to be mostly a lot of two- and three-day sex marathons whenever they could get together. Mostly when she came to see him. The relationship had been heavily weighted on her side. She took the brunt of his inability to get away from his job. He regretted that more than anything.

But while the perception from others was that they were just having a lot of sex, they'd taken the time to have deep, meaningful conversations, too. They talked about their pasts, what they wanted for the future. Maybe they hadn't made plans because of his demanding job, but they were doing that now.

"Is your dad okay with you moving in with me?" The last thing he needed was an irate father after his ass. Though he and Wade got along great.

"He wants me to be happy. And he likes you. He thinks if you get your priorities straight you might actually make me happy." She grinned and winked at him.

"I'm working on it. Didn't I put you first today? Twice. And then I gave you some more."

"You are very generous." For that, she pulled him a beer from the tap and set it in front of him. "I've got customers. Finish your food." She blew him a kiss, then headed down the bar, filling drinks and talking to customers. Most of them were asking when we were going to tie the knot. Soon, if he had anything to say about it.

He needed to move her in, buy her a ring, and marry her.

And he could accomplish all that a hell of a lot faster if he didn't have Lopez out there complicating the whole thing. Nothing he could do about it until IA cleared him from the shooting.

Mason came up beside him and slapped him on the shoulder. Nick winced as it made him pull something where he'd been stabbed.

"I heard you and Aria made up and are moving in together."

"Yeah. You want to follow me home and help me unload?"

"Wish I could, but I'm taking Lyric home and rubbing her aching feet. She's not going to be able to stand over a stove for hours at a time for much longer."

"How is my niece coming along?"

"Getting bigger by the day. Doc says everything looked good on the ultrasound. Now it's just waiting for her to pop out."

Nick eyed his brother. "I think it's a little more involved than her just popping out."

"I know." Mason looked a bit worried about the whole birth thing. "We've got birthing classes coming up."

Nick felt a pang of envy for his brother. "I'm happy for you both."

"Happy for you, too. I called Stacy earlier today. Lyric wanted to check on her. We had a good chat. Stacy seems like she's hanging in there."

"I hate that she's stuck in protective custody with no answer to where she'll go once it's over. It's like her life is on hold."

"I suppose she'll go into foster care. Hopefully she'll get a good family to take care of her."

Nick wasn't sure that was good enough for Stacy. She deserved a loving family. One she knew she belonged to after everything that happened to her.

Right now, he hoped she continued to heal, but knew there would be setbacks and dark periods where her past overwhelmed her. She needed people who'd support and love her through it.

The uncertainty of her future weighed on him. He needed to think about it and what could be done to ensure she had a safe and happy future.

Nick glanced over at Mason and sighed. "Did you ever think we'd end up marrying sisters, having kids, any of this?"

Mason shook his head. "Not me. Not until her."

"Exactly." Nick raised his beer to Aria as she walked by. "To the Wilde women."

Mason clinked his glass. "To the Wilde women." He raised his voice so Lyric would hear and lifted his glass to her.

Aria and Lyric exchanged a look, then shook their heads at them, like they were sweet but nuts.

Nick just grinned and sipped his beer.

"What was that about?" Aria asked.

Nick leaned over the bar and kissed her. "I just love you, that's all."

"That's a lot," she shot back. "And I love you, too."

Yeah. It didn't get better than this.

Chapter Thirty-Three

Nick woke up in heaven, wrapped around Aria, her head on his arm, her sweet ass pushed into his hard dick as he spooned her from behind. "I could get used to this," he whispered, nuzzling his nose into her hair. He breathed in her scent. Beer, booze, and peaches. He wasn't trying to wake her. Not at this hour. He simply couldn't help himself.

She needed her rest. She'd gotten home around two a.m. and snuggled into bed beside him.

Their first night officially living together.

He had a list of things they needed to buy for the house, starting with a dresser for her. He'd put away some of her clothes in the massive walk-in closet. Of course he gave her more than half of it. His suits and casual clothes barely took up 40 percent.

But just seeing her stuff with his made him so damn happy.

He gently untangled himself from Aria and eased out of bed. He couldn't resist kissing her forehead before he headed to the kitchen to get a cup of coffee and check his work emails. He might be on leave, but that didn't mean his cases stopped. He had agents who reported to him and needed his guidance or approval to move ahead, depending on the case or situation.

The coffee was ready and he poured himself a cup. As he took his first sip, he noticed something stuck to the sliding back door that led out to the backyard. He set his coffee aside and walked up to the door and read the note staring back at him.

I bet I'd make a lot of money off your pretty girlfriend. She rides your cock like a rodeo queen. Perhaps that's the best revenge. You not knowing where she is or how many men are fucking her. One way or another, you'll pay.

The ugly words sank into the pit of his stomach, making him feel sick, even as his rage grew to monumental proportions. Every muscle in his body tensed, ready to kill the bastard.

That asshole came to his house and threatened his girlfriend. The woman who would be his wife, the mother of their kids. No fucking way.

Javier was not going to take her from him. Nothing and no one as ugly as Javier Lopez and his dirty business would ever touch her.

They already have.

He's watching me. He was watching us.

Fuck!

He couldn't let Aria see that note. He couldn't tell her what Javier had seen. But he did need to warn her. He needed to tell Mason and the team of agents keeping an eye on all of them.

He hung his head and took a moment to compose himself. That's when he spotted the phone on the ground. His head shot up and he scanned the area. In the early morning dawn, shadows still covered the backyard. He waited, watching if anything moved.

When he was certain enough that he was alone, he opened the door and snatched up the phone, then he closed and locked it again.

The burner phone had a full charge and one number programmed into it. He hit dial and waited as the phone rang, once, then twice.

"You're up early. I thought you'd be fucking that sweet piece of ass all night now that you finally have her in your bed. You two look so happy in your bliss. Moving in together suits you." His malicious voice and taunting words made Nick see red.

"Fuck you. You touch her and you're dead." Nick wanted to kill him. Slowly.

"You know what you took from me. I thought I could trust you, then you betrayed me. The whole time you were just trying to take me down. You failed. Now I will take my revenge. And once I've crushed your heart, I will take your brother, then kill you."

"Not if I kill you first." Nick hung up and let Javier choke on that.

The phone rang immediately. He didn't answer. Javier was the kind of guy who let his rage get the better of him.

Nick was more controlled. More calculating.

Javier was in town. Or at least close by. He couldn't hide in a small town like this for long. Nick would find him. He'd stop him. Before that monster got close to Aria again.

Chapter Thirty-Four

Nick walked into the new FBI offices upstairs and across from the Blackrock Falls PD. Of course, there was no sign announcing it as the FBI offices. They had four thousand square feet of space. One large conference room, two small ones, two interrogation rooms, four cubicles, and six offices. There were two bathrooms, one for men, one for women, with multiple stalls in each. The galley-style kitchen boasted a large double-door fridge/freezer combo, two microwaves, a toaster oven, and two coffee pots, plus an electric kettle. He'd seen the specs and layout his boss sent him last week. Whoever set up the offices did a good job of getting them the equipment and furniture they needed, along with the necessities for working long hours.

He wondered how long this had been in the works.

"What are you doing here?" Agent Monroe asked, coming out of his office holding a folder and a mug.

"I left Aria with extra protection and thought I'd come in and check out the space. See what I need for my office before I'm back on duty." Nick hid his black mood behind professionalism in front of his subordinate.

Monroe held up his mug. "Can I get you a cup?" Monroe was new to being under Nick's command, but they'd met on multiple occasions in the past. This transition should be a smooth one.

"No thanks." Nick held up the note he'd found on his window. He'd put it in a plastic bag. "Mind putting this into evidence on the Javier Lopez case? That fucker left it at my house this morning." Nick seethed. "He's also been watching me."

Monroe's eyes went wide. "No shit. Fuck. Did you see him there?"

"No. I called him on the burner phone he left outside the glass door." Nick pulled it out of his pocket. It hadn't rung again since he called Lopez and they had their little pissing match. It would come in handy when he was ready to face off with Lopez.

Agent Monroe eyed the phone. "Damn. What did he want?"

"To let me know he's coming for my brother and girlfriend. Retribution for his sister."

"So he's here. In town. Maybe close by." Agent Monroe turned thoughtful. "He's keeping tabs on you, your brother, and your girlfriend. She lives at the bar, right?"

"Not anymore. She moved in with me yesterday. There's no way I can get her to stay away from the bar, so she'll spend most of her time there."

He nodded. "We've got agents watching her."

Nick wanted to believe that would keep her safe. He knew better. All Lopez needed was a moment's distraction to take her. It soured his gut and made his blood run cold. "Lopez is gunning for her."

"Does she know that?"

"She knows he's a threat to me and everyone close to me. She was still asleep when I left. But I texted her about the note. She'll see it when she wakes. And the agents guarding the house." As much as he'd like to keep her locked up at the house, he knew that wasn't any safer than her being at the bar, surrounded by agents and patrons, along with everyone she worked with who knew to watch out for Javier Lopez. "Where's Agent Bateman?"

"Running down a lead on a banking case. Something about wire transfers, Medicare, and defrauding the government."

"Great. More corruption in the system meant to help those in need." Nick rolled his eyes. "And Mason?"

"He got a call about that doctor in your case. Pike, I think he said. Dude's attorney wanted to meet to discuss what his client has to offer. Apparently, Lopez has the guy take care of lots of his victims. Doc is ready to give specifics for immunity."

"Why didn't Mason fill me in on that? I would have gone to the meeting."

Agent Monroe gave him a pointed look. "Because you're on medical leave and haven't been cleared by IA."

He hated being sidelined. "Yeah, well, you all should continue to keep me informed, so I can hit the ground running when I'm cleared to return to work."

"Don't you have the final interview about the shooting today?"

Another pain in his ass. "Yes. I'll do it from home." That way he didn't have to relive it in front of everyone in the office. While the shooting was righteous, it still left a stain on him. One he'd never lose.

Julia had done some terrible things, but that didn't mean she deserved to die. She'd given him no choice. Though he'd rather have locked her in a cell the rest of her life. Punishment enough. Time to reflect on her bad deeds and how she made others suffer. Time to think about how life went on for others while hers shrank to a cell and just surviving, instead of really living.

Agent Monroe sipped his coffee. "How's the new place? You like it here?"

"Perfect, because *she's* here."

Agent Monroe smirked, a twinkle in his eyes. "So it's like that."

"It's more than that. I'm going to marry her."

"Does she know that?"

He nodded, knowing exactly what kind of ring he wanted to get her. "She knows, I just haven't popped the question yet." Soon. He didn't want to wait much longer, but he needed to get Lopez locked up so they could move on with their lives without looking over their shoulders.

"What are you waiting for?"

"Nothing now, except Lopez's arrest. We're finally in the same place, with the same roof over our heads."

"Well, then, congrats, even if it is premature." Agent Monroe held up the letter. "I'll put this into evidence and add a copy to the file. Anything else?"

"Where's my office?"

"Mason said to give you the one with the best view because you spend too much time indoors. So it's the first one on the right. Overlooks a park and a bunch of trees. You can see part of the street, too. Shops and restaurants around here are good. There's a place a block up that has really good coffee, bagels, baked goods, and donuts. None of the places are open past ten, so if you're working late, you're shit out of luck. We've been taking turns stocking the fridge and cupboards with some snacks and staples."

Nick liked that the guys were working well together and turning this small office into a place where they could collaborate on cases, hang out, and decompress. This job took a lot out of you. It was good to have people around who knew what you were going through. And he was glad Mason was getting to know the other two agents. He was too used to being undercover and on his own for the most part.

This would be a good change for him.

As for Nick, he only had three guys right now to oversee, plus their cases. That was a cakewalk compared to the twelve agents he supervised back in Montana.

They'd be backing up the Blackrock Falls PD on any cases that overlapped their jurisdiction and working wider in the state, but this would be home base. Here. With Aria. With their extended family.

He and Aria would find a routine that worked for them.

Nick walked into the office Monroe pointed him to and immediately hated the way the desk had been positioned facing the door, his back to the windows. That wouldn't do.

So he rearranged the credenza on the right-side wall, shifted the desk in front of it, then put the two chairs in front of his desk. It left quite a bit of space on the other side of the room, but at least now he had the wall of windows on his right, the office to his left, and plenty of room to add a table or cabinet, something where they could spread out documents or maps or whatever to go over when needed. Maybe a magnetic whiteboard where they could put up pictures and notes about a case on the wall.

Yeah, this was going to work out well.

He sat behind the desk, checking out his new chair. Comfortable. That was good, because he'd be here a lot.

He picked up the phone and called Aria at home.

"Hey there. You left before I got up. Should I be worried?"

"Why?"

"Because the guy who doesn't have time to date, let alone ever live with someone, left me sleeping alone when he didn't have to go to work. So either there was an emergency, or you're already regretting asking me to move in."

Fuck me. I suck at this.

"No. That's not it at all. In fact, it couldn't be farther from the truth. I wanted to wake you up this morning. I almost did. In the good kind of way. But you looked so peaceful sleeping there. In *our* bed."

"Tell me the truth. Were you watching me sleep?" Her teasing tone let him know she'd let go of her upset.

"Maybe. But not in a creepy way. More like in a, *I can't believe she's here and mine* kind of way."

"Okay. But if you're having second thoughts..."

"I'm not. Put that out of your mind." In fact, he'd like to fast-track a few things. "With our schedules kind of opposite, we'll have to get used to missing each other sometimes so the other can sleep."

"True. I just didn't expect you to be gone this morning after you were so excited to have me in your bed."

"*Our* bed. *Our* house. *Our* life together."

"I like the sound of all that." It wasn't hard at all to hear the smile in her voice.

"Good. Me, too. And, hey, I'm at the new office. Save this number, so you can call me here, too."

"Okay. So how is it? Do you like it?"

"It's nice. I was just thinking this is going to be a good change of pace. Less people to manage, more time to be with you." It would be an adjustment. And he'd need to let go of some of his control over everything he was leaving behind at his old job. But he'd do it. He was ready for it. Plus he'd have more time to settle in with Aria and find a new routine, which he hoped included more family time with his brother and the Wilde family, too. He didn't want to keep missing out on events and celebrations.

"Hey, I just saw your text about the threat from Javier Lopez. Do you want to tell me more about it?"

He hated the anger and worry in her voice. "You don't need to know the details." He didn't want to scare her more by telling her Javier had been at the house. Or that there were double the agents there protecting her. "Just be careful. Keep the agent assigned to you close." There would be others she didn't see.

"Two are walking the perimeter of the house as we speak."

The other two were probably doing a wider sweep. "Good. How'd you sleep?" Having her in bed with him made his night.

"Better than I have in ages."

That's what he liked to hear. "Then you'll be well rested for what I have in store for you later."

"I can't wait. Um…"

He didn't like her hesitant tone. "What is it?" He wanted her to know she could tell him anything.

"If I send you a pic of the grocery list, could you do the shopping while you're in town and save me a trip? I need a few things."

He grinned and got a light feeling in his stomach. "Sure. I'd love to do the grocery shopping for us."

"You would?" She sounded surprised and dubious.

"This is the first time you've asked me to do something like I'm your boyfriend. Like we live together. It just makes this all finally seem real."

She chuckled. "My stuff all over the bathroom counter wasn't real enough for you?"

"I like seeing your stuff mixed with my stuff."

"I'm glad, because I worried that you'd never lived with a woman so it might be off-putting to have me invade your space."

"That's just it, sweetheart. It's *our* space. We moved into a new place so we could make it ours."

"Does that mean I can start decorating? Because the walls are bare and so are most of the rooms. And while I love the hardwood floors, some big rugs would add color, texture, and warmth to the spaces."

"Let's plan to do it together over the next couple of weeks I'm off."

"Sounds good."

His phone dinged with the incoming text Aria sent of the grocery list followed by a heart emoji.

"I'm headed out now. Be home before you leave for work, so I can kiss you goodbye and you'll remember it. Unlike when you were asleep and I kissed you before coming here."

"Lucky me."

"No. I'm the lucky one to have someone like you."

"Let's call and check on Stacy when you get home so she can see us together, here."

"Great idea. She'll love that." It was all coming together. Finally.

Chapter Thirty-Five

Nick was just finishing up with his interview about the shooting when his brother knocked on the front door. Nick saw him on the new video doorbell he'd installed when he returned from town. He'd gone by the hardware store, the garden center, and then hit the grocery store. He hoped taking care of a few things around the house showed Aria that he really was excited about buying the house, making it theirs, and being with her.

"Please excuse me for a second, my brother is at the door."

Agent Whitson nodded as he typed in more notes from their conversation.

Nick went to the front door and opened it to his scowling brother. "I hate that piece of shit."

Nick assumed he was talking about Javier and his early morning call. "Join the club. Come in. Be quiet. I'm finishing up my interview with Agent Whitson." Nick waved Mason toward the kitchen. "Help yourself to whatever, I'll be done soon." He took a seat at the dining table he'd moved from his apartment and unmuted his side of the video call. "I'm back. Thank you for waiting. Did you have any further questions?"

"After Javier Lopez threatened you, you said he used Toby as a shield to get away."

"That's right."

"Why didn't he take the child with him?"

Nick shrugged, relieved all over again that Javier had left the boy behind. "I don't know. Because it would add another level to a manhunt for him if he had the kid. Toby was also severely injured. He needed medical help. Lopez probably didn't want to deal with that. When I find Lopez, I'll be sure to ask him." Thank God Lopez left Toby behind. Nick didn't want to think what might have happened to him if he hadn't.

"And since Javier Lopez escaped after issuing the threat, have you had any further contact with him?"

"First of all, like I already said, I didn't have a shot with him holding a kid in front of him. And I was in no condition to run after him with a bullet through my leg. But as to your question...yes. This morning Javier Lopez contacted me. He left a note on my back door and called me on a prepaid cell phone he left on the ground."

"What did the note say?"

"Basically, that he planned to kill my brother and girlfriend to get back at me for killing his sister."

"And on the phone?"

"He wanted me to know that he's been watching me and Aria. I've submitted the note and details of the call into evidence."

"Perhaps you should be officially off the case, since you are so personally involved in it."

"Whether I'm on it or not, Javier Lopez has fixated on me and the people closest to me. He will not stop. His threat is as real as it gets."

"Yes. I know. That's why the FBI has provided protection."

"Exactly. Now if we're finished, I'd like to get the update my brother came to deliver regarding the case."

"Do you feel remorse for shooting Julia Lopez?"

"I wish it didn't have to go down that way. She gave me no other choice when she came at me with a knife after she'd already stabbed me."

"Her mother feels that you could have disarmed her."

"Her mother forgets that her son had a gun on me as well. I didn't have time to disarm either of them. I had him at my front and her at my back. There was nothing else I could do but defend myself. She would have lived if she'd simply let me take her brother into custody. Instead, she tried to kill me so he could get away." That's what happened. That's what he had to live with.

"Thank you for your time, ASAC Gunn. I appreciate your candor. I'll file the report and my findings. You'll be advised of the official standing of the case soon."

The process sucked.

"Thank you." Nick mashed his finger on the mouse to click the End Call button and sat back in his seat, taking a second to breathe and let go of all the feelings swirling inside him about the shooting, his job, and fucking Javier Lopez, that asshole who kept getting away. Not to mention being questioned about his actions.

He hated having his decisions second-guessed. But the checks were in place to ensure he did things by the book and innocent people weren't hurt in the course of him doing his job.

But having to relive it was another kind of trauma that he'd have to deal with and learn to live with.

He was a good agent, he reminded himself. He'd done what was necessary to defend himself.

Lopez wanted his revenge. Nick wished he and Mrs. Lopez knew how sorry he was for taking Julia's life and that he wished it hadn't come to that in the first place. He understood their anger and upset. He wished they could see things from his side, too.

A cold beer appeared in his line of sight.

Nick grabbed it and took a deep pull. "Thanks."

Mason dropped into the seat next to him. "I know that sucked, but we have business to discuss, so I need your head back in the game."

Nick took another deep sip, then met Mason's cold eyes. "What did you find out?"

"Hell is too good for people like Javier Lopez and Dr. Pike. They deserve the worst kind of punishment for the atrocities they've carried out. And yet, Dr. Pike is only getting half the years he should spend in jail and losing his license to practice medicine. Not that it will stop him after he gets out. I doubt anything will stop him from doling out his brand of *help*."

"It's that bad, huh?"

"Worse. When we met with him, he arrived in a van that he'd converted into what you'd assume was like an ambulance, except his vehicle was equipped to help Lopez's victims. He uses the van to follow the circuit, basically a circle from Montana to Wyoming, through Utah, back up through Idaho, and back to Montana. Lopez has about fourteen stops along the way. He's got people below him taking groups of kids from one place to the next. The doctor is brought in when kids are beaten, have broken bones, get sick, or need an abortion."

Nick's eyes went wide.

"Yeah. Kids getting abortions in some dump of a motel or in the back of that fucking van. The good doctor also admitted that Lopez 'put several kids down.'" Mason cringed. "Those were his callous fucking words, not mine."

Nick's stomach knotted. "How many is several?"

"Seven. Some were hurt too severely to be helped without being in a hospital, a couple had threatened to go to the cops, and one the doctor killed to keep Lopez from finding out that he'd been fucking her without paying. She was fifteen."

"Fucking bastard. I can't believe we gave this guy a deal." Sometimes to get the evidence to put someone like Lopez behind bars, you had to use people like Dr. Pike. It still made him sick.

Mason gripped his beer bottle so tight, Nick wondered if it would shatter soon. "Yeah, well, he knows where all seven of the bodies are buried."

That was good news. "How does he know that?" They could return the remains to the victims' families.

"It was one of the services he provided. He told Lopez that he had a guy he used at a crematorium and it would cost Lopez ten grand each, but the doctor just pocketed the money and buried the kids on a piece of property his sister owns. Collateral in case Lopez tried to harm or eliminate him. He gave us a map."

"And did the doctor admit to anything else besides pedophilia, murder, disposing of bodies, and not reporting child sex trafficking, all while dispensing medical care to children he should have actually saved instead of sending them back into hell?"

"While he's licensed in Montana, he's not licensed in the other three states, though that's kind of a minor point after all the rest."

Nick smacked his hand on the table. "I hate these cases."

"Me, too. But you found four of the children. We know where Lopez is operating now thanks to that fucking doctor. We'll find the rest of them. We're already putting together agents in every state to start taking these assholes down. We know Lopez is here, so our group will focus on getting him."

"Aria and Lyric are safe, right?" They couldn't be safe enough in Nick's estimation.

"They have agents on them. Lots of people at the bar. No one can get to them."

"That's what I keep thinking. How is he going to do it?"

"We're most vulnerable at our houses, even with all the security I've installed. You need to get this place wired up."

"I'm working on it. I have a guy coming in a few days." He hoped that wouldn't be too late.

"Good. Until then, I assume you're armed."

Nick nodded, feeling the gun at his back. "And then some." He'd hidden a couple of weapons throughout the house, guns and knives.

"We'll get him," Mason assured him. "He's going to lose his shit when we take down his network."

"When is it happening? I assume you'll try for a coordinated roundup."

Mason grinned with glee. "That's the plan. But it's being done by people higher up than me and you. We'll get the credit for uncovering all of this, but we're sitting out of the takedowns."

Nick settled back in his chair. "Maybe it's better that way. It keeps us here, where Lopez can find us. And he will. Especially when he loses everything. He'll blame me. He'll want that revenge so badly he won't be able to stop himself from coming for me."

"That means we need to be prepared, and we can't let him see that we're getting ready for him."

"I know. I just wish this didn't involve the people we love."

"We can't help that now. And they love us enough to trust us to keep them safe."

"Maybe you should take Lyric and go somewhere safe. Don't tell me. Don't tell anyone. Just go. You've got a kid on the way. If something happened…" He could barely swallow the lump in his throat or bear to think about it. "I couldn't live with myself for bringing this on you."

Mason nearly growled. "Bullshit. You think I haven't put a target on you in the past because of my undercover work? It's not your fault, like you always told me it wasn't mine. And I am going to send Lyric away tonight. I already have it set up. If you want Aria to go with her, just say the word."

Nick wondered where he'd send Lyric. "Hawk coming to get her?"

"Yes. He's got a friend who has a remote cabin. No one will know she's there with him."

Nick needed to thank Hawk for always coming through for them. "Hawk will keep her safe."

Mason nodded. "With his life."

Frustration rose in Nick's whole body. "Aria's made it clear she's ready to face any threat to be with me." He didn't deserve her or her trust in him.

Mason leaned in. "We need to make him play our game."

Nick met his deadly gaze. "Do you have a plan?"

"Not yet."

"Yeah, well, it needs to be fucking foolproof before I risk one hair on her head."

Mason fell back in his seat. "That's why I don't have a plan, because nothing is foolproof. I don't want to risk her any more than you do. I don't want to do anything that risks your future happiness. Or the wrath of my wife."

Fuck. They were screwed.

Maybe they'd catch a break and find Lopez's hiding spot before he came after the ones they loved.

Chapter Thirty-Six

T he bar was bursting with customers. Every seat in the place was filled. Couples were packed tight on the dance floor. The music was loud, the booze flowing, and everyone was having a good time. Aria hadn't had a break all night. She loved it when the customers were shoulder to shoulder in front of her and the waitresses were running ragged.

But none of that made her forget there was a man out there who wanted to hurt Nick by hurting her. The seven texts she'd received from him tonight reminded her that he didn't like her away from him. But she had to have faith in the agents protecting her. She had to have faith in herself.

Mason had picked up Lyric two hours ago, to send her away. Aria hated that it was necessary. She'd miss her sister. But understood Mason's need to keep her and their unborn daughter safe.

Aria had thought about going with her sister to ease Nick's mind, but ultimately decided she was needed at the bar and didn't want to spend any more time away from Nick. She trusted those protecting her.

Aria was filling orders for the waitresses while Jax and Parker covered the rest of the bar. She filled two glasses of chardonnay, two Bud Lights, and four margaritas, then sent the waitress off as someone sidled up to her at the end of the bar.

Suddenly, there were several loud cracking sounds outside. Everyone in the bar froze, wondering if it was gunfire, and stared toward the windows and door facing the lot.

The agents watching her headed for the door to check things out.

"Come with me if you want your boyfriend to live."

It sounded like a line from a movie.

Aria went still as her gaze collided with the man, who had to be Javier Lopez, though his hair was cut short with some wave at the top. In the picture she'd seen, he'd had shoulder-length hair and a goatee. He was clean-shaven tonight with a few acne scars on his chin and cheeks. The look in his dark brown eyes was the same deadly one she'd seen in the picture.

He flipped up the pass-through, reached out, and gripped her throat. "I don't have time for this. Move." He tried to drag her forward but she pulled back, countering his move.

He cut off her breath to scream, so she picked up the paring knife next to the condiments she used to garnish drinks and slashed it across his arm to get him to release her.

He hissed at the nasty gash she left across his forearm, but he didn't let her go. She desperately needed to breathe. So she swung her hand in an arc and this time stabbed him in the side of his bicep. She hoped the lime juice on the knife burned like hell.

He released her, took a step back, then stared at the knife sticking out of his arm.

She sucked in a deep breath. "Fuck you," she screamed at him.

He looked at the customers closest to them staring at him in horror, then he ran through the kitchen and out the back door, three agents running after him while one rushed to her.

"Are you okay?"

"Fine. Go help them." Aria pointed to the kitchen, but the agent shook her head, kept her gun down at her side, out of sight from everyone out in the bar, and remained by Aria's side. She tried to catch her breath.

Jax wrapped her in a hug and held her close. "That was too fucking close." He held her away from him and checked out her throat.

It hurt, but it wasn't that bad. "I'm fine." She brushed her fingertips over the sensitive skin. "Was someone shooting outside?"

The agent shook her head. "Firecrackers. Must have been a distraction so he could snatch you and take you out the back."

Jax put one hand to her cheek. "Call Nick. You don't want him to hear about this from anyone else."

She pulled out her phone and, though her hands were shaking, she managed to make the call.

He answered on the first ring.

She didn't give him a chance to say anything, she just blurted out, "I'm fine. I promise. He didn't hurt me."

"Who?" The calm word didn't hide the intensity behind it, because he already knew what she was going to say.

"Javier Lopez just tried to kidnap me right from the bar with a crowd of people around me. I stabbed him and he got away."

"What the fuck!"

Jax hugged her tighter. "That's what I'm talking about. No one lays a hand on you."

"Say it again," Nick demanded.

"I stabbed him in the arm with a paring knife."

"No," Nick said. "Tell me you're okay."

"I am. I'm fine. I swear it. Just a little shook up." Her hands were trembling. Okay, her whole body was shaking, but she was alive and in one piece.

Jax confirmed it. "She is, man. She's fine. I've got her," he yelled into the phone. He kissed her on the head as people around the bar were staring and asking each other what happened while they eyed the agent standing close to Aria and watching the crowd back.

"Where the fuck were the agents?" Nick's voice practically growled through the line.

"He set off some firecrackers out front. Sounded like gunfire. Everyone turned that way. He was just there in front of me all of a sudden. Then the agents rushed over, in like a minute. That's all the time it took." She sucked in a breath. It happened so fast. She'd barely had time to think, let alone react.

Jax poured her a shot of her favorite Gunn Brothers caramel vanilla vodka. "Drink that."

She downed it.

"I'm on my way. You're coming home with me."

"You don't have to do that. I'm fine and I mean it."

"He just tried to... He could have... I need to see you. I need...you."

She needed him. "Come and get me." She couldn't wait to feel his arms around her. "But be careful."

"Stay right there. And there better be at least one fucking agent watching you."

"Three went after Lopez. One is right in front of me."

"I want to talk to him."

"Her," she corrected, then handed the phone over to the woman. "Sorry. It's Nick. He wants to talk to you." She hated that she'd forgotten the agent's name. The woman was ready to take a bullet for her, and Aria forgot her name.

"This is Agent Valent." She listened for a moment. "I won't leave her side." She listened some more.

Aria could only imagine the orders—she hoped not threats—he was issuing after she'd scared him.

Agent Valent gave Aria a nod that everything was all right. "I understand. I know my duties."

Aria gave her credit for not rolling her eyes. Aria snatched the phone from the agent. "Nick. Stop. I'm fine. Agent Valent is literally a foot away from me. She is armed and I'm sure a damn fine shot. No one is getting past her. And if they do, I have another knife." Jax had just jammed it into her boot. She hoped that settled him down.

Agent Valent grinned at her. "And you know how to use it."

Nick wasn't in the mood. "A knife. He could have... If I lost you... If..."

"Nick. Baby. Sweetheart. I. Am. Fine. And I will prove it to you when you get here." She hoped that calmed him down.

Jax gripped her shoulder, shook his head like he couldn't believe what she'd done but was proud of her for defending herself, then went to calm patrons and fill drinks for those who hadn't seen what happened and were getting impatient.

Nick sighed. "I'm already in the car. I'll see you soon. Please, stay with the agent."

"I'm not going anywhere without her, not even to the bathroom. She's my new best friend."

Agent Valent gave her another smile. "I would like to get you out of this crowd and somewhere more secure."

She checked out the crowd. She shook her head. "I'll see you soon, Nick. Drive carefully," she pleaded with him.

"I am. But nothing is keeping me from you."

"I love you."

"I love you, too. You took ten years off my life."

"Hold that against him, not me. I was just pouring drinks, minding my own business."

"A fucking knife," he said in awe. "Damn but you're tough."

"Don't you forget it." She loved his praise. It went right to the heart of her.

"Never. I can't believe I almost lost you. Again. You're mine, Ari. I love you so much. And I need you in my life."

"I am yours. And I'm not going anywhere. Let's hope Lopez got the message, too."

Nick actually laughed. "I think you drove the point home."

CHAPTER THIRTY-SEVEN

Javier ran to his truck, jumped in, and sped away before the three guys following him caught up. They had to be agents.

He hit the heel of his hand on the steering wheel, once, twice, three times, then stared at the knife sticking out of his arm and the blood soaking his shirt. It hurt like hell. The cut across his forearm stung like a thousand bees.

He'd get to the place he rented, pull out the damn knife, and bandage himself up with the leftover supplies Dr. Pike had given him after he fixed up Javier's gunshot wound.

He never expected the woman to fight him like that.

And now he wanted to teach her a lesson all the more.

Agent Gunn would think he'd won this round. He'd be proud of his girl for standing up for herself. But she was still dead. Nothing had changed. She'd only made him more determined to take her out.

And he'd make it hurt.

She better watch out, because he was coming for her.

Half a mile down the road, he started thinking more clearly. Now was the time to go after them. Now was when they'd think he'd retreated.

What the fuck was he waiting for? He'd been in this town too long. He had other things to do, a business to run.

He didn't hide. He didn't give his enemies time to plan. He struck the deadly blow swiftly, so everyone knew they couldn't fuck with him.

And if a fucking agent duped him, that motherfucker died a painful death.

One way or another, this ended tonight!

So he considered his options and came up with the perfect plan, anticipating Nick's next move.

Oh, yes, he'd get that girl for what she did to him. And in doing so, he'd hurt Nick, right before he took the fucker out.

Chapter Thirty-Eight

Nick had been frantic to see Aria after Javier tried to kidnap her. If he'd gotten her out of the bar... Well, he didn't want to think about what would have happened.

The thought of losing Aria scared him to death. Without her, the rest of his life looked bleak. He didn't even want to contemplate it.

"Nick, honey, you're squeezing my hand too tightly."

He eased off and took his eyes from the road for a brief second. "Sorry, baby. I just..." He didn't know how to finish that sentence. He just couldn't live without her. He couldn't believe how incredible she was. He couldn't love her any more than he did right now.

"It's okay." She squeezed his hand. "I know how you feel. If he'd hurt me... If I couldn't get back to you... I can't." A tear slid down her cheek. She hadn't cried after she'd been attacked, but thinking of not being with him anymore, that brought her to tears.

Nick brought her hand to his mouth and kissed the back of it. "I love you. Nothing is going to happen to you. I won't let it."

"You're not sending me away like Mason did with Lyric tonight."

"If you went with her, this wouldn't have happened."

"It's not your fault. And who's to say he wouldn't have followed us."

"Hard to follow a helicopter out of here."

Aria sighed out her frustration. "I'm not leaving you. Not when I just got you back. Not when we are finally doing this."

So fierce. So resolute about being with him.

"We can't do anything if you're dead." He stared ahead at the dark road, his hand clenched on the wheel, his thoughts as dark as the night.

"I can protect myself. I did tonight."

She sure did. He was so damn proud of her. "If he'd simply pulled a gun and shot you before running from the bar, he'd have gotten exactly what he wanted and I'd be even more of a wreck than I am right now."

"I don't want to fight with you. I don't want to be away from you. I know the risk. I accept it, because it's worth being with you."

He shook his head. "It's not." Didn't she understand? He couldn't live without her.

"I say it is, but I understand that you can't concentrate and do what you need to do to stop Lopez with me here."

"Are you saying you'll join your sister until he's caught?"

She kissed the back of his hand. "Yes. I'll go first thing in the morning. Tonight, I want to be with you."

Relief washed through him. "I should get you out of here as soon as possible."

She shook her head. "You should start thinking about how good it's going to feel when I get you home and into our bed and make you forget everything that happened tonight. Because I need you to do that for me, too."

Nick brought her hand to his chest, right over his heart. "Whatever you need."

She smiled and it eased his heart if not his worries. They could talk more in the morning before he sent her away to safety. Tonight, they both needed each other to block out the world and this trouble dogging them.

He pulled into the driveway. The FBI agents following them parked along the side of the house on the left. They'd sweep the property and make sure nothing was out of the ordinary, while he checked the house.

Nick climbed out of the car and met Aria at the front. He took her hand and they walked up to the house together. The motion light on the porch lit the way to the front door. He hadn't gotten any notifications about anyone coming near the front of the house from the doorbell camera, but that didn't mean they were in the clear.

He couldn't wait for the guys to come the day after next to install the security system. Right now, he had two agents covering the house, so he let his guard down a little, even though he still flicked on the lights inside the entry and surveyed the space, looking for anything out of place.

"Relax." Aria kissed him softly. "We're home." She released his hand. "I'm going to get a glass of water before bed. Want anything?"

"No. I'm good. Meet me back there when you're done." He'd check out the rest of the house, make sure everything was secure.

She kissed him one more time, this one a little longer, deeper, a prelude to what was to come.

He reluctantly left her after she ended the kiss and gave him a look that said everything about what she wanted. Him.

He checked out each of the empty rooms as he made his way to the primary suite. He was just about to pull off his shirt when he noticed the draft coming from the window that looked out to the backyard. The window Lopez had probably used to spy on him and Aria in bed together.

Just then, one of the agents appeared, staring down at the ground with a flashlight. His head snapped up and their gazes locked through the broken window.

Nick whispered, "He's probably got her in the kitchen."

The agent pulled his gun at the same time Nick pulled his.

The agent walked forward to go to the sliding glass door that opened into the dining area next to the kitchen.

Nick headed for the hallway, calling out, "Aria, what's taking you so long?"

She didn't answer him.

The second he stepped into the hallway, he spotted her. Javier had one arm banded around her neck, her head right next to his face, her body shielding his as he stood with his back to the wall, the dining area to his left, the living space on his right.

His right arm was covered in blood. He'd cut his sleeve off and used it as a bandage over his bicep where Aria had stabbed him earlier.

Nick stayed as calm as could be expected and fell back on his training. "Let her go and put your hands up. This doesn't have to end the way it will if you so much as flinch."

Javier raised the gun in his hand and pointed it at Aria's head.

She didn't even balk. Her gaze held steady on him.

"Don't move, sweetheart. He's not going to hurt you." Nick's heart pounded against his ribs. Sweat broke out on his brow.

Javier's face contorted into disdain and rage. "I'm going to fucking put a bullet in her like you did to Julia."

Nick shook his head. "She hasn't done anything to you. You want to shoot someone, shoot me."

"No!" Aria went limp in Javier's hold, taking him by surprise and pulling him forward as her knees bent and her weight dropped toward the floor.

Everything seemed to happen at once.

In his peripheral vision, he caught one of the agents coming in through the front door, gun drawn.

Aria reached down to her cowboy boot and extracted a knife, the blade gleaming, right before she palmed it and shifted sideways to break the hold Javier had on her neck.

The second agent on duty lined up a shot at Javier just outside the sliding glass door.

Aria used her free hand to push the gun in Javier's hand away from her as she stabbed him in the same arm, pinning it to the wall. She scrambled back and fell to the floor, giving him and the agents a perfect shot.

Javier wailed in pain and lost his grip on the gun. It dropped to the floor with a thunk and it skittered across the floor toward Aria. She left it where it landed.

Nick rushed forward, his gun leveled at Javier's head. "Don't fucking move."

"What the fuck is with her and fucking knives?" Javier grimaced as he looked at his arm, blood trickling down his skin and dripping onto the floor.

Nick loved that she wasn't afraid to defend herself.

Javier hissed some more. "It fucking hurts. Get it out."

Aria stood up beside Nick. "My brother gave me that one before I left the bar, so I'd like it back."

The agent who came in the front door holstered his gun, pulled out cuffs, and approached Javier. He hooked up his free hand first, then raised a brow about how he was going to free Javier from the wall.

Aria looked at him. "You shouldn't pull the knife out of his arm. Not until he gets to the hospital where they can stop the bleeding. Shall I?"

Nick couldn't believe how well she was handling this. "Go for it."

She approached Javier. Pain etched lines in his face and filled his eyes, but he still remained a threat. And he took advantage of Aria's proximity and tried to headbutt her. She clocked him, right in the eye with her fist, busting open a cut at the corner of his eyebrow. "That's for Stacy. You want some more? Because I'd be happy to make you bleed all night."

The agent holding his cuffed hand took hold of Javier's injured bicep where Aria had stabbed him earlier and squeezed. Fresh blood soaked Javier's shirt and arm as he yelled and bared his teeth. "Fuck you."

Aria wiggled the knife in his arm up and down, slowly easing the knife out of the wall, but also adding to Javier's pain. "Your fingertips are starting to look a little blue. You don't get that looked at soon, you might lose your hand." She pulled his hand toward his other one and the agent cuffed him. The one-and-a-half-inch blade was about six inches long with a deer antler handle. The tip of the blade was sticking out the back of Javier's arm about two inches.

Nick shook his head in awe. "Damn, sweetheart, you amaze me."

"I have Jax to thank for making sure I had the means to defend myself."

"You had me, too. I would have shot him in the head if he hurt you again." He didn't like the bruises that were darkening on her throat from earlier when Javier had wrapped his hand around her neck at the bar.

Aria looked right into Javier's cold eyes. "You are a piece of shit human being. You deserve everything that is coming to you and more. Now get out of my house."

The agent carried out her order and pushed Javier through the living room and out the door, where their backup was just pulling in along with an ambulance.

Nick cupped Aria's face and looked deep into her eyes. "Are you okay?"

"I am now that he's going to prison for the rest of his life."

Adrenaline was still riding her hard. She'd crash later. What she'd done, what she'd been through would hit her all at once. He'd be there to help her through the crash and rush of emotions.

Him, too. Right now, all he wanted was to hold her close and thank his lucky stars that she was okay. They were both alive. And finally, they could start their lives together, get married, and start a family.

Chapter Thirty-Nine

A ria tossed the last flower pot onto the grass behind her, then gently plopped the root ball into the hole she'd dug and scooped the remaining dirt into the space around the roots and top of the plant, patting it down until it was properly planted. She poured some mulch around the new plant, then stood and surveyed her work.

Nick had bought some really lovely plants to fill in the garden space out back. She didn't know the names of all of them, but they sure were pretty. He'd taken a picture of the garden space before going to the nursery, where the lovely employee who helped him pick out plants also told him where to plant them in the space based on how big they'd grow.

Nick had laid out the potted plants days ago according to the plan the garden employee had laid out for him on paper. He'd even managed to plant the largest ones already. She needed to thank him for digging those huge holes.

Since she barely slept after all the excitement last night and she needed something to blow off some steam and keep her from thinking about what she'd done at the bar and what happened here at home, she'd come out here after her morning coffee and started planting. It helped. A lot. More than she thought it would.

But it felt great to look at her work, see how it all came together to create this pretty and serene spot, to know it would make Nick happy and that it made her happy to do it for herself, them, and their home. The weight of what happened yesterday just seemed to fade away.

She was looking forward, not back.

This was the start of something wonderful. This was the first day of them living their lives free of Javier Lopez and the nightmare he brought into their lives.

From now on, they were free to live their happy, healthy, and love-filled lives as a family. Here.

Aria looked out over the beautiful garden at the yellow, white, blue, pink, red, and fuchsia colored flowers amongst the lush green leaves and bushes. She looked up at the sprawling branches of the trees at the back. She loved the crushed gravel path that meandered through the space.

"I think we should add a fire pit out here, so we can roast marshmallows and look up at the stars." Nick's hands swept around her waist and overlapped on her belly as his chest met her back, and he held her as he surveyed the garden.

"We could string some lights out here, too. That way we can see the garden at night."

Nick nuzzled his nose into her hair. "Did you sleep at all?"

"Some." Then she'd woken from a nightmare, her mind spinning after that.

It had taken a couple of hours last night to answer questions, for the forensic team to do their thing for the report, and for everyone to finally leave.

Nick had taken her into their room, where someone had cleaned up the glass from the broken window and put up cardboard to cover the window and keep the bugs out, and they'd undressed and fallen into bed exhausted. It hadn't stopped him from sweeping his hands over every inch of her skin, slowly. Sensually. Where his hands went, his lips followed. He made love to her in the same way with deep kisses, his body telling her how much he loved her. Worshipped her. Needed her.

She loved the attention, the care, the connection he reinforced with every stroke of his body into hers, making them one as their hearts beat against each other's and their breaths mingled as they breathed each other in.

It was the most romantic, erotic, lovely thing she'd ever shared with anyone.

She snuggled back into him and sighed out her contentment. "I love you. I love this place. I love that after everything we've been through to get here, that we're even more connected to each other. The past is done. It's time for us to really start living the life we dreamed."

Nick kissed her on the head. "I'm in." He held up his phone. "Are you up for a serious talk?"

She gave him her full attention. "Of course. What is it?"

"I just got an email letting me know that Stacy is being moved out of protective custody today."

Her heart beat faster. "Where are they sending her?" She wanted Stacy safe.

"To a foster home. I have the details. We can check in on her later."

"Okay. That's good. She might be scared in a new place with new strangers." Aria wished she had family who could take her in, someone who cared.

Nick took her hand. "So I was thinking about her situation. This foster home might be temporary. She could be moved again."

"They might even put her in a group home because of her age. Finding adoptive parents for a ten-year-old won't be easy."

"Unless..." Nick held her stare.

She tried to read his face. "Are you thinking we should take her?"

"We could give her a good life. A mom. A dad. A big-ass family."

Aria grinned. "You don't mean foster her. You want to adopt her?"

"Why not? I saved her. I feel responsible for her. And...I really want to do this. With you."

Her heart couldn't take how compassionate and kind he could be. "You know I adore her."

"Are you sure though? You said you wanted to wait a year before we tried for a baby..."

"Stacy is special. You saved her. She's ours."

"I just can't get that feeling out of my chest." Nick rubbed his hand over his heart.

"Because she's a piece of you already." She wrapped her arms around him. "She needs us. I'm in."

He brushed his fingers along the side of her face. "You're going to be an amazing mother."

"Thank you." Really, her heart couldn't take much more.

"After all that's happened on this case, the too many close calls we've had, I don't want to waste any more time."

She gripped his sides tighter and smiled up at him, excitement fluttering in her belly. "Well then, let's not leave her with strangers longer than she has to be there."

"You're sure. You want to adopt her and make her ours?" Hope filled his eyes.

"She's already ours." The relief in his eyes made her grin even wider. "We can be her safe place."

Nick cupped her face and kissed her with such tenderness, it brought tears to her eyes. "You've always been mine."

"She needs us. We can give her a good life. Certainly better than the one she's had so far. Between your family and mine, she'd have all the help and support she needs to grow into a new version of herself that looks nothing like the girl she was."

He brushed his thumbs over her cheeks. "With a role model like you to show her how to be a strong, independent, loving, and amazing woman... Yeah. She couldn't do better than you."

"Nick." His praise set off a love bomb in her heart. He made her feel all of those things.

He touched his forehead to hers. "I mean it."

They held each other for a long moment.

This was good, standing in the garden together, the bright morning sun on their backs, the birds chirping, and the flowers showing off their beautiful colors, and her and Nick planning what would come next for them.

She could get used to mornings like this. With him.

Chapter Forty

It felt like Bring Your Partner to Work Day, having Aria at his workplace. Nick showed her his new office and introduced her to the guys working under him.

They both sat down with an agent to give their official statement about what had happened last night at the bar, and then at their home.

It dawned on him this morning, standing in the backyard, that he'd spent very little of his mandatory leave not working this case. Yes, he'd done his physical therapy, given his statement about the shooting at Julia's house, and started his mandatory therapy because of the shooting. But he'd spent very little time actually being with Aria, alone in their house, making it theirs, and strengthening the bond between them.

He'd nearly lost her twice last night.

And if something had happened to her, he'd have looked back at the last many months they were together yet apart, and he'd have considered all that time lost, wasted. Because nothing in his life was more important than her. Nothing gave him greater joy or made him more content than her.

He vowed to stop wasting time and spend more of it with her.

Behind his desk, he was contemplating what to do next when she walked in the door.

"Hey. You okay? You look a million miles away." Aria closed the distance between them and stood in front of his desk.

"We've been talking about what we need to do, but we've barely gotten anything done."

Her head tilted. "We've both been busy, but you got us both moved into the house. The garden looks amazing. We'll tackle the decorating and spending time together now that this case is over." She bit her lip. "Well, once you go see Javier Lopez?"

"Technically, I'm still on leave."

She raised a brow. "That hasn't stopped you so far. I don't see why that would change now." A hint of a smile tilted her lips.

Yeah, she understood he couldn't turn it off. Not when this case had become personal.

He stood and rounded the desk to her. Instead of saying anything, he took her into his arms and kissed her, brushing his lips over hers in a soft caress. A warmup to him plunging in, sweeping his tongue along hers, telling her without words that he loved her for understanding him. "I don't deserve you."

"Yes, you do. You're a good man, Nick. The best. You care. So much so you want to adopt a little girl who had everyone in her life turn their back on her. But not you. If I knew nothing else about you but that, I'd love you. But you're so much more than just that one act of decency, kindness, and love. And I am so lucky you love me the way you do."

His heart felt too big for his chest. "How do you always amaze me?"

"I just love you so much, Nick. I never want to lose you." She wiped away a tear.

He kissed her again, letting her feel every ounce of want and need and love pour out of him and into her.

"You two are going to set this place on fire."

Nick growled out his frustration that his brother interrupted them. But he couldn't hold a grudge when Aria's whole face lit up when she saw her sister Lyric pressed to Mason's side.

Aria sighed out, "You're home."

"I was only gone overnight." Lyric looked Aria up and down. "You okay?"

Aria looked up at him with a soft smile and love in her eyes. "I'm great. Though I think I scared another ten years off Nick's life last night."

Mason stared at Aria, his sharp gaze dipping to the bruises on her neck. "I can't believe you stabbed him twice."

Aria smirked. "He shouldn't have put his hands on me."

Lyric chuckled. "Damn straight. I heard Jax armed you before you left the bar."

Aria shrugged. "He wasn't letting me out of there without some protection. And it came in handy."

Nick pulled her to his side and kissed her on the head. "Sure did. But I'd really love it if you never had to do anything like that again."

"Me, too." She squeezed him hard around the middle.

Nick focused on Mason. "We're headed across the hall and downstairs to talk to Lopez. You want in on that?"

"Absolutely."

Nick looked down at Aria. "You and Lyric can observe from the attached surveillance room."

They headed over to the Blackrock Falls PD offices, where Javier Lopez was being held after his visit to the ER last night. Nick got the update this morning that he'd been patched up and refused to talk to anyone but him.

More than likely, Lopez simply wanted another shot at hurting him.

Javier could bring it.

Nick was the one walking out free and clear, while Javier faced the rest of his life behind bars with inmates who didn't look kindly on scum who hurt kids.

Chapter Forty-One

Nick and Mason walked into the room and stared down at Javier Lopez's pale face and tired eyes. It looked like he hadn't slept at all.

His arm was swollen and bandaged.

Nick assumed it hurt like hell, along with the stitches over his eye and the black and blue shiner Aria gave him last night when she slugged him. He couldn't help the swell of pride inside him that Aria had defended herself and taken this piece of shit down. "You thought she was weak. Just a woman. Someone you could easily take out in front of an entire bar of people and you'd just walk away. But she's made of steel. She's strong and smart and fierce. You thought you had her. Twice. And twice she handed you your ass."

"Stupid puta." He spit on the floor.

"She's no whore. But that's what you think of all girls and women. They're nothing but things to be used. Well, let's see if you even love your mother."

Lopez's eyes rose to his and the death glare he leveled on Nick would make many shrink away.

Not Nick.

"I will kill that bitch." The softly spoken words held a world of intent behind them. All of it aimed at Aria.

Javier had the connections and associates to carry out that threat.

Nick wasn't taking any chances with Aria's life. He had leverage. "No. You won't ever touch her again. Because we're going to make a deal. You leave Aria, me, and my family alone, and your mother receives a suspended sentence. If not, then she will be charged with an accessory to every crime you're facing concerning those four children we found in her cellar. She'd spend the rest of her life in a cell, just like you."

"And what do I get?"

Of course he was only thinking about himself.

"You can work that out with the DA. He'll want to know where the rest of the children you've kidnapped and prostituted out are." Not that it would help him much, since the seven bodies of the children he killed were being exhumed today from Dr. Pike's sister's land. Those seven murder charges would keep Javier Lopez locked up for the rest of his life. But he could give back the kids he'd kidnapped to get some concessions in prison. He could choose a better place to be, though he'd still be locked up wherever he went.

But he better act fast, because the FBI was on the hunt and ready to raid a few of Lopez's underground places where he did business thanks to Dr. Pike's information.

"This offer is only good for as long as I'm in this room. And my patience is running short."

Mason folded his arms and stared down Lopez. "You should also know that the FBI has been rounding up as many clients as they can identify from surveillance at the Snowcap Resort. If those men know anything about any other children you've supplied to them, where they might be, or where else they've indulged their sick fantasies, then they're going to use it to get a better deal for themselves. They've got money and influence and information to bargain with, and they'll bargain quickly to save their necks and reputations."

Nick waited to see what Lopez did next. The man was ruthless. Would he save his own mother? Or let her rot in a cell?

Nick tried to sway him. "If it helps, I didn't want to hurt Julia. I admired her for changing her circumstances and working her way up to the manager position she held at the resort. I thought she'd done well. And your mother...well, she didn't really have a say, did she. You used her like you use everyone."

Lopez leveled his cold stare on Nick again. "You think you know something about me, my life, what I've had to do to survive."

"I know you didn't have to use children to survive. I know you could have done a lot of different things to better your life that didn't involve hurting innocent people. So don't bullshit me about how your life was so hard the only thing you could do was kidnap children and sell them into the sex trade. You wanted to make as much money as you could and you found a lucrative way to do it, because your customers would pay dearly to keep their secret hidden. And I'm sure you made them pay a lot. You'll probably keep that money train going even from prison."

Lopez's lips pulled back in the slightest of grins. "You have your deal. My mother goes home to her house and property. You will not take that from her."

"And you won't take anyone I care about from me. This is done between us."

Lopez nodded. "So long as you stay out of my life and business from now on."

"I have better things to do."

"And I have bigger battles to wage, so I better not find out that you're still digging into me."

"Not me. But the FBI will until they're satisfied there aren't more children out there under your thumb. I'll have the paperwork delivered to your attorney."

Lopez's decisive nod ended their discussion.

Nick and Mason walked out of the room and closed the door behind them. For Nick, it felt like closing the door on the case and his past and finally stepping into his future.

Mason dropped his big hand on Nick's shoulder and squeezed. "It's over."

"Thank God."

Mason asked the question Nick was asking himself. "Do you think Lopez will keep to his end of the bargain?"

"I have to believe, somewhere in his cold heart, he said yes because he truly loved his sister and mother. So, yeah, I think he'll back off now." But he'd be ready to defend and protect those he loved if Lopez came after them again. "It's not like we won't be on guard in our line of work. In his world, his word means something, so I think we're safe."

He wouldn't bet his life, or the lives of the ones he loved, on it, but he wasn't going to obsess over it either.

He was going to live his life to the fullest now, because he had so much to live for. Aria. His family and hers. The children they hoped to have soon.

They were going to be happy and together.

Nick tilted his head toward the door. "Let's go." Nick led Mason to the room where Aria and Lyric had watched them talk to Javier.

They stepped inside and found Aria and Lyric sitting close together, so Stacy could see both of them in the call screen.

"So he's really locked up for good?" Stacy stared back from her foster home, earnest and hopeful.

"Yes," Aria and Lyric said at the same time.

"He won't ever hurt you again," Aria assured her.

"But how?" Stacy asked.

Nick didn't hesitate and said, "Aria took him down, then punched him in the face for hurting you."

Stacy's eyes went wide. "You did? Wow."

"I did it for you, sweetheart. I did it for us." Aria looked up at him, her heart in her eyes.

"And you're going to come and visit me, right?"

"Yes," Aria assured her. "Nick and I will be there tomorrow."

Nick left Aria with her sister and Stacy and pulled Mason into the hallway. If they were going to adopt Stacy, he needed to marry Aria soon.

He turned to his brother. "Want to go shopping with me?"

Mason looked like he'd rather do anything but that.

Nick raised a brow at him and smirked.

Mason quickly caught on. "Yeah. Let's go shopping."

Nick left all his concerns about the case, the children still out there, and whether or not Javier Lopez would stay true to his word, behind him. The FBI would hold Javier accountable and find those associated with him.

Nick was free to move on and focus on what was most important. His new life with Aria.

Chapter Forty-Two

Later that evening, Nick found Aria in the backyard. She'd bought four turquoise-painted Adirondack chairs and placed them in a circle around a new fire pit in the garden. She was seated in one of the chairs, reading a book, and didn't seem to see him walking toward her.

He and Mason had found what he was looking for downtown, then he'd taken a drive out to her parents' ranch to talk to them before coming home.

He wished Stacy could be here for this, but thought it better that they start their new life together, just the two of them.

Well, and Mason and Lyric, who were coming up behind him, recording everything.

God, Aria looked beautiful in a simple pink T-shirt and a long deep blue skirt that hugged her curves. Her feet were bare, her hair hanging past her shoulders in loose waves.

The second she spotted him, her bright blue eyes lit with joy and her smile nearly made his heart stop.

He was so nervous, but excited. He leaned down and handed her the huge bundle of flowers and kissed her, long and deep. "I missed you today."

She buried her nose in the blooms and inhaled deeply, smiling with joy and contentment. "I didn't think you'd be gone so long after you left with Mason this afternoon." She studied him. "Everything okay?"

He brushed his hand down her long hair. "Better than okay. I have you."

She smiled again. "And I have you."

He took her hand and tugged, silently asking her to stand with him.

She set her book and the flowers on the arm of the chair, then stood. She spotted Mason and her sister in the distance. "What's going on?"

He touched his finger to her jaw and turned her face back to him. "Just look at me, sweetheart."

She grinned, a sultry look in her eyes. "I never get tired of looking at you."

"I love you so much. More than I ever thought possible to love someone."

"I love you, too. It's why I can't stand to be apart from you."

"Then let's never be apart." He sank down on one knee, ignoring the ache in his injured thigh, and instead looked up into Aria's astonished face, the tears brimming in her eyes, her smile as happy as he'd ever seen it. "I don't want to spend another day without you. I want to wake up to your loving smile and fall asleep to your beautiful face. I want to build a life and a family with you. So, please, make me even happier than you already do and say you'll be my wife. Will you marry me?"

She'd been nodding since his knee hit the ground. "YES!" She leaned down and kissed his lips. "Yes." She kissed him again. "Yes." She really kissed him, sliding her tongue along his, and sinking into the moment and the way they both loved to be this close, this connected. "Yes," she whispered against his lips and kissed him again.

Nick stood and took her into his arms, holding her close and loving how desperately she clung to him. Then he realized he'd made a mistake and stepped back, holding her at arm's length. "I forgot the ring."

He pulled the black velvet box out of his pocket and held it up in front of him, then flipped open the lid.

Aria's eyes went wide. She looked from the ring, to him, and back again. "Nick, it's beautiful."

Nick plucked the ring from the cushion, took Aria's left hand, and slid the ring into place. It fit perfectly. He kissed her knuckle right over the ring, then stared into her beautiful blue eyes. "I love you."

"I love you, too."

They fell into another kiss, her arms wrapped around his neck, her fingers in his hair.

He was so excited and happy, he picked her up off her feet and spun her around and yelled, "She said yes."

Aria laughed. "Of course I said yes." She buried her face in his neck and hugged him hard.

Mason and Lyric rushed to congratulate them. They shared a round of hugs, then Lyric held up her phone and showed them the picture she'd taken. "I've got your engagement announcement right here." In the photo, Nick and Aria were kissing and Aria's hand was on the back of his head, her engagement ring sparkling in the sunset light.

It was perfect.

It was beautiful.

And anyone looking at them would see what Nick saw. They really and truly loved each other.

"We need to send it to Stacy." Aria squeezed his hand. "I can't believe you proposed. I mean, I knew you would. I just didn't expect it now. Like this. But it was so...perfect." She went up on tiptoe and kissed him again. "You're amazing."

"So are you. And I have one more question."

She eyed him. "What's that?"

"Will you marry me three weeks from Sunday?"

Her eyes went wide. "Are you serious?"

"I don't want to wait. You won't have to close the bar. It's already closed. Melody and Fox can fly in on Saturday. I already asked. Your mom and dad would love to have the ceremony on the ranch. I talked to the florist next door to the jeweler downtown. They're waiting for your call to tell them what kind of flowers you want. All you need to do is get a dress. My family can't wait to come down."

"You already talked to them?"

"Yes, right after I talked to your parents about asking you to marry me."

"You did?" Aria's eyes filled with tears. "That's really sweet, but you didn't have to get their permission. You already knew I'd marry you."

"I wanted to do it right, even if we are doing it fast. I want you to have everything you want for the wedding, but I don't want to wait. Please, say yes."

"What about Stacy?"

"I spoke to her foster mom, Anne. She's happy to bring her down. Stacy's case worker approved it." Hopefully, they'd get Stacy's decision about them adopting her tomorrow. He had already requested a meeting with her father and his attorney the day after that. But first, he wanted to make Aria his wife.

"Anne will stay with her here, in one of your parents' cabins, until we return from our honeymoon. Stacy will have a chance to get to know both our families. My parents are going to stay there, too."

"You've already set this up?"

"We leave on the Monday after the wedding for our honeymoon."

Her eyes lit up. "Where?"

"Hawaii. An oceanfront cottage with a really pretty and private beach."

"That sounds expensive."

"It's our honeymoon. And like Mason, I invested in Gunn Brothers Distillery. Not a lot, but enough that I've got a chunk of money saved up for our wedding, even after I paid for this house. So say yes again and make me the happiest man on the planet."

Aria's smile nearly knocked him to his knees. "I already said I would. I don't care how or when as long as I get to say you're my husband."

"No title needed, sweetheart. I'm yours. Have been since the second I saw you." But he needed to be sure this was how she wanted to get married. "You've probably been thinking about your wedding for a long time."

She put her fingers over his lips. "I always wanted a simple ceremony with my family and friends. I already have the dress."

"You do?" That surprised him, but then he remembered why she'd have a dress. "Because you were going to marry that asshole?"

She shook her head. "No. I bought it after him because I'd seen it and knew it was what *I* wanted. All I needed was the love of my life to show up. You did the day after I bought the dress."

"That's..." He couldn't believe it. "Amazing."

"I like to think it was fate." She kissed him softly. "So I guess we have a lot to do over the next few weeks."

"You're sure?"

She nodded. "I was the moment I met you."

He crushed her to his chest and kissed her like he'd never get to do it again, like she meant everything to him, like he'd never get enough of her. Because that would never happen.

Aria hugged him close. "Thank you," she whispered in his ear.

"For what?"

"Making my dreams come true."

"You are my every dream and fantasy, sweetheart." He held her tighter, his heart so full it felt like it might burst with happiness.

She'd changed his life. She made his life worth living.

Every day wouldn't be easy, but with her by his side, they could get through anything. And together, they'd be happy.

He picked her up and spun her around again just so he could see her smile and hear her laugh. Best thing he'd ever seen or heard in his life. He felt lighter than he'd ever felt in his life.

Now all he had to do was make them official.

Chapter Forty-Three

Aria and Nick had flown to Montana to see Stacy in person. They wanted to check on her and ask her a big question.

Nick pulled up to the house with the weathered paint and shutters. Maybe the house needed some work, but the yard was green, and it had a basketball and soccer ball on the lawn to go with the purple kid's bike on the driveway. Flowerpots lined the three steps up to the porch. The bright, cheerful blooms welcomed everyone. So did the sign on the door. "This Mess Is Blessed."

It made Aria smile and feel like this was a good place for Stacy. For now.

Nick put his hand over her thigh. "This place seems nice. Kid friendly."

The front door opened and Stacy came rushing out, bounding down the stairs and across the small yard to the curb.

Aria's smile notched up and her heart beat faster. She climbed out of the car and opened her arms to Stacy, letting Stacy come to her for the hug if she wanted it.

Stacy leapt into her arms. "You're finally here. I've been waiting for you."

Nick climbed out of the car, hurried around it as best he could limping on his bad leg, and caught Stacy around her back as she wrapped her arms around his legs. He winced when she hit his injury, but he didn't complain. His smile and bright eyes said he didn't care.

Happy tears gathered in Stacy's eyes. "I can't believe you're both here."

Aria looked into Stacy's pretty green eyes and saw the joy and excitement there. "I missed you. How are you?"

"I'm good." She turned back toward the house, where the foster mom, Anne, sat on the top step keeping watch.

"You look great." Aria loved her adorable black coveralls, white T-shirt, and black sneakers.

Stacy's smile faltered. "I miss the others."

Aria put her hand on Stacy's shoulder. "I know you do. You've seen them during your therapy, right?"

"Yes. It's just not the same." Stacy dug the toe of her shoe into the grass.

Nick held his hand out. "Let's sit on the stairs and talk."

Stacy walked with them and took a seat with her foster mom. Aria and Nick exchanged hellos with Anne and sat with Stacy between them.

Nick started the real conversation they were here to have with her. "Do you like it here?"

"Yeah. It's okay. But it's temporary, right?"

At ten, Stacy had more life experience than most her age. She'd been through so much. But she understood she couldn't go back to her father.

Nick continued. "Foster care is supposed to be temporary, until you either return to your family, or you get adopted to a forever home."

Stacy shook her head. "I don't want to go back to my dad. Besides, he's in jail for what he did to me. Right?"

"Yes, he is. But you still have a couple of options." Nick looked at Aria.

She gave him a nod to keep going.

"Maybe you'd like to check out Wyoming and Aria and my new house."

"Really?" The excitement made Stacy vibrate.

"Really." Nick took a deep breath. "We came here today so we could ask you what you want to do next. After we leave here, we're going to see your dad and I'll tell him your answer. You have a few options. Number one: You can stay in foster care until your grandmother settles her legal troubles and can take you in to live with her. Number two: You can stay in foster care here in Montana, hopefully with Anne, but you could be moved to another home, even several more homes depending on the situation."

Aria's heart ached that this was so many children's reality.

Stacy shook her head to both those choices.

Nick went on. "Number three: If your father gives up his right to be your parent, then you could be adopted by a forever family." Unfortunately, the odds of her being adopted at her age were small. "The last option is one Aria and I talked about and hope you choose. If you want, you could choose us."

She nodded, tears running down her face. "I choose you." She threw herself into Nick's chest. "Yes. Yes. Yes. You."

Nick hugged her close.

Aria had tears trailing down her face as she softly rubbed Stacy's back.

Nick tipped up Stacy's chin, so she was looking at him. "It's not going to be right away. We have to talk to your dad about giving us custody and letting us adopt you. That means, for right now, you'll have to stay in foster care with Anne."

Stacy looked from Nick to Aria and back again. "How long?"

"I'm not sure yet. We will try to get everything sorted out as quickly as possible."

Aria tapped Stacy's forearm to get Stacy to turn to her. "We have to ask a judge to make us a family. It takes time to do all the paperwork and get everyone to agree, but if this is what you want, Nick and I will work really hard to make it happen as soon as we can."

Nick hugged her to his side. "In the meantime, we have Anne's phone number and can call and video chat with you. We'll update you with everything that's going on, so you know what's happening." Nick hated to bring her past into this, but there was something else she needed to know. "I have something to tell you about the case. The man your dad gave you to..."

"Perry." She screwed her lips and nose into an ew face.

"Yes. Him. He was arrested and is in jail. He can't ever hurt you again. In fact, he confessed to everything, so you won't have to testify in court about him."

Tears gathered in her eyes. "What about my dad and grandma?"

"Your dad confessed as well. He's already plead guilty and will be sentenced and taken to prison very soon. Your grandma made a deal to get an easier sentence that means she won't go to prison. Instead she'll do community service and have a suspended sentence, which means if she does anything wrong again, she'll go to prison."

"But she can't see me, right?" The shake of her head told him she didn't want to see her.

Nick asked anyway. "Do you want to see her?"

"No. She hates me." Stacy's gaze dropped to her feet.

Aria touched her chin with her finger and gently pushed to get Stacy to look at her. "I don't think that's true. I think she resented your father for being such a bad parent, making her have to help out, and she took out her resentment on you."

Stacy bottom lip puffed out. "She never wanted me around."

Aria's heart broke. "That's her loss. Because you're amazing. So much so that we want to be with you all the time, sweet girl." Aria nodded vigorously, so Stacy would see and take in those words.

Stacy stared up at Nick. "I wish I could just go with you."

"Me, too. But I promise it will be soon. And when it's all done, you'll have a forever family."

"A really big one," Aria added. "With grandparents and aunts and uncles."

Stacy finally smiled. "And Lyric's baby."

"My brother Jax is having one, too." Aria grinned. "Wildes and Gunns. That's who you'll belong to, sweetheart. And we can't wait."

Stacy nodded. "Okay. Yes. I choose you."

Nick looked over Stacy's head at Aria, a sheen of tears in his eyes and joy on his face. "We're getting a kid."

She brushed a tear from her cheek. "Some things are just meant to be."

"Like you and me."

Her grin widened. "Definitely you and me and her."

"Can we get a dog?" Stacy asked, and he and Aria laughed.

"Let's start with getting you home with us first." He hugged her to him.

Stacy looked up at him. "If I go live with you guys, will you be my parents?"

Nick nodded. "Eventually, yes. Why?"

"So I'll have a mom and dad?" She looked so earnest and hopeful.

Aria could see plainly by the look in Nick's eyes that this little girl had stolen his heart and owned it. "Yes."

Stacy turned and looked up at Anne. "I'm getting a new family."

Anne smiled down at her. "It sounds like a really good one, too."

"We're so lucky that you chose us." Aria couldn't let this little warrior girl grow up in foster care. Not when she and Nick could give her a home and the love and kindness and decency that had been lacking in her life.

Stacy deserved all of that and more.

Anne stood on the step. "Would you like to join us for lunch?"

She and Nick exchanged a look, saying yes to each other, all without a word.

Aria nodded and stood with the others. They went inside and enjoyed the lovely meal Anne had put together for them. Turkey sandwiches, parmesan pasta salad, and fresh fruit. After lunch, they checked out Stacy's room, made a list of things she'd need if she moved in with Aria and

Nick, and showed her pictures of the house so she could pick out her room.

Maybe they were getting a bit ahead of themselves, but Aria wanted everything to be ready when Stacy arrived. She wouldn't even consider that they wouldn't get Stacy. If nothing else, they could become foster parents and keep her that way. But she and Nick really wanted to make things official. They wanted Stacy to know she would always have a place with them.

They ended the day after playing a board game, which Stacy and Nick won together against her and Anne.

Aria waved goodbye to Stacy and Anne from the bottom of the porch stairs. "I'll call you tomorrow, Stacy. Thank you, Anne, for taking care of our girl."

Stacy blushed.

Anne waved and said, "My pleasure."

Nick took Aria's hand, but stared up at Stacy. "Is there anything you want us to say to your dad when we see him tomorrow?"

She ran down the steps and wrapped her hand around Nick's wrist, her eyes pleading with him. "Tell him I want to go with you. He has to let me go with you."

Nick nodded. "I'll tell him." He kissed her on the head.

They climbed into the car, determined to do exactly what she asked of them, and what they promised they'd do: make her theirs.

Aria couldn't wait. She loved her life. Having Nick made it infinitely better. And now they had a chance to raise Stacy as their daughter. Life really couldn't get any sweeter.

She couldn't wait to call Stacy her daughter.

Chapter Forty-Four

Nick walked into the holding area, Aria right behind him, where Stacy's father was locked up. Karl sat at a scarred table with his lawyer, knowing exactly why Nick was there. Nick had spoken to the lawyer yesterday, letting him know that he'd planned to speak to Stacy and offer her a life with a family who would protect and care for her to their dying breath.

I'm going to be a father.

That thought had run through his mind a thousand times since yesterday. Thoughts of what that meant crowded his mind, the awesome responsibility weighing on him, but not deterring him in any way. He welcomed the job. He wanted it. He was excited to see Stacy grow into herself.

He thought about all the things they could do together. School functions. Camping trips. Visits to his family. Little things like having breakfast and dinner together, grocery shopping, doing homework, watching movies, and introducing her to new things. A whole life where he was Dad and she was his little girl. Which meant he'd have to make time for those things by prioritizing her and Aria. How could he not when he wanted to be there for all those things.

He couldn't wait to have her with them, to take her to school, to teach her how to do things, to kiss her skinned knees and banish the imaginary monsters from her nightmares. He couldn't wait to be there for her firsts, whatever they might be, like riding a horse. He'd be the one to walk her down the aisle to the person she loved.

But first, she'd be the flower girl at his and Aria's wedding.

"Should I be worried that you look so damn happy?" Dark circles and two days of beard scruff didn't help Karl's wrinkled, gaunt face. The man looked like he'd been rode hard and put away wet.

Nick stepped into the tiny room, holding Aria's hand, noting two of the three lights overhead were burned out. This place felt oppressive and dreary. Nick took the lead, because he'd been there to help Stacy take her father down for what he did to her. "You're going to thank me for what I'm about to tell you, because you owe Stacy after what you did to her. This will not erase the pain and suffering you've caused her; it won't even get you her forgiveness. But maybe...just maybe...she won't hate you every day for the rest of her life. One day, she might even have a kind thought, that you did this for her, to make her happy, and then she'll go on with her day and probably never think of you again, because she'll have people in her life who matter. Who take care of her. Who love her so much, the thought of ever hurting her breaks their hearts."

Karl looked to his quiet lawyer, then glared back at Nick. "What do you want?"

"I want you to relinquish your parental rights and allow me and my fiancée to adopt Stacy. We will help her through this terrible time, help her to heal, all while we give her the love and family she deserves." *Please say yes, you prick. Do this for her.* Nick wasn't leaving until he got that yes, no matter what.

Karl perked up. "And you'll drop the charges?"

Of course that was his first thought. Selfish asshole.

Karl grinned at his lawyer, who didn't say anything.

Aria practically growled under her breath.

This was Nick's show. He'd already spoken to the lawyer and had him draw up the papers on behalf of his client. All Nick needed was his signature. Was that too much to ask for his daughter? To do one good thing for *her*?

Nick narrowed his gaze on the dirtbag. "You broke the law and that little girl."

Karl winced. But that tiny bit of remorse wasn't enough.

"You don't get a free pass. But this is your chance to do something selfless. For her. The question is, are you man enough to do it? Do you deserve that title of father? Will you sacrifice for your only child, simply to give her a better life than the one you brought her into?" Nick stared him down, daring him to be the selfish prick he'd always been so Nick could hurt him. Oh, how he wanted to punish the fuck out of this asshole.

But he also hoped that Karl would finally, for once, do the right thing by Stacy.

All he had to do was find that one shred of decency inside him.

Karl sat back heavily in the plastic chair and hung his head. "I never meant for this to happen."

Nick's hands clenched into fists. "Bullshit. You knew what you were doing when you handed her over to that deviant prick. You knew what he wanted and you hand-delivered her to him without a thought to the damage he'd inflict. You were supposed to keep her safe. You were supposed to protect her. You were supposed to take a bullet for her and you didn't. You betrayed her in the worst possible way. You did it to save yourself an ass-kicking you more than deserved. And all for what? Money. A forgiven debt. A lifetime of nightmares and pain for her."

Karl crossed his arms on the table, laid his head down on them, and silently wept.

Nick rolled his eyes at the lawyer, who simply shrugged. The court-appointed lawyer probably saw this shit all the time. People being regretful after the fact. After they'd ruined someone else's life with their careless deeds.

Nick sighed, just trying to get through this without sinking to Karl's level and doing something he'd regret if it cost him adopting Stacy. "You let her go once. All I'm asking is that you do it again, only this time for the right reasons. Aria and I can give her the life I hope you once thought you wanted for Stacy. A home. A mother and father who would do anything for her. An extended family of aunts and uncles and cousins. Grandparents who will spoil her, not look the other way when she's being abandoned and hurt."

Nick gave Karl a moment to think about that, to imagine the life Stacy could have. "You know this is the right thing to do. Make it easy on her. For us. Because even if you say no, I will still make it happen. It will just take longer to get her out of foster care and permanently placed with us. Don't put her through that, Karl. She needs you to do right by her this time, to show her that she matters."

Karl's tearstained face rose. "What if she thinks I abandoned her again?"

"You've already done that. You're going to be in prison. Who will take care of her? Strangers? Or me, the guy who saved her. The man she trusts, despite what all those other monstrous men did to her. She'll have Aria, the sweetest, kindest woman you will *never* see again. She loves that little girl. She will be the one to show Stacy how to be a strong woman. She will bake her cookies, hug her when she's happy and sad, she'll cheer for her at every school event, sport, and dance recital. Whatever Stacy decides to do, we'll be there."

Aria hooked her arm through his and hugged him tight.

Karl looked straight ahead, his gaze desolate, and bobbed his head.

Nick's frustration grew. "Is that a yes? You'll sign the paperwork? You'll let her go, so she gets what she needs and deserves?"

Karl raised his bloodshot eyes to Nick. "I knew the second I gave her up, I'd never get her back, even if I found her again. I knew what I'd done would make her hate me and never want to be with me again."

Nick seethed. "But you did it anyway."

Anguish drew lines across his forehead. "I didn't want to. But I couldn't see another way out."

Nick barely refrained from shaking the guy. "Give her this way out of the mess you made of her life. She needs it. She deserves it. I promise you, Aria and I will give her a good life. One where she feels safe and loved. One where she can forget the past and truly start over."

Karl gathered himself and leveled a steadier gaze on Nick. "Does she know her mother passed away while she was gone?"

"No. I don't think now is the time to tell her." Nick hated the idea of giving Stacy more bad news.

Karl nodded. "We hadn't seen her in years. She didn't reach out when she got sick. Maybe she felt like I do, that she didn't deserve Stacy after she'd left her." Karl let out a heavy sigh. "So much loss. So many mistakes." Tears dripped down his ruddy face. "Okay. I'll sign the papers."

Nick let out a huge sigh of relief. "Thank you for making this easy. I don't want her in foster care longer than she needs to be."

"Me either." Karl took the pen his lawyer offered.

The lawyer held up the papers. "Do you understand that by signing these, you relinquish your parental rights? That you will no longer legally be responsible for Stacy, or have any rights to make decisions about her life, that you in fact want Aria Wilde and Nick Gunn to be her legal guardians, until they marry and legally adopt Stacy and assume all the rights of parents?"

Nick raised a brow at the stipulation the lawyer had added. It didn't matter. They were weeks away from their wedding.

"I understand. Yes. I want him and Aria to adopt Stacy." Karl looked up at them. "It's what my little girl wants, right?"

Nick nodded. "We spoke to her yesterday. She was very sure, otherwise we would have given her more time to decide."

The lawyer set the papers down in front of Karl. "I also spoke to her by telephone before I arrived. She confirmed, she would like to live with Aria and Nick. Forever, she said."

Nick's heart beat faster and melted all at once. She'd be theirs. Forever.

Karl glanced at Aria's engagement ring. "Are you getting married soon?"

"A few weeks from now," Aria confirmed.

The lawyer put his hand on Karl's shoulder. "Agent Gunn is fast-tracking this process. I just thought you'd want some assurance that what he says he and Aria will be to Stacy actually comes to fruition."

Nick relaxed, letting Karl and the lawyer see that he didn't have any reservations about meeting the terms. "I love Aria. I know my life is with her. That's why I moved to Wyoming to be with her. We want Stacy home with us as soon as possible. After everything she's been through, we want her to have a place she knows she's safe and that's hers."

Karl took the pen and signed the documents. "Thank you, Agent Gunn. I know you'll do right by my Stacy. But maybe you or your girl could do something for me."

Nick tensed. "What?"

"Send me a picture of her once in a while. Tell me how she is. So I know she's doing okay. That she's happy."

Nick relaxed. "We will. If you agree to let *her* decide if and when she sees you again."

Karl nodded and signed the papers. "Thank you. You didn't have to do this." He pushed the papers to Nick.

He took them in hand, feeling like he won the lottery. "I want to do this for her. Thank you for making me a dad. I don't take that lightly. I mean to be the best one I can be."

Karl nodded. "I believe it."

"Thank you," Aria said, standing to leave.

"Teach her to stay away from gambling men like me."

Aria stared right back at him. "I won't have to. She'll see how Nick treats me and she won't settle for anything less than someone who looks at her like she's their everything."

Nick pulled her to his side and kissed her forehead.

They left with what they came for, ecstatic and hopeful, leaving the past behind for a brighter future as a family.

He headed out of the depressing building with the love of his life at his side and toward his car and his new life with Aria.

He couldn't wait to call Stacy and dialed the second his ass hit the driver's seat. He cranked the engine just as she answered the phone.

"Did you get it?" The anticipation and stress in her voice made him smile. She wanted this as much as he and Aria did.

"I got it. You're ours. Or at least you will be once a judge signs off. Guardianship should go through in a couple of weeks. The adoption in about six months." Maybe he could get it faster. He knew a couple of judges. Neither of them wanted to make Stacy wait to be with them a second longer than was necessary.

He had a lot to do and very little time to do it.

Luckily, he was still on leave from the FBI.

"I can't wait to go back to school." Stacy sounded excited about all of it.

"Soon," Aria replied. "Until then, keep working with the tutor they lined up for you, so you can catch up. I know you've been working hard and passing all your tests."

"I like school." She hesitated, then admitted, "I miss my friends back home."

Nick frowned, sad for her. "I know you do, sweetheart, but you'll make new friends in Wyoming. Aria already started the enrollment process by getting your records from your old school sent to the one in Wyoming. You can start as soon as we move you to our new home."

Stacy sighed. "Maybe it's better to start over somewhere new, Anne says. No one will know what happened to me. I can just be me. No one will stare at me or say bad things."

Nick's heart couldn't take her unhappiness and trepidation about others judging her. "You know what happened isn't your fault, right?"

"Yes. But I still did it."

That softly spoken confession tightened his chest. "No. You were *forced* to do it. That's different. You didn't have a choice."

"Yeah. Still. I miss Nicole and Emma and Toby."

"You get to visit with them during group therapy, right?" He'd set that up for them before he moved to Wyoming.

"Yes. And Nicole has her own phone, so she's called a couple of times just to talk."

"Well, that's nice. See, you haven't lost touch with them. And Aria and I will make sure you can contact them anytime you want."

Stacy seemed satisfied with that and asked, "About my room...the bedroom that looks out over the back garden." The one closest to the primary bedroom.

Nick figured it made her feel safe to be closest to them.

"The flowers are so bright and cheerful. And I love the bench seat in the window. I could sit and stare out the window all the time. It would feel like being outside."

Scratch Nick's first thought. She wanted to feel like she had space and freedom. After being locked in a cellar for so long, she deserved the prettiest view and feeling like she wasn't closed in.

"Anything special you want for the room? Besides a dog." He foresaw a trip to the nearest animal shelter in his future.

"Books, so I can read by the window."

Aria leaned into his side so she could talk through the speaker. "I'll get you a bookcase and you and I will go to the bookstore and pick out books together."

"I'd like that." The enthusiasm was back in her voice. "Anne says it's time for me to do homework."

"Okay. Keep working hard. We'll call you tomorrow."

"Bye, Aria. Bye, Nick."

"Bye, sprite."

Stacy giggled when he called her that nickname. He'd be sure to call her that again if she liked it so much.

"Talk soon." He hung up and thought about how much his life was about to change.

He and Aria would have to start a whole new routine. "When she moves in, I can get Stacy up for school in the morning, while you sleep in." He pulled out of the lot and kept talking as he drove them to the airport, so they could fly home. "Maybe you can pick up Stacy after school and get her settled at home. We'll need a babysitter. Or maybe Stacy could hang out with Lyric while she's on maternity leave, or stay with your parents at the ranch after school. They'd love to dote on their new granddaughter."

He turned to her. "The more I think about her with us, the more I want it." Excitement fluttered in his gut and made him anxious to move things along as quickly as possible.

Aria smiled so big he couldn't help but smile back. "They'd love that. I can't wait go shopping and get her some new clothes, everything she'll need for school. I want everything to be ready for her when she gets here. I want her to see how much we want her to feel at home."

"She will, because she knows she's wanted now. She knows we'll take care of her and keep her safe."

Every person deserved that, and Nick aimed to make sure Stacy felt it for the rest of her life.

CHAPTER FORTY-FIVE

Aria, Nick, and Stacy walked up the path to Aria's parents' front door. This was their second Sunday family dinner after a judge signed off on their guardianship of Stacy. They'd passed their home visit and interviews. The social worker had given the judge a glowing review, letting him know Stacy would be lucky to have them. Really, they were lucky to have her.

Last Sunday, Stacy had been nervous. She barely spoke to anyone, except Aria and Nick. This time, she seemed more confident and put her hand on the knob and opened the door, just like Aria had done last weekend. This was home. Just like her place with Nick. This would always be a place where she was welcomed and loved. Nick and Stacy were a part of that, too.

It was what they wanted Stacy to feel every time she walked in their door and this one.

Her mom, Robin, rushed to them as they entered. "I'm so happy you guys could make it." She bent down to Stacy. "Hello. I made you another batch of double-chocolate brownies because you said they're your favorite."

Without prompting, Stacy enveloped Robin in a hug. "Thank you, Grandma."

Robin's eyes glassed over and she held Stacy close. "Oh. Well. You're more than welcome."

Stacy stepped back and smiled, though she clenched her hands in front of her like she didn't know what to do with them.

Aria's dad, Wade, moved closer, keeping some distance because Stacy had been especially shy around him and her brother, Jax.

Stacy took a step closer to him. "How is the baby cow that got sick?"

Wade dropped to a crouch and pulled out his phone. He swiped the screen, then turned it to Stacy. "I took a picture of her this morning. She's doing just fine. Back with her mama. See?"

Stacy took two more steps closer to him for a better look. "She looks much better. She's so cute."

"Hey, munchkin, do you have a hello for me?" Jax bent forward and held out his fist.

Stacy bumped, then shied away and backed up into Nick, who kept close to her because he knew how hard it was for Stacy to relax in big groups.

Lyric was sitting at the table, her hand over her baby bump. "Want to feel the baby kick?"

Stacy rushed over and threw her arms around Lyric, then put her hand on Lyric's belly. Stacy let out a squeak. "I felt her, Auntie."

Mason walked over to her, looming large like all the other men. But Stacy didn't shy away.

"Hi, Uncle Mason."

"Hey, sprite." Mason had started calling her that after he heard Nick call her by the nickname. "You still working on your dad about that dog?"

Stacy grinned. "He says I have to wait until after the wedding."

Mason brushed his hand over her head. "That's just another week away."

Stacy let out a huff. "But they'll be gone on their trip."

"And you'll be spoiled by both sets of grandparents. Plus, our cousins are coming. You should call them all uncle and make them feel old." He winked at her.

"Is Uncle Hawk flying everyone here, like he brought me?" Excitement filled her voice.

Once the judge signed off on the guardianship, Hawk had volunteered to fly Stacy home to them. Since she was familiar with him from the hospital after she was rescued, she'd been excited and eager to fly with him.

Nicole, Emma, and Toby heard about it during one of their group therapy sessions and wanted their turn, too.

Mason nodded. "You're going to meet the whole crew. Your grandma and grandpa can't wait to see you in person."

They'd been having video chats with everyone in the family, so Stacy would know each of them at least a little bit before there were so many people surrounding her at the wedding. She and Nick were trying to ease her into things, but with such a big family, it was hard not to overwhelm her.

She was doing well in school. The teacher had paired her up with a different girl from her class each day, so she could make friends and navigate the new campus. Stacy had made a couple of friends, who invited her to lunch with them every day. Her teachers said she was bright, but quiet in class. So far, she'd brought home nothing but high scores on all her classwork and tests.

They were nurturing her love of books. She liked getting lost in another world. Aria and Stacy had bought a stack of books at the bookstore and put them on the shelf in her room, right next to her favorite spot on the window seat, which Aria had cozied up with a soft pillow and blanket for her to snuggle up. She even found a cute little table with carved legs to put next to her. Stacy loved to drink hot chocolate and read on weekend mornings.

Stacy walked around the table and hugged Layla. They'd spent last Saturday in Layla's art studio after Stacy asked about her aunt's talent. Layla gave her some lessons on drawing, but it seemed Stacy had a talent for it.

Stacy pulled out the sketchpad from her bag and opened it on the table, showing off what she'd drawn this past week.

Jax came up beside Aria. "They have a special bond. Layla hasn't stopped talking about what a fantastic artist she is. How there's something raw and bold and some-times sad in what she creates."

"She's been through a lot."

"She's warming up to us. She'll be ready to babysit Lay-la's and my munchkin before we know it." Jax hooked his arm around her shoulders. "You did a really good thing. An amazing thing. She's already better for being with you and Nick."

"She's got a long way to go."

"She's got a lot of love and support to get her there." Jax looked down at her, a twinkle in his eyes. "And if that's not enough, Dad and I found her a pony. He'll be here next week."

Her eyes popped wide. "What? Are you serious?" It warmed her heart that they'd do something so sweet.

"Mars will be for all the kids. But he's mostly hers because she's so much older than her cousins."

Nick brought her a glass of wine. "Why are you grinning like that?" Nick pulled her from Jax and into his arms.

"Because our girl is getting a pony from her uncle and grandpa."

Nick chuckled. "I'm surprised it took you two this long to get her one," he said to Jax.

Stacy was in the kitchen now with Robin, helping her mash potatoes in a pot at the stove, standing on the same step stool she, Lyric, Jax, and Melody used to use when they were kids.

Nick kissed the side of her head. "She's happy."

Every day, she got a little bit farther away from the pain. One day, it would fade into the background, a distant memory of where she'd come from and how she'd survived.

Aria loved being a mom. It made everything else pale in comparison. She still loved the bar, but she loved being with her family more. Right now, she got to shower Stacy with all her attention and love. Stacy needed it. But Aria couldn't wait to make her a big sister, too.

But first, she and Nick were tying the knot.

"What's that smile for?" Nick held her close in the warmth of her family home.

"I was thinking about how excited and anxious I am to marry you."

"Yeah. Me, too. I can't wait to call you Mrs. Gunn." He kissed her right there in her mother's kitchen, their family around them. Their soon-to-be daughter was surrounded by just some of the many people who would love and protect her always.

She'd never felt more humbled and appreciative to be a part of the people here who made this place home.

She held up her wine. "To the Wilde Gunn family."

Everyone around the room held up a glass. "The Wilde Gunn family." They all drank.

Stacy clinked her soda can to her grandma's glass of wine, then they hugged each other, and Stacy announced, "Dinner's ready."

The family gathered around the table with their plates piled high and their hearts full.

EPILOGUE

Aria couldn't believe how fast the days passed until their wedding and her standing in front of the full-length mirror in her old bedroom at her parents' ranch, staring at herself in her gown. It was a wish when she bought it and a dream come true today. She loved it.

"Nick is going to pass out when he sees you in this dress." Her mother smiled from behind her. "You are breathtaking." Tears gathered in her mother's eyes.

"Don't cry, or I'll start crying." She blinked to hold back the tears and smoothed her hands over the full lace skirt. The sweetheart neckline and cap sleeves made her look and feel like a princess. With every move she made, the skirt swished.

The door flew open behind her and Stacy ran in ahead of Lyric and Melody. "It's time! It's time! It's time," she shouted.

Aria turned to them and got a bunch of oohs and ahhs.

"That dress…" Lyric said. "I see why you had to have it."

"It's perfect," Melody agreed.

"You're so pretty, Mommy." Stacy looked up at her with pure joy.

Even now, weeks after Stacy had started living with them, hearing Stacy call her that made her heart melt and her throat choke up.

Three days after she'd started living with them, Aria and Nick went into her room to say goodnight and she asked them if it was finally okay to call them Mom and Dad. She and Nick had both choked up and said yes.

Then, right before they walked out of her bedroom, she'd said, "See you in the morning, Mom and Dad." They'd both teared up and gone back and hugged their little girl one more time.

Aria would never forget it.

"You look beautiful, too."

Stacy's pale pink satin dress with flutter sleeves and a full skirt made her look like the young lady she'd turned into over the last weeks. She'd been twirling around in it since she put it on and couldn't wait to be their flower girl.

Since Mason and Nick were brothers and she and Lyric were sisters, she and Nick decided to just have them stand up for them.

Lyric wore a dusty-rose-colored dress with flutter sleeves like Stacy's dress, a V-neck, and a full asymmetrical skirt that showed off her baby bump.

Nick and Mason had chosen to wear black suits. Simple and timeless.

"Ready?" her dad asked as he walked into the room, then stopped short when he saw her in her gown. "Oh." He shook his head. "Oh, wow. You look amazing, sweetheart. He's not going to know what hit him."

Her blush heated her cheeks. "Let's go. I'm more than ready."

Nick and Mason arrived at the very cool glass-topped cabin Jax's wife Layla used as a studio when she stayed at the ranch to paint her masterpieces. Now, the Wildes used the open cabin space for wedding ceremonies and a honeymoon getaway, depending on how they decorated it.

Today it was decorated with green garlands with pinecones and white roses, pink floral bouquets lining the aisle between the guest chairs, and large lanterns filled with white candles. The whole space felt warm and inviting, especially with the large tree branches overhead as the forest surrounded them.

Nick loved it as much as Aria did. She'd told him about Jax and Layla's wedding as well as the many others she'd helped her mom and dad set up for guests at the ranch. It turned out better than she'd described to him.

"You ready?" Mason asked before they stepped inside.

"I've been ready almost since the day I met her." Nick walked up the steps and greeted his mom and dad.

"We're so happy for you," his mom said, hugging him close.

Nick kissed her cheek, then turned to his dad and hugged him.

His dad put his hand on Nick's shoulder. "You're making a beautiful family, son."

Stacy had his dad wrapped around her little finger. His parents didn't know what it was like to have a daughter. His three cousins were all boys, too.

"I can't wait to expand it, too." Nick would give Aria the year she wanted, then he wanted to work on the next Wilde Gunn addition.

His father squeezed his shoulder again. "That's what the honeymoon is for."

His mom swatted his dad's chest. "Take your time, Nick. Enjoy being together for a while."

"We will. We want to give Stacy some time to settle in with us, too."

"I'm looking forward to spoiling her while you're away." His mom would happily rain affection down on her the whole time.

He hoped Stacy was ready for all the attention.

More likely she'd talk her uncle Jax into letting her ride her pony again. She'd had her first riding lesson yesterday. He and Aria hadn't wanted to miss her first time up on a pony, knowing she was going to have this whole next week to help out her grandparents and Jax on the ranch.

"She's going to be in great hands with all of you. Just be careful not to overwhelm her."

His mom nodded her understanding. "We'll take it slow and easy. Now go say hello to your aunt, uncle, and cousins."

Nick made his way over to Mason, who was between his cousins, Lincoln, Hawk, and Damon.

Hawk came forward first. "Congrats, man. I'm happy for you." He actually looked it.

"Thanks for always helping out when Mason and I need you."

"I'm always there for you and the family, bro." Hawk and his brothers truly were like brothers to them.

Lincoln and Damon both gave him a hug and slap on the back, congratulating him.

"None of you brought a date? What's with you guys? You can't work all the time," Nick teased, knowing he'd been guilty of doing just that. But not anymore. Now he made it a point to be home for dinner. Weekends were family time, unless something truly urgent came up.

Damon groaned. "I'm hardly ever in one place long enough for one date, let alone a follow-up." Damon traveled around the globe promoting the Gunn Brothers Distillery brand.

Lincoln rolled his eyes. "I don't want to hear any complaining from the guy who gets texts from every area and country code around the globe asking if he's free tonight. They don't even know you're not even in the same time zone as them."

Damon grinned. "I hardly ever know what time zone I'm in. But I can tell you where to find the best-looking women in over twenty countries."

Hawk smacked his younger brother on the back of the head. "Don't brag when you can't even remember the name of the last girl you slept with."

Aunt Donna glared at her boys, then shushed them. "We're here to celebrate Nick and Aria. This is not some bar where you get to boast about your conquests."

Damon snickered. "It's not boasting if it's true."

Aunt Donna shook her head at her boys. "One of these days a woman is going to knock you off your feet, like Aria did Nick. Then you'll know what real love feels like and what it's like to be with someone who matters."

"Listen to your mother, boys," Uncle Mac admonished. "She speaks the truth. You'll see."

"Nick had to go and bring the first grandchild into the family," Lincoln complained with a note of lightheartedness to it. "Lyric and Layla are delivering two more soon.

Mom and Dad are just hoping for some grandbabies of their own."

Nick grinned. "Not my fault, boys. I fell in love with the kid the way I did Aria. Best thing to ever happen to me, those two."

"She's here," Aria's mother, Robin, announced as she stepped into the room.

"It's time." Lincoln gave him a nudge toward the front.

Mason walked up with him to their position and gave him a hearty pat on the back. "No going back now."

"I only want the future I know I'll have with her."

Judge Kerrich stood beside them, ready to perform the ceremony. "It starts right now."

"Thank you for doing this for us, Judge. I appreciate you taking the time."

"This is one of the nicer things I get to do in this job. I like making families, especially for good people like you and the Wildes."

Judge Kerrich was a good friend of Aria's father. They'd known each other since grade school. The judge was kind enough to preside over their wedding and sign off on the adoption after he'd had a conversation with Stacy earlier in the day.

Was he getting special treatment because he was an FBI agent and he had this family connection? Yes. But the judge had made it clear, too, that Stacy had been through enough in her short life and if the one thing she wanted was for him and Aria to be her mom and dad, then the judge was going to make that happen so that she could move forward with her life as a Gunn.

She and Aria would belong to him now.

He couldn't wait.

And he didn't have to, because Jax escorted Robin to her seat in the front row beside Layla. Melody and Fox sat behind them. Several of Aria's friends filled out the rest of that side.

His parents were right up front on his side, along with his aunt and uncle behind them, with his cousins. He'd invited several of his buddies from work with their partners, too.

These were the people who mattered most in their lives.

"Can't Help Falling In Love" by Kina Grannis from the movie *Crazy Rich Asians*, one of Aria's favorite movies and love songs, started playing and Nick fell into the sultry tune and beautiful lyrics.

It was the perfect song for them, because neither of them had been able to help falling in love with the other. It was inevitable and meant to be and all those things Nick had always thought were too sappy for him until he felt it all.

She made him feel, like he'd never felt before.

The song eased him into taking in this moment and what it meant to marry the woman he loved. She was everything. His whole world. Today was the luckiest day of his life.

For more than one reason.

His sweet little Stacy walked up the steps at the back in her pretty pink dress, a joyous smile on her face, carrying a white basket filled with pink rose petals. She walked into the room and called out, "Hi, Dad," lighting up his heart.

She walked forward in the patent leather sandals with a little heel that she'd loved so much because they were so grown up and tossed handfuls of the petals out in front of her as she walked up the aisle to him.

His heart melted. "Good job, sprite."

Stacy beamed and took her position opposite him.

He and Aria wanted her to be part of the ceremony, because today they became a family of three.

Lyric stepped into the room in her beautiful pink dress, looking radiant with her baby bump. She held a bouquet of pink roses and smiled as she walked down the aisle, timing the end of her walk to the music.

Mason whispered behind him, "That's my beautiful angel." He called her "angel" all the time. And even though they'd been married for some time now, you'd think they were still newlyweds.

Lyric took her place beside Stacy and then the music changed to the traditional wedding march.

Nick held his breath, waiting to see her.

She didn't disappoint. The second he saw her face, she smiled so big, her cheeks pinked and her eyes lit up, seeing him. And then he saw the dress as she stepped into the room, and wow, she blew his mind. All he could do was say, "Gorgeous."

She must have read his lips because her smile went up to megawatt.

Her father walked Aria to him. Her mother had tears in her eyes as Aria passed her. His mom and dad both looked overwhelmed with joy.

And then she was right in front of him.

Her dad put her hand in his and said, "Take care of each other." Then he went to take his seat beside Robin.

Nick stared into Aria's eyes and felt every beat of love coming from his heart. "You're stunning."

"I'm going to say this one last time, since I only got to say it for a few weeks, but my *fiancée* is gorgeous."

Their loved ones all laughed.

"Let's turn that into husband and wife, shall we?" Judge Kerrich asked.

Aria handed her flowers to her sister Lyric.

Nick held his hand out to Stacy, who moved in between him and Aria and held both their hands. They made a circle. Unbroken. A family.

"You look so pretty, Mommy."

Aria bent and kissed Stacy on the forehead. "So do you, my sweet girl." Aria turned to the judge and nodded for him to go ahead, then her beautiful blue gaze held his with so much love, sincerity, and certainty, he knew she was thinking the same thing he was. *We're forever.*

"Love is magical. That chemistry combined with kismet brings people together. In this case, love brought Aria and Nick together. And that love expanded when Stacy came into their lives. Because of love, they will become a family here today."

It felt like Nick blinked and the I dos were done and he had a platinum band on his hand and Aria had a diamond eternity band around hers. The best part, he was kissing her again and again as everyone clapped.

"Can I say it now, Daddy?" Stacy tugged on his pant leg.

He reluctantly broke the kiss with his *wife*. "One second, sprite. We have one more thing to do."

She looked at him, confused, because they hadn't practiced this part. Even his new wife didn't know about this.

Nick took Aria's hand and kissed the back of it right above her new ring. "Our first wedding gift is the one we both want more than anything."

Aria eyed him curiously, but didn't say anything.

Nick turned to the judge. "If you'll do the honors, please."

Judge Kerrich held up the papers so everyone could see them. "We have just witnessed the union between Nick and Aria, but there is someone else here who wants very much to be a part of their union. Isn't that right, Stacy?"

Confusion filled her eyes. "What?"

"Do you, Stacy Elizabeth Cabot, want Nick and Aria Gunn to be your forever mom and dad?"

She nodded her head over and over again. "Oh, yes. I do."

"Do you, Aria and Nick, want Stacy to be your daughter?"

Nick squeezed Aria's hand.

Tears fell down her cheeks. "This is happening right now?"

Nick nodded. "I asked the judge if he'd make an exception and allow us to become a family together at the same time."

"That's why we had the surprise home visit?"

Nick squeezed her hand again. "Yes. Though I knew it was coming."

Despite the tears, she smiled at him. "You did this."

"I'd do anything for you and her."

Judge Kerrich leaned in. "Do you want Stacy to be your daughter?"

Aria, his kindhearted wife, looked at the judge and spoke the truth. "She already is."

Stacy's wide smile matched Aria's.

"We do," Nick answered the question for both of them.

Judge Kerrich went on with the little ceremony they'd planned to make this special for Stacy. "And will you love, honor, cherish, and keep safe this beautiful child? Will you be the light that outshines the dark? Will you be the parent, teacher, and protector she deserves?"

"We will," Nick and Aria said in unison.

Judge Kerrich put his hand over Nick and Aria's joined hands. "Then from this day forward, you will be a family, a bond that shall never be broken, a place that you shall always be held in each other's hearts." He looked past them to their guests. "I present to you, Nick, Aria, and Stacy Gunn."

Judge Kerrich signed the papers.

Their family and friends clapped and cheered, many of them brushing away their own tears.

Nick picked up Stacy, wrapped his free arm around Aria, and held his girls close.

"So that's it, she's ours?" Aria asked, stunned.

Nick looked into Stacy's pretty green eyes. "You're ours, sprite. Forever."

She threw her arms around both of them. "I love you so much."

"We love you, too." Aria held her close, her eyes locked on him, and he saw everything she didn't say out loud to him. She loved him. She thanked him for making this happen. She adored their child. She couldn't wait for them to start making a million memories together.

Nick released Aria for a moment and pulled out the silver chain from his pocket. He held it up in front of Stacy. "Mommy got a brand new ring today for our wedding. So I thought maybe you should get something special, too, for your adoption day."

She grabbed hold of the small silver disc with the three gems on it with her new initials—SG—and today's date.

Aria grinned. "Nick, you put all our birthstones on it."

Stacy's smile kicked up a notch. "That's so cool. I love it."

Aria took the chain and put it around Stacy's neck.

"So a little piece of us will always be with you." Nick kissed her cheek.

Aria kissed him. "You're incredible."

Stacy hugged them both tight and it was perfect.

Bonus Epilogue

Two weeks later...

"Hey, sprite, how was school today?"

"Dad!" Stacy ran across the backyard and right into his arms.

Nick scooped her up and kissed her cheek. He'd taken an extra week off work to spend time at home with her and Aria after the honeymoon.

Stacy had loved spending time with her grandparents and aunts and uncles. But she missed them.

And even though Nick had kept them busy the whole time they were gone, he and Aria missed her, too. They even felt guilty for leaving her at home. So they made sure to bring her a few gifts from the island.

She was wearing her dolphin ring right now.

"Mom says you have something you want to show me."

Nick kissed Aria as she joined them near the backyard fire pit. He held both his girls in his arms and looked into Stacy's pretty green eyes. "Aria and I have something to tell you."

"Is everything okay? The adoption is done. You said so." Her worried gaze made his heart clench.

Aria put her hand on Stacy's cheek. "Yes, sweet girl. The adoption is done. It can't be undone. You're ours."

"Stuck with us forever," Nick added, hoping that reassured her.

It was taking Stacy a little while to process everything that happened to her. Therapy brought up a lot of emotions for her. They took things one day at a time, always checking in with Stacy to be sure they were giving her the help and support she needed.

She'd been through so much in her short life. And unfortunately, Nick only had more bad news for her today.

But they'd promised her they'd always be open and honest about the case, her father, and anything having to do with her.

"Then what is it?" she asked, wariness in her eyes.

"It's official. Your father made a deal with the prosecutor. He plead guilty to the charges against him and agreed to spend the next five years in prison. They're going to move him tomorrow."

Stacy sucked in her lips and looked from Aria to him. "Did he say anything?"

"I didn't talk to him, sprite. His lawyer called me to tell me."

Aria brushed a lock of Stacy's hair behind her ear. "Do you want to talk to him?"

Stacy shook her head. "No. I..."

"What is it, sprite?" he asked.

"I just...I like it here so much I forgot."

"You forgot what?" Aria asked.

"Him." Her bottom lip trembled. "Is that bad?"

Nick hugged her close. "No, sweetheart. It's been a long time since you saw him. And when you did, it scared you.

And I get that being here lets you kind of forget the bad things. You want to focus on the good things."

"I can't forget that other stuff though."

Aria rubbed her hand up and down Stacy's back. "We know, sweet girl. And it's okay when those memories come back and you're sad and angry and just want them to go away. Those things happened and you will deal with them as they come in the best way you know how and with our support and with your therapist. As for your dad...he hurt you. You can be mad and upset and hurt as long as you want to be about it."

Nick nodded. "I asked him to do something for you."

"What?"

"I asked him to wait to talk to you again until you were ready. You get to decide when and if you talk to him again." Nick wanted her to know she had control. No one, not even her father, could force her to interact with him.

She'd been forced to do things against her will far too many times.

Stacy breathed a sigh of relief. "I have nothing to say to him." Maybe not now, but in the future, she might have a lot to say to the man who turned his back on her and handed her into the arms of a monster.

"Okay," Nick agreed. "If you ever change your mind, you just let us know and we'll make it happen. If you never change your mind, that's okay, too."

"You're my parents now. I like it here. I don't want to go back."

Aria brushed her hand over Stacy's head. "You don't have to, sweet girl."

Nick wasn't sure how she'd take the next bit of news he'd been holding on to since he met with her father. "There's one more thing you need to know, sprite. Do you remember your mother?"

"Kinda. Why? I haven't seen her in a long time. She left us. Is she back? Is she going to try to take me from you?" Her hands trembled as she clasped them together.

Nick and Aria both shook their heads, trying to stave off Stacy falling into a panic attack.

Aria cupped her face. "No one is taking you from us. Ever. Not your dad. Not your mom. She can't, sweet girl, because she got sick with cancer and she died."

Tears welled in Stacy's eyes. "She did?"

"Yes. It was several months ago. Before I found you," Nick explained.

Stacy looked at him with her sad eyes. "I used to wish that she'd somehow find me and save me, even though I knew she didn't want me. She just wanted out. She used to say that all the time."

Nick didn't understand how the two people in her life both wanted to unburden themselves of her. Such selfishness. So much damage they inflicted on her.

Aria tried to turn things around. "Your dad and I thought that perhaps you'd like to say goodbye."

Nick set Stacy down and took her hand. "Come see." He led her over to the garden, where he'd left a rose bush and the rock with MOM engraved into it.

Aria kneeled next to the hole he'd dug earlier. "We thought as a remembrance of her, we'd plant a white rose bush and place this marker for her."

"Like a funeral."

"A memorial. And anytime you feel like you want to talk to her, you could come out here and visit her. Even if you just want to sit and think about her."

"I don't want to do that. She left me. She never came back. She didn't care." Tears welled in her eyes and spilled over.

"Tell her," Nick encouraged. "Whatever you want to say to her."

Stacy looked from him, then at the rock. "You left me with him. Why didn't you take me, too? Why did you let him do that to me?" she yelled. "I hate you!" Her whole body vibrated.

Nick's heart cracked. He hated seeing her upset.

Aria's eyes were filled with concern, but also admiration. "That's it, sweet girl. Let it out. She can take it, because she's your mom and she knows what she did was wrong. She knows she hurt you."

Stacy was all out of anger. "Why didn't you come back?" The softly spoken words were so filled with pain, Nick felt the ache of them in his bones.

"We'll never know the answer to that question, sweet girl. But what if she did want to come back and just didn't know how after she hurt you so much? What if you could find a way to believe that answer, knowing that she ran out of time when she got sick? And maybe if you could believe that, you can believe that she regretted leaving you, that she thought about you all the time, and that she wished she was with you. And now, maybe, she's looking down on you and watching her little girl not just survive, but thrive in her new life. Maybe you can look up to the sky and tell her, 'I'm still here. I made it. I survived. I did it.'"

Stacy tipped her head back and said, "I'm still here."

"Say it louder, sprite, so she can hear you."

"I'm still here," she yelled.

"Louder, sweet girl. Let her know you mean it."

Stacy sucked in a deep breath, her tears drying on her cheeks. "I'm. Still. Here!"

Nick scooped her up and held her close. Aria hugged both of them, making a Stacy sandwich.

"That's my girl." Nick grinned at her. "You are still here."

"You made it, sweet girl. You overcame the odds. You kept fighting. You never gave up. Your mom, your dad, all those people who hurt you, none of them are as strong and resilient as you."

"Because you're amazing, sprite." Nick buried his face in her soft hair and hugged her hard.

Stacy's smile bloomed soft and sweet on her face. "Thank you for saving me. And keeping me."

Aria squeezed them both tighter. "You're ours, sweet girl. Forever. We will never let you go. We will never walk away. We will always be yours."

"I know."

Nick didn't know what to do with all the emotions inside him.

She trusted them.

They would never betray that trust. They'd give her a good life. They'd be her everything, the way she was theirs.

Which meant he had a promise to keep.

Nick got a call last night from his boss, asking one more time, "Don't you want to lead one of the raids?"

Nick didn't have to think for even a moment. "No, sir. I need to be with my wife and daughter when it all goes public. They need me."

The morning news broke the story across the country with FBI arrests happening in multiple states. Tech moguls, millionaires, corporate executives, government officials, influencers, and even a couple of celebrities were taken into custody, linked either to one of the four children who hadn't forgotten a name or to Javier Lopez's operation. The coordinated arrests were a warning to other traffickers and those who preyed on children. The FBI was coming for them. The case was the largest of its kind in holding pedophiles accountable for destroying the lives of children.

And the arrests would keep coming as they went through the digital files and linked the people they'd arrested to others who liked to share child pornography.

Nick felt especially good about himself and his job today. He felt immense pride in the four children standing in front of him in the middle of a field on Wilde Wind Ranch where Nicole, Emma, and Toby's families were staying for a few days, so all the kids could spend some time together.

So he could tell them that the men who'd hurt them were all under arrest. And give them a special surprise.

He spotted their special guest in the distance and signaled all the parents it was time as he asked the kids to join him in the field. "I hope you're all having a good time on the ranch." They'd arrived yesterday and spent this morning on a trail ride with Jax and Aria.

They were expecting a dinner by the campfire and s'mores later.

But first… "I made you guys a promise, that the FBI would hunt down every single person on your lists. They hurt you. And you wanted to hurt them back. And that's the reason I wanted you all together today. This morning the FBI started arresting all the people connected to Javier Lopez's operation. Every. Single. One. Of. Them."

The kids all started looking at each other, then turned back to him, smiling.

"All of them?" Nicole asked.

"Yes. Because you had the brilliant idea to make sure you each remember the names." He met her gaze, letting her know how much he meant those words. "It took some time to gather the evidence and identify the men you only had first names on, but we did it, because we wanted you four to know that you hadn't survived that hell for nothing. We didn't want a single person to get away with what they did to you. And from those arrests, there will be others."

"How many today?" Emma asked.

"A staggering three hundred and fifty-seven across the country."

"Will they stay in jail forever?" Toby asked. He'd had the hardest time transitioning at home. He'd been taken so young. Used and abused, until he simply didn't know anything but that horrible world.

Nick gave him the truth. "Not forever, Toby. Not for all of them. But now people know who they are. People know they're monsters. They will never escape that."

"So what now?" Stacy asked.

"It's over. Javier's operation has been toppled. He's in prison for the rest of his life. And because of you four, sixty-two minors have been rescued, most returned to their families." Nick looked at each one of them. "You did that. You saved them. You stopped a very bad man from taking and hurting anyone else.

"So when things seem hard, when you feel really down, I want you to think about the sixty-two young people, who are just like you, that you saved. I want you to remember that you helped each other, and then you helped people you didn't even know. That's who you are. That's the amazing thing you did. That's part of the story of the life you survived. When all you can think about is the bad, I want you to remember the good you did, the courage you showed, because you guys are the real heroes, not the agents who carried out the arrests. You made it happen."

The wind kicked up along with the roar of the helicopter coming in for a landing behind him.

"Is that Hawk?" Toby grinned from ear to ear.

"Yes, it is. Remember how I promised you all a helicopter ride? Well, here we go." Nick took Toby and Stacy by the hand.

Aria rushed over and took Nicole and Emma's hands, and they all walked out to the helicopter, ducking their heads against the downwash of the blades.

He buckled in Toby and Stacy while Aria helped Nicole and Emma. They all put on their headsets, grinning so big their cheeks were going to hurt later.

Nick caught Aria before she rushed back to the parents all waiting to wave their kids off for the ride Hawk had planned to let them see some of the beautiful country surrounding them.

He pulled Aria into a kiss. "I love you," he mouthed, because it was too noisy to even try to yell over the chopper's engine and blades.

"I love you, too. See you soon."

Yeah, he'd been in heaven every day since she moved in with him.

He loved having her as his wife. He loved the life they were making together.

Most of all, he loved how much he loved being part of their family.

They were happy.

He kissed her one last time, then climbed into the copilot seat and fist-bumped Hawk, mouthing, "Thank you."

Hawk handed him a headset, verified that Aria had sealed the back door and gotten clear of the helicopter, then he turned to their honored guests. "You guys ready to fly?"

These kids were ready to soar. One day soon, they were going to be okay again. One day, they were going to use all that strength and perseverance and live as warriors.

**I'm so excited to introduce you to something differ-
ent and new.
The SHE'S MINE duet. SEE ME and LOVE ME.**

**The duet begins with SEE ME, a dark and twist-
ed romance that will hit you in the heart. It ends
on a cliffhanger and continues in LOVE ME to a
hard-won happy ever after for Brooke and Cody.**

SEE ME

Brooke has only loved one man. Cody's
smart, gorgeous, perfect.

Except he's older. Taken.

Oh, and her step-brother.

If only she could prove to him they are meant
to be.

Cody has the perfect life.

A sophisticated, supportive girlfriend, a career on the rise.

And an amazing best friend and stepsister. If only he could stop noticing just how beautiful Brooke is. How she gets him. How he hates any other guy near her.

When one night of passion turns into a morning-after disaster, Brooke is left to face the future alone. And pregnant.

But little does Brooke know, she's not alone. Someone else has been watching. Waiting.

Stalking her every move. And they only want one thing.

Her.

4th of July picnic at Brooke's home...

Brooke Banks stared out at the crowd of people milling around the garden and seated at the picnic tables on the patio. Her best friend Mindy Sue was holding court by the pond with her boyfriend, Marco, and several of their college friends. They were entertaining themselves playing cornhole and horseshoes on the grass. They'd all come to support Brooke through this happy but difficult event.

"Brooke! Is that really you!" Mrs. Ellis's mouth hung open as her gaze went from the tips of Brooke's cowboy boots, up her legs and her slightly curvy body, to her green-eyed gaze. "Wow! You were always a pretty girl, but now you're a beautiful young lady."

She appreciated the praise. At least someone had noticed. "Thank you."

"I'm so sorry about your stepfather. We've missed him these last two years." Mrs. Ellis's husband, the mayor, had been friends with Harland since they were boys in school.

Two years ago, her stepfather had died of a sudden heart attack. He'd held the annual picnic for all his friends, fellow ranchers, and community leaders. She missed him every day. She, her mom, and his son, Cody, hadn't been ready to carry on the tradition after Harland's passing. But this year, Brooke insisted they revive it. It was important to keep Harland's memory alive. Traditions mattered and kept them together.

Plus she hoped it would help Cody look toward the future and see this place as *his* now, because he was the one carrying on in his father's absence.

And it didn't hurt that some of the most influential people in the state were here.

As a lawyer, Cody could use the connections with his father's cronies. One never knew when they'd need a favor from someone with the kind of clout many of the individuals here today flaunted.

She nodded to the governor and his wife, who were chatting with her mother, Susanne, nearby. Mindy Sue's father, Doug Wagner, was one of the most highly respected and successful defense attorneys in the state. There were three judges, plus the district attorney and several of his associates here, too, along with most of the business owners from three nearby towns. Everyone they'd invited showed up out of respect for Cody and his father.

And she'd been the one to pull all of this together, from the invitations to the catering, decorations, the music, games, and fireworks show. Every detail, she'd conceived and executed.

She hoped it showed everyone on the ranch that she'd grown up, because from the second she'd arrived home, she'd had to remind everyone she was twenty, not ten.

It started with their ranch hand the day she arrived home for summer break...

"Little one, let me saddle the horse for you."

That nickname. Paco didn't mean anything by it. He'd been calling her that since she came to live at the ranch.

But right now, it grated.

She shook her head. "I've got this." All she wanted was some time alone out on the property. Wide-open spaces. No classes to stress over. Freedom. Just her on a horse, the wind in her face. Somewhere she didn't run into Cody and Kristi.

Paco tried to take the saddle from her. "It's too heavy."

She held tight. "I've got it. I'm twenty, not ten," she snapped, then caught herself and apologized.

Paco sighed. "You shouldn't ride alone. Why don't you ask Cody to go with you? You two always ride together."

Not lately. Not since she started coming over all the time. "He's busy."

And I need to not look like a lovesick puppy and have a little respect. For him. And myself.

And Cody also never missed an opportunity to exercise his overprotective streak when it came to her.

Brooke poured half a glass of white wine for herself in the kitchen, walked out to the dining room, and took her seat across from her mom, who eyed the glass but didn't say anything but, "You grew up way too fast.

Cody walked in with her, the girlfriend, and plucked the glass out of Brooke's hand and took his seat beside Miss Perfect. "You're not old enough to drink."

Kristi gave a firm nod. Team Cody all the way. UGH! Of course she sided with him to score points.

"I'm twenty, not ten. And it's not like you didn't help drain a few beer kegs when you were my age."

"I'm just looking out for you." Like always.

And she appreciated it most of the time. Not tonight, when he made her feel like she wasn't as much of a woman as the one sitting beside him.

Cody drank her wine.

Mrs. Ellis pressed her hand to her heart. "Time passes so quickly. We blink and..." She waved her hand up and down in front of Brooke. "Little girls turn into young ladies. Friends pass." She waved at her misty eyes. "Sorry. I miss Harland."

"Me, too."

"And I haven't seen enough of your mother. How is Susanne doing? She must be so proud of you."

"She is." Brooke was lucky to have such a supportive mom, even if she was having trouble giving Brooke her freedom. "And she's well. It was hard in the beginning, but now we're all just trying to keep Dad alive in our hearts."

Mrs. Ellis patted Brooke's forearm. "That's the way, now isn't it? You must be close to finishing college."

"One more year to go until I graduate with my bachelor's degree." She couldn't wait.

Mrs. Ellis leaned in. "And is there a special young man?"

Brooke's cheeks warmed. "No." Just Cody. But he wasn't hers. No matter how hard she tried or wished it were true.

"Well"—Mrs. Ellis nudged her shoulder—"the right one will come along soon enough."

Yeah, I already found him. He's just not into me. Not in that way.

Her mom, Susanne, made her way over to them. "Betty, don't you look lovely."

Mrs. Ellis's sleeveless, fuchsia-colored sheath dress complemented her dark hair and green eyes while showing off a nice pair of toned arms. Mrs. Ellis must work out, because she was in good shape.

Mrs. Ellis waved off Brooke's mother's compliment. "Thank you, Susanne. You're as beautiful as ever. That turquoise dress just makes you glow." The women shared a quick embrace and kiss on the cheek.

"I've missed you," Susanne confessed.

Her mom had retreated from her friends after Harland's death, lost in her grief. But over the past year, she'd slowly started to really live again and reconnect with old friends.

Brooke loved that the party had brought these two back together.

Mrs. Ellis held her hand out toward Brooke. "I nearly didn't recognize your beautiful daughter."

"They grow up so fast." Her mom smiled, even if a bit of sadness crept into her eyes that time had passed too quickly and soon Brooke would be off to school again.

"Yes, they do." Mrs. Ellis was probably thinking of her two children. "Thank you for inviting us to the party."

"Oh," her mother said, "I'm so happy you're here, but the event"—Susanne looked around at all the people, decorations, and buffet nearby—"this was all Brooke's doing."

And today Cody would see she could handle a party of this size and scale and make it enticing for all these people to show up and be here for him. All she'd had to do was call up the governor's wife and tell her how much she hoped she and her husband would attend, and that her stepfather Harland had loved her pecan pie. Mrs. Harris had won first place in the state fair three years in a row and took great pride in showing off her version of the official state pie. She had graciously agreed to not only come to the picnic but to bring a dozen of her homemade pies herself. From there, it had been simple to let others know the governor would be attending, and the RSVPs had rolled in. Not that these people wouldn't come because they respected Harland and Cody. They would. They did. But it never hurt to have a little incentive for those who thrived on being seen in the right circles.

And she'd do anything for Cody.

Mrs. Ellis's smile grew as her gaze shifted to Brooke. "I should hire you for the mayor's next event."

Pride swelled in her heart. She'd worked hard on this picnic. And Mrs. Ellis's approval meant a lot. She attended a ton of events each year. She'd know if something was done well, or fell short. "Unfortunately, I'll have my nose stuck in books for the next couple semesters."

"You should think about becoming an event planner."

Mrs. Ellis's suggestion was nice, but Brooke had other plans. And they included running the ranch with Cody.

Unfortunately, she wouldn't have Cody all to herself. His girlfriend, Kristi Randall, beelined it across the patio toward her and she inwardly cringed.

Kristi barely got out, "Sorry to interrupt, Susanne, Mrs. Ellis." She turned to Brooke. "Have you seen your brother?" Kristi stood before her, searching the crowd with barely a glance for her.

Kristi had never liked her. The feeling was mutual. Kristi wanted all of Cody's attention on her. Brooke? Same. Still, you'd think Kristi would want to befriend Cody's best friend.

Not Kristi. She saw other women as competition.

And while Brooke loved Cody, she also knew she wasn't in the running to be anything more than what she already was to him.

And referring to him as her brother. Yeah, no. She and Cody didn't call each other brother and sister. Their seven-year age gap meant they hadn't been raised together. Brooke and her mom arrived on the ranch when she was ten. Her mother hired on as the cook before Harland fell hard and fast for Susanne and they married. And while Harland had felt like the father she'd never had, she and Cody treated each other like good friends, not siblings.

She'd never, not once, thought of the charming, temptingly hot Cody as her brother.

Kristi huffed out her frustration. "I've been looking for him everywhere." In her long, flowing white dress, pink strappy kitten heels that Brooke hated to admit were super cute, and a tan sunhat over her long golden hair, Kristi made Brooke look like a ranch hand and not the hostess of one of the most sought-after invitations in the state.

Brooke should have put more thought into her outfit like her mother suggested. Suggested not once, but like four times.

She never really paid much attention to what she wore on the ranch or at school. She went for comfort over fashion.

Today she'd thought she'd upped her game by wearing a faded denim skirt that hit mid-thigh and showed off her tanned, toned legs, a short-sleeved, fitted red T-shirt that had lace detail around the arms and hemline but now felt like it wasn't anything special, and her black cowboy boots. She'd pulled her hair up into her usual ponytail to keep it out of the way and off her neck in the hot sun. She could have tried something different. Maybe keeping it down and using some pretty clips to keep it out of her face, even if it would be heavy and hot draped down her neck and back.

Compared to Kristi, she looked plain.

Not exactly showstopping for this who's who party.

Standing next to Kristi, seeing how everyone else around her had dressed in what Mindy Sue would probably call resort chic, suddenly made her uncomfortable. Nervous butterflies battled in her belly as her cheeks heated with embarrassment. She'd tried so hard to make today perfect for everyone. Now, she felt out of place. Not the first time.

Changing now would look too obvious. So she let it go with a heavy heart and tried not to let herself think about it again.

Brooke glanced at Mindy Sue and her other friends out on the lawn, all of them in sundresses or skirts and pretty blouses, hair done, makeup on. Brooke had swiped on some ChapStick and mascara and called it done.

Even the guys were in khakis and slacks with short-sleeved button-up shirts.

She scanned the crowd again and noticed the ranch hands had put on their finest boots, dark denim, and cowboy shirts with pearl buttons, belt buckles shining.

She sighed, thinking that instead of spending the whole morning helping the caterer set up, she could have taken time to actually think about what she wanted to wear and put together something a bit more...sophisticated. Maybe then Cody would look at her like he looked at other women. And she wouldn't feel like the lovesick shadow who followed him around all the time, hoping he'd see how much she loved him.

Ugh. Pathetic. And yet she couldn't squash the undying hope that lived inside her that one day...

Kristi tapped her on the shoulder. "Brooke. Hello. Cody?"

Right. Brooke looked out across the patio, gardens, and grass area where the just-over-two-hundred guests were mingling. "I haven't seen him since we came out to greet everyone."

Kristi huffed out a breath.

Trouble in paradise?

One could hope. Because Kristi had this way about her. She liked getting what she wanted and seemed to be the kind of person who'd do anything to get it.

An only child. Spoiled.

But Brooke had also gotten the sense that pleasing her parents really mattered to Kristi. Brooke got that. You wanted them to be proud of you. It just seemed like Kristi really needed it more than most.

Still, Brooke recognized the longing in Kristi's eyes. She felt it in herself every time she thought about Cody or even looked at him. He had this quality that drew her in.

Kristi and others weren't immune to it either.

But Cody was different with Brooke than he was with the other women who came and went. They could talk for hours or just chill and watch a movie with nothing said. She knew him so well, she could read him like a book. And he was always there for her. Since the day she arrived at the ranch with her mom, they just clicked.

They were friends.

She wanted them to be more.

He ignored all her attempts to get his attention in that way.

She had half a mind to tell Kristi he was off talking to some ex, but that was petty and immature. She'd long since grown past trying to sabotage Cody's girlfriends by conveniently forgetting to deliver messages, or telling them Cody liked something that he hated. He always caught on and gave her a disapproving look that made her feel terrible. She didn't want to be on the wrong side of Cody. She definitely didn't want to lose the amazing connection they shared.

And now, she was really trying to be the grown-up no one on the ranch saw her to be, including her mother and Cody.

Maybe she could do a better job by thinking things through first, like dressing appropriately for the party and presenting herself as the adult she felt like on the inside. Then everyone would see it. Right?

It sucked that everyone still treated her like a child. Well, at least a teen with no sense, despite her stellar grades and the twenty years she'd kept herself alive and well, thank you very much.

Maybe she'd made some mistakes along the way. Thinking Jamie was her friend at middle school summer camp, only to find out that Jamie had hidden a bottle of vodka in Brooke's bag and she got caught during inspection the first day and sent home. Luckily, her mom believed her that she hadn't stolen it from the bar at home. It was a cheap brand they didn't keep in the house. Then there was the time she'd played spin the bottle at Brent's house freshman year with a bunch of friends. She really wanted her first kiss to be with Cody, but Joe came in second, and then the bottle landed on Chris. She'd been disappointed but game to kiss him just to get it over with. But Brent, the asshole trickster, who she'd turned down in front of several of his friends for the spring dance, told her to close her eyes. She did and puckered up to kiss Chris but got a face full of dog tongue instead. Brent got his revenge. Everyone laughed at her. The next day at school, everyone snickered behind her back about her French-kissing Brent's mini poodle. Yeah, high school was not fun with that hanging over her head.

Kristi frowned as she continued to scan the crowd. "If you see him, please send him to me. Tell him my father would like to have a word with him? It's important."

The demand wrapped in the request rubbed Brooke the wrong way. "We're supposed to give a speech while everyone is eating. The lines are forming now. I'm sure he'll find me soon."

"That can wait. This can't. It's an opportunity Cody won't want to pass up. Not if he's smart."

Cody was the smartest guy she knew.

"What's it about?"

"The future. One I think Cody wants, which is why I worked so hard to set this up."

Brooke cocked her head, concerned and suspicious. "What did you set up?"

Kristi huffed. "My father is waiting. Will you just help me find him?"

Mrs. Ellis and Susanne both raised a brow, though Kristi didn't see their curious gazes.

Brooke couldn't let the snappish tone go. "You know, a straight answer would get better results."

"Cody wants to make a name for himself. I can make that happen." Smugness was not becoming on Kristi.

The muscles in Brooke's shoulders tensed. "He doesn't need anyone to make him look good. He's smart, driven, and good at everything he does."

Kristi smirked. "Oh, I know he is."

Brooke didn't like the innuendo. She avoided Mrs. Ellis and her mother's stares. "Whatever." She tried to walk away, but Kristi snagged her arm and halted her.

"Don't mess this up for him."

She turned and looked Kristi right in the eyes. "I want what's best for him."

Kristi grinned again. "Good. Then send him over to me." She smiled smugly and walked away.

Brooke wanted to tear Kristi's pretty blonde hair out.

Mrs. Ellis gave Brooke the same sympathetic look as her mom. "Don't let her get to you. Women like her end up with no friends, wondering why no one likes them."

"I guess. Excuse me. I have to find Cody." She decided if whatever Kristi was talking about would really help him, then she'd do the right thing.

She found him in the garden, sitting in an Adirondack chair next to his buddy Brad Whitlock, the district attorney's son. They'd grown up together and went to college together.

Brad saw her coming and grinned. "Hello, beautiful." He took her hand and tugged, putting her off-balance so that she landed in his lap. He hugged her close. "Where have you been all my life."

"Right under your nose. But the B word you use for me is usually brat." She elbowed him in the gut, making him laugh as she smiled back at him. Brad was like a brother to her.

Which was weird to think of him as when she'd never seen Cody that way.

And the object of all her desires frowned at his friend.

Brad ignored it. "I think gorgeous suits you better now."

Cody pounded his fist into Brad's shoulder with anger in his eyes as he reached out and took Brooke's hand, pulling her up and out of Brad's lap and into his. "Hands off, asshole."

Brad held up his hands. "I was just saying hello."

Cody narrowed his gaze. "You know the rule. No flirting with *her*."

Brooke cocked a brow. "Is this like the bro code?" She had to admit, she liked seeing Cody possessive over her. And sitting in his lap gave her all kinds of shivery feelings and indecent ideas.

Brad chuckled. "You don't mess with your best friend's sister."

Cody nudged her off him. "Is it time for the speech you want us to make?"

Brooke stood beside him, knowing he'd changed the subject on purpose, but not understanding the wince he'd given at Brad's words or the strange look in his eyes when she left his lap. Regret?

No. That's wishful thinking and my imagination.

She tamped down her hormones and adoration for him and focused. "Uh, Kristi ordered me to find you."

"Excuse me?" Cody didn't look happy about that.

Brooke let it go. "Her father wants to talk to you. Something important."

"Better hop to it," Brad teased. "Don't want to keep the future Mrs. Jansen waiting."

"What?" Brooke nearly choked on the word and the idea that Cody planned to propose.

Cody punched his fist into Brad's arm again as he stood. "Stop joking about shit like that."

She grabbed his forearm and stopped him from walking away. "Are you..."

"No," he said emphatically.

She breathed a sigh of relief that he wasn't planning on asking her to marry him.

Yet.

She wanted to shut that voice up.

Cody glanced at the crowd. "Where is she?"

Brooke looked past him. "By the bar."

"How about I get you a drink, Brooke?" Brad offered.

"No," Cody snapped. "Brooke isn't of age."

Brad shook his head. "Come on, old man. We were drinking way younger than she is now."

Cody met Brad's taunting eyes. "Go find one of the couple dozen available women here today. She's not for you."

Brooke wanted to break the tension between these two friends. "I mean, I could do worse."

Cody's lethal gaze landed on her. "Are you serious?"

She rolled her eyes. "No. I'm going to make sure everyone is heading to the buffet line." She walked away, but not before she heard Brad tell Cody, "I was just messing around."

She knew it was to keep his friendship with Cody on good terms, but it kind of pinched her heart, too, that he wasn't serious about her being beautiful, or that he would be interested in her.

Not that she wanted to date Brad. It would just be nice if he thought she was worth Cody's wrath.

You're being ridiculous.

She knew that.

Still, the whole interaction with all of them felt weird. Like maybe Cody didn't want her with anyone but him.

Now that's really ridiculous.

Or was it?

She really needed to stop this train of thought and get a grip.

She made it through the garden and to the buffet line just in time to catch the moment Cody found Kristi and slipped his hand around her waist, pulling her close to his side as he used his free hand to shake her father's hand.

Kristi looked up at him adoringly.

Cody glanced down at her and smiled. People close to them noticed the happy couple.

Was he really thinking about marrying her? Or had Brad really just been joking?

Brooke's heart sank. She was too used to this feeling when it came to Cody. Maybe one day he'd see her as the woman she'd become.

The one who wanted him and only him.

ACKNOWLEDGEMENTS

I hope you enjoyed Aria and Nick's story. For more information about upcoming releases and sales, please sign up for my newsletter.

I'm so pleased I finished the Dark Horse Dive Bar series and everyone got their story. I know, you're probably waiting for Hawk's story next. Me too! I have an outline for his HEA and hope to write it soon, though I am working on some new and different things, too.

This book could not have been completed without the wonderful people who helped me put this book together.

Thank you to my amazing editor Susan Barnes (www.susanbarnesediting.com) for your amazing insights, comments, and suggestions. Your reaction comments were the best! Every book we work on together is better because of you – even when you ask me to rearrange the book. LOL.

Melissa Frain (www.melissafrain.com), thank you for making sure all the hyphenated words I never hyphenate got hyphenated and fixing all my grammar mistakes. There are some things I just need an expert like you for. Your reaction comments were the best. I appreciate your love for the story.

Angela Haddon (www.angelahaddon.com), you are an amazing cover artist. You took the picture I sent you and turned it into a beautiful cover that seamlessly complements the other books in the series. I love working with you.

To my amazing agent, Suzie Townsend, thank you for always having my back, guiding me through this crazy business, sharing your insights and expertise, and always cheering me on. I couldn't, and wouldn't, want to do this without you.

Steve, I love you. What else is there to say after 33 years of support and encouragement, kids, laughter, fun, and everything else that goes into a life together. I can't imagine doing any of this without you by my side.

ALSO BY JENNIFER RYAN

Stand-Alone Novels
Summer's Gift – The One You Want – Lost and Found
Family
Sisters and Secrets – The Me I Used to Be
The Dark Horse Dive Bar Series
Wilde In His Arms – Wilde Abandon
Wilde For You – Wilde Love
The Wyoming Wilde Series
Max Wilde's Cowboy Heart
Surrendering to Hunt – Chase Wilde Comes Home
The McGrath Series
True Love Cowboy
Love of a Cowboy – Waiting on a Cowboy
Wild Rose Ranch Series
Tough Talking Cowboy
Restless Rancher – Dirty Little Secret
Montana Heat Series
Tempted by Love – True to You
Escape to You – Protected by Love
Montana Men Series
His Cowboy Heart – Her Renegade Rancher
Stone Cold Cowboy – Her Lucky Cowboy
When It's Right – At Wolf Ranch

The McBride Series
Dylan's Redemption
Falling For Owen – The Return of Brody McBride
The Hunted Series
Everything She Wanted
Chasing Morgan – The Right Bride
Lucky Like Us – Saved by the Rancher
Short Stories
"Close to Perfect" (appears in Snowbound at Chrstmas)
"Can't Wait" (appears in All I Want for Christmas is a
Cowboy)
"Waiting for You" (appears in Confessions of a Secret Ad-
mirer)

*N*ew *York Times* and *USA Today* bestselling author Jennifer Ryan writes suspenseful contemporary romances about everyday people who do extraordinary things. Her deeply emotional love stories are filled with high stakes and higher drama, family, friendship, and the happy-ever-after we all hope to find.

Jennifer lives in the San Francisco Bay Area with her husband and three children. When she isn't writing a book, she's reading one. Her obsession with both is often revealed in the state of her home and how late dinner is to the table. When she finally leaves those fictional worlds, you'll find her in the garden, playing in the dirt and day-dreaming about people who live only in her head – until she puts them on paper.

Please visit her website at www.jennifer-ryan.com for information about upcoming releases.